Morning for Dove

MARTHA ROGERS

Most Strang Communications Book Group products are available at special quantity discounts for bulk purchase for sales promotions, premiums, fund-raising, and educational needs. For details, write Strang Communications Book Group, 600 Rinehart Road, Lake Mary, Florida 32746, or telephone (407) 333-0600.

Morning for Dove by Martha Rogers
Published by Realms
A Strang Company
600 Rinehart Road
Lake Mary, Florida 32746
www.strangbookgroup.com

This book or parts thereof may not be reproduced in any form, stored in a retrieval system, or transmitted in any form by any means—electronic, mechanical, photocopy, recording, or otherwise—without prior written permission of the publisher, except as provided by United States of America copyright law.

Unless otherwise noted, all Scripture quotations are from the King James Version of the Bible.

Cover design by Nathan Morgan
Design Director: Bill Johnson

Copyright © 2010 by Martha Rogers
All rights reserved

Library of Congress Cataloging-in-Publication Data:

An application to register this book for cataloging has been submitted to the Library of Congress.

International Standard Book Number: 978-1-59979-984-1

First Edition

10 11 12 13 14 — 9 8 7 6 5 4 3 2 1
Printed in the United States of America

To my dear husband, Rex, who has given me loving support throughout my years of writing.

To my critique partner, Janice Thompson, who spent a lot of time with Dove and gave me great advice for making this a stronger book.

To my agent, Tamela Hancock Murray, for having faith in me and not giving up.

To my writing friends, DiAnn Mills, Kathleen Y'Barbo, Linda Kozar, and Marcia Gruver, for their encouragement and support.

To Wanda Shadle, for forming the Inspirational Writers Alive! group at our church that started me down the path to publication.

Weeping may endure for a night, but
joy cometh in the morning.

—Psalm 30:5

Chapter 1

Oklahoma Territory, June 1897

Today was not a good day for a wedding. It was Lucinda Bishop's wedding day, and he wasn't the groom. The sun may be shining outside, but Luke Anderson's insides rolled and tumbled like the dark clouds before a storm. His feelings should have been under control by now, and they had been up until this moment. Now Lucy's image rolled through his mind like pictures on a stereo-optic machine.

He shook his head and snatched off his tie. Anger filled his heart. His eyes closed tightly, and he prayed for God to take away his negative feelings. All thoughts of Lucinda must be put away as part of his past and not his future.

Calm swept through him as he felt the Lord's peace take over. Still, he'd rather do anything else, like stay behind and keep the store open. Pa didn't worry about the business he'd be losing by closing down for the day because most of the townsfolk would be at the church. Luke shrugged his arms into the sleeves of his jacket. He hated having to wear a suit in this heat. With his tie now securely back in place, Luke headed downstairs to meet his parents.

His mother tilted her head and looked him over from head to foot. "I must say you do look especially handsome today." She nodded her approval and turned for the door.

Luke tugged at his collar and forced himself to smile. She must have thought he'd come down in his work clothes.

His sister beamed at him. "You are handsome, even if you are my brother."

Luke shook his head and followed her outside. "You look very pretty yourself, Alice."

She looked up at him and furrowed her brow. "Thank you, I think."

Luke relaxed at his sister's comments. He usually ridiculed or teased her, but she did look pretty today with her blonde curls dancing on her shoulders. At sixteen, she had the notice of a few boys in her class at school.

The tightness in his chest loosened. He'd get through this day.

Since the church was only a few blocks down the street, they would walk, but his younger brother, Will, ran ahead. When they reached the churchyard, wagons, surreys, and horses filled the area. Pa had been right. People from all over were here, paying tribute to the niece of one of the most powerful ranchers in the area, Mr. Haynes.

He followed the rest of his family into the church and down to a pew. The sanctuary filled quickly, and the music began. Instead of paying attention, Luke tugged once again at the demon collar and tie and wished for relief from the early summer heat. The organ swelled with a melody, and everyone stood. Dove, Lucy's best friend, walked down the aisle followed by the bride.

Never had Lucy looked more beautiful. Mrs. Weems, the dressmaker, had made many trips to the store for the ribbons and laces that adorned the dress and slight train now trailing behind it. The white satin enhanced Lucy's dark hair and fair face, and her eyes sparkled with the love she had for Jake.

Luke had to admit deep in his heart that she'd never been his. Even when he courted her, her heart had belonged to Jake. Luke should have known he'd never make her forget that cowboy.

Then his gaze fell on Dove, and his throat tightened. Although he'd known her for years, he'd never seen her as any more than the part-Cherokee daughter of Sam Morris. Now her bronzed complexion and dark eyes glowed with a beauty that stunned him. He had looked right through her when they had been at the box social last spring and on other social occasions. At those events, she'd been with someone else, and he'd seen only Lucinda. Dove was quiet and didn't say much when around others their age, and he had spoken directly to her only a few times at church. Today he saw her with new eyes.

When Lucy reached the altar on the arm of her uncle Ben, Luke sat down, as did the congregation. Ignoring the words of the minister, he stared at Dove. How could he not have noticed her before?

Luke glanced to his left and right. Pa had been right when he said most of Barton Creek would attend the wedding. Even Chester Fowler had come. He'd been less than friendly with Ben Haynes and Sam Morris the few times Luke had seen them together. Something about the man bothered Luke, but he couldn't quite put a finger on it.

From the corner of his eye he noticed Bobby Frankston staring to the side of the altar. Luke followed the boy's gaze to find Becky Haynes at the other end. She stood with Dove beside Lucy as an attendant. Her attention had been drawn to Bobby, and a faint bloom reddened her cheeks. That blush didn't come from the heat. Luke chuckled to himself. It looked to him like another boy had fallen in love.

When the ceremony ended, the couple left the church and headed to the hotel where the Haynes had planned a lavish celebration for their niece.

When Luke joined the other guests there, tables laden with thin slices of beef, chicken, and ham, along with a variety of breads, vegetables, and fruit, filled one end of the room and beckoned to him. After filling his plate, he moved to the side of the room and bit into a piece of chicken. At least the food tasted good.

His gaze swept around the room. The hotel dining hall had been cleared of almost all its tables, and people milled about talking with one another and balancing plates of food.

In his perusal of the room, his gaze came to rest on Dove Morris. The pale yellow dress she wore emphasized her dark hair and almost black eyes. He'd never seen such a flawless complexion on anyone besides Lucy. But where Lucy's was fair, Dove's reflected the heritage of her Indian blood. As she chatted with a guest, a smile lit up her face. At that moment she turned in Luke's direction, her eyes locking with his and widening as though surprised to see him. A sharp tingle skittered through his heart. Before he could catch his breath, she turned back to the woman beside her. The tightness in his chest lessened, but he still stared at her even though she no longer looked at him.

Twice now something had coursed through his veins as he observed her. An explanation for those feelings eluded him because nothing like that had happened with Lucy when he was with her. Whatever this feeling happened to be, one thing was certain—he had to speak to Dove. Still, after what happened with Lucy, he would take his time and not rush into a relationship so quickly this time.

He made his way in her direction, not allowing his eyes to lose contact with her face. When he stood by her side, her head barely reached his shoulder. He had never truly paid any attention to how tiny and petite she was, even when he'd seen her in the store and at church. A sudden urge to stand taller and make a good impression overcame him.

Finally he caught her eye. "Miss Morris, what a pleasure to see you this afternoon," he said.

Her lips quivered then broke into a smile. "Luke Anderson. It's a pleasure to see you too. Wasn't the wedding lovely?"

"Yes, it was." But not as lovely as the girl standing before him. "Would you like some refreshment?"

"I would like that; thank you." Her soft voice melted his resolve. He had to know more about this beautiful young woman. How her beauty had escaped his notice was something he didn't understand. He straightened his shoulders and grasped her hand to tuck it over his arm. She'd certainly grown up while he had been so smitten with Lucy Bishop.

The warmth of Luke's arm beneath Dove's hand sent a shiver through her body despite the heat. He was the last person she expected to pay attention to her today. As long as she had known him and wanted his admiration, he had spoken only a few words directly to her. His noticing her today sent currents of excitement through her as well as questions about why he chose this day to show any interest in her.

He offered her a cup of punch, and the sunlight streaming through the windows glistened on the crystal in her hand, turning it into shimmering sparkles. In fact, everything about the day had become brighter. She sipped from her cup then smiled at Luke. "This is very good." Her face warmed. Not a very exciting topic of conversation.

Luke raised his cup to his mouth and swallowed. "Yes, it is." He glanced around the room. "Would you save a dance for me, Miss Morris?"

Words first stuck in Dove's throat and then came forth in a squeak. "Yes, I will." Her face grew even warmer. She would like nothing more than to be whirling across the dance floor with Luke's arms about her, and he would probably be her only partner except for Martin, who had asked earlier.

At that moment the young man in question stepped up. "Don't forget you promised me a dance today, Miss Morris."

"Of course I won't forget." Two young men seeking her companionship today was twice as many as she had even imagined. Because of her Cherokee heritage, she never expected young men to take much notice of her or spend time with her. Today would be a more lovely day than she had believed it would be.

Martin glanced at Luke. "Miss Morris, if you'll excuse us, I must speak to Luke alone."

Dove nodded as the two young men made their way across the room. With both being so tall, she had no trouble seeing them as they stopped by the door. Once their gaze turned toward her, and she averted her eyes. Her cheeks once again burned at the thought they could be discussing her. Luke was the one she wanted by her side, and she prayed he wouldn't back out of his request.

An arm slipped around Dove's shoulders. Turning to find Clara Haynes beside her, she beamed at the elderly lady everyone called Aunt Clara. "Oh, didn't Lucy look lovely?"

"She certainly did, and Mellie and Mrs. Weems did a wonderful job with the dress, but you look just as beautiful."

The compliment unnerved her because no one but Ma or Pa

had ever called her beautiful before. "Thank you." Her hand trembled, and she had to set her punch cup down. "It's been a wonderful day for a wedding, and so many are here to honor Lucy and Jake." Anything to change the topic.

The ploy didn't work with Aunt Clara, who leaned close and whispered, "Next thing is to find a suitable young man for you, and that may be sooner than we think."

Dove blinked. The elderly woman meant well, but no young man in town wanted to court a half-breed girl. Men like her father were few and far between. With his prominence and wealth, he had paid no attention to what others thought when he chose his Cherokee bride. He'd said more than once that a man should be judged on his treatment of others, his honesty, and his reliability, not on his race or skin color. If only Luke could see her that way.

Aunt Clara squeezed Dove's arm then patted it. "I believe it's time to get some life into this party." She headed toward the newly married couple.

Dove wished she were more adventuresome like Lucy, who had left her native Boston to come west to live with the Haynes family. Everything here was new and strange to Lucy, but she adapted, even shortening her name from Lucinda to Lucy. Dove sighed, wishing for some changes in her own life.

At that moment, Luke returned, and her hopes rose in anticipation. Perhaps those changes could begin in a friendship with Luke.

As Bea Anderson stared across the crowded room, she nudged her husband. "Carl, look over there. Luke's talking with Dove Morris."

Carl nodded in their direction. "She looks very pretty today."

"She does, but that still doesn't mean I like his talking with her." Indeed her son could do much better than the half-breed Morris girl. As pretty as she may be, she wasn't the kind Luke should even think of courting.

"Now, Bea, they're just having a polite conversation."

Polite conversation or not, this would not go any further if she had any say in the matter. All her childhood memories of Indian raids and attacks could not be erased by a few years of peace with one tribe. The horrors she'd seen were forever etched in her memory, and the very sight of Dove and her mother or her brothers sent them all flooding into her soul again. No matter that everyone else recognized the girl's mother as Emily Morris—she'd always be White Feather to Bea.

She had tried to be civil, but always the images that couldn't be forgiven lurked in the background. They were as much a part of her being as every thought or emotion she ever had.

Now she simply avoided the Morris family as much as possible and let Carl take care of their needs when they came into the store. She had chosen to keep her distance and ignore them. Even though most of the town knew her story and would understand her feelings toward the Morris family, Bea didn't want to say something that might embarrass the Andersons in front of strangers who might be in the store. That wouldn't be good for business.

Carl placed his arm around her and hugged her close. "Bea, Luke is a grown young man. He's all ready to take over the store when the time comes. He's smart, and he's a good son. You have to let him make his own decisions and choose his own life."

Bea swallowed hard. Knowing and letting it happen were two different things. She wished Luke had been the one to marry the Bishop girl today, but Lucy chose Jake, a cowboy turned rancher who had joined the ranks of men like Ben Haynes and Sam Morris.

Carl patted her arm. "See, Martin Fleming is drawing Dove's attention now. We don't have to worry about Luke. He'll make the right decision."

"I should hope so. He knows our history, and any Indian, especially a half-breed girl like Dove, would never fit into our family."

Chapter 2

Dove gazed out the window to the morning sun beyond. No matter how dark the night, daylight brought new hope. It reminded her of the verse in Psalms that said, "Weeping may endure for the night, but joy cometh in the morning." And joy did fill her heart this new day.

Although it had been almost a week since the wedding, she still reveled in the attention Luke had paid to her. She finished her chores and sought out her mother. She found her sitting in the parlor working on a new crochet project. "Ma, wasn't Lucy's wedding just wonderful?"

"Yes, it was." She laid the shawl in her lap and peered at Dove. "And that's the fourth time in as many days that you've mentioned it. Is there something else or someone else you're thinking about?"

Heat rose in Dove's cheeks. How like Ma to see through her comment. Of course she had mentioned the wedding more than a few times the past few days. Her gaze shifted to the floor. "Luke Anderson. He looked so handsome in his suit." His face with eyes more green than brown and hair the color of caramel filled her mind. She could still feel his arm about her as they danced.

"Luke is a fine young man. Someday he'll run the mercantile with his father." She reached over and grasped Dove's arm. "My dear child, I must caution you to not let your dreams of the future become too wrapped up in Luke Anderson."

"Ma, I know his mother doesn't like us because we're Cherokee, but why can't she let Luke and me be friends?" They had been only casual acquaintances until the wedding when he'd looked at her with a different light in his eyes, and the attention had enchanted her.

"Friendship is one thing, but Mrs. Anderson and I are both aware how friendships can turn into something else entirely. That's what she fears."

"I don't understand why she would be afraid of that. She even seems to be afraid of you and me. She never talks to us when we go into the store, and Mr. Anderson always waits on us."

Ma closed her eyes and took a deep breath. Dove bit her lip. Had she said something wrong? After all, she wasn't blind and could see exactly how Mrs. Anderson eyed them and then ignored them in the store.

"It's a long story, my dear, and one we should have told you long before now, but it never occurred to me or your pa that something like this attraction to Luke would happen."

"Oh, Ma, please tell me what happened. It must have been terrible."

Her mother's answer didn't come right away. Her mouth set in a firm line, and a faraway look filled her eyes. All the stories Dove had heard about Indian raids and killings raced through her mind.

Finally Ma shook her head. "I'm sorry. My thoughts wandered there for a moment." She rolled crochet yarn between her fingers. "Most people in town know the story, but we shielded you from it. Back when Bea Anderson was a little girl and living in Nebraska, I think around 1864, Indians attacked ranchers and settlements somewhere near Little Blue River. Cheyenne, Sioux, and Arapaho massacred many people, including Bea's parents. From what Mr. Anderson told your father, Bea was seven when her mother fell. She shielded Bea's body with her own. Bea's older sister was carried off, but the rest of the family lay dead all around Bea."

Tears sprang to Dove's eyes. The image of a little girl and her dead mother sent chills through her veins. Dove hugged herself and rubbed her arms. "Oh, Ma, how awful for Mrs. Anderson. Who took care of her?"

"Mellie Haynes told me that some folks in town found Bea and took her in. After she married Carl, they came down to Oklahoma for the land rush and set up a store for the settlers in Barton Creek."

"You and Pa came then too. I remember how happy Pa was to get the piece of land he wanted." She had been only ten years old, but it had been the most exciting thing she could remember. Pa staked his claim and said he was going to build a fine house on the best ranch land in the territory.

"Yes, but Bea has never forgotten what happened to her, and I'm afraid she never will. She can't find it in her heart to forgive what was done to her and her family. Those feelings have grown stronger over the years to the point of hatred for anything associated with Indians. Even if Luke defies his parents and seeks your favor, you'd have a most unhappy relationship."

The statement sat like lead in Dove's heart, but it held a truth neither of them could deny. No home could be happy if the husband and wife went against their parents. She'd have to be content with seeing Luke on Sundays and the few times they went into town.

Ma picked up her crochet hook and secured it in the yarn. "Not just members of white families were killed. Our villages were attacked and our people killed too. I was afraid of white men just as Bea is afraid of us. When your pa found me, I was all alone with no family. He was like no other white man I had seen. You remember I told you how he took me out of the camp where we'd been kept, and I fell in love with him and his gentle ways right at that moment."

"I'm glad I didn't live back then when life was so hard."

Ma smiled. "Child, life is always hard." Then she laughed. "One thing I learned is that Sam Morris is one who will fight to his death to defend those he loves and what he thinks is right. I believe that's why he and Ben Haynes are such good friends." She paused a moment. "I do remember that the Sioux tribe that joined us had several white girls among their captives. We learned about them later because they were kept hidden from the soldiers."

"Oh, that must have been a terrible thing for them."

"I don't know what happened before they were brought to our camp, but I met one girl a little older than I am, but she didn't speak our Cherokee language, and I didn't understand hers. She did learn my name, White Feather, and I called her Yellow Hair. The women at the fort were very kind to the women and children in our tribes. The colonel's wife took great interest in me because I had no family."

"Why haven't you ever told me about this before?"

Emily picked at a few crochet stitches. "I haven't wanted to talk much about those days. If not for the kindness of the officers' wives, we would have been miserable. Anyway, let's not talk about it anymore."

Dove stood then leaned over and hugged her mother. "All right, Ma, but thank you for telling me about your own experience, and thank you for listening to me and telling me about Mrs. Anderson. I understand more about Luke now and will be patient. Perhaps God will allow us to be friends at church." Although the idea tore her heart in half, having Luke as a distant friend would be all she could hope for or expect as long as his mother felt as she did.

She turned to leave the room, but Ma grabbed her hand. "Dove, you are right in that this is a matter for God to take care of. We both must pray about your relationship with Luke. If it's in God's plan, then all will work together to bring good. Remember that."

"Yes, Ma, I will." She would do what Ma suggested, but being patient and waiting for God to work would be difficult.

As Luke checked off new inventory, he tried to keep the image of Dove out of his mind. But her dark brown eyes held his thoughts like a hook in the mouth of fish. No matter how hard he tried, the deeper it sank into his heart.

The bell over the door jingled to announce a customer. Luke shoved the last can on the shelf and turned to find Martin Fleming standing a few feet away.

"Good morning, Martin. What brings you in so early in the morning?" His best friend grinned and shrugged his shoulders. Although Martin was taller by an inch or two, Luke outweighed him by a good fifteen pounds or more.

Martin's Adam's apple bobbed when he spoke. "I came in to see if you'd be free for some fishing this afternoon. I usually stay another hour to help balance the books, but Father said he'd let me go after the bank closes. I figured fishing would be a good way to spend the rest of the afternoon."

The idea of fishing appealed to Luke. He studied the paper in his hands. All the new merchandise had been counted and shelved, Thursdays were rather slow, and if they caught a mess of fish, it would make a good dinner. "Don't see why I can't go too. What time you thinking about?"

"Oh, around three, I s'pose. It'll be cool down by the creek in the shade."

"I'll be ready." Sitting under a shade tree with a fishing pole certainly beat stacking and selling goods in a hot store. Besides, he wanted to ask Martin about his feelings for Dove. Martin escorted her to the box social and danced with her at the wedding last week. If his friend sought Dove's favor, then Luke would have to consider stepping back. He frowned. No, he'd done that once and lost out. Still, Martin was his friend, and friends didn't betray each other.

Martin purchased a bag of hard candy and then left as another customer entered the store. It was Chester Fowler, one of the most disagreeable men around. Luke scanned the shelf in front of him as though busy. He wanted no part of that man. Let Pa wait on him.

Fowler's words rose as he ranted on about farmers and their fences. Luke listened as he worked, his ears tuned to the anger bursting from the rancher.

"Those sod busters are ruining grazing land, and it's time the law put a stop to it. This is free-range land, and I aim to keep it that way." He slammed some coins on the counter as Pa filled the order for supplies.

"Chester, I don't see why that's bothering you seeing as how your land is surrounded by the Haynes's and Morris's spreads and nowhere near the farmers. I haven't heard Ben or Sam complaining."

Fowler let go a stream of tobacco juice that pinged in the brass container by the counter. "That's the problem. Those two ain't got no sense of what's right. That Morris and his half-breed sons ain't ranchers. Why, they're even helping the farmers with their fences. He says it's to keep the cattle out of the crops, but that's a poor excuse."

Luke bit back a retort. The Morris spread was the wealthiest along with Ben Haynes's ranch. Those two men and their cowboys were obviously doing something right. Besides, he'd heard Mr. Haynes and Mr. Morris both complain about Fowler's cattle always mixing in with their herds and his claiming some of them as Fowler cattle.

That man never liked anything anybody did unless he had suggested it first. Luke sneaked a glance at the supplies Fowler wanted. Wire cutters sat on top of rope, as well as regular supplies of coffee and tins of beans.

Pa wrapped the order in brown paper. "You planning on cutting a few fences or putting up a few yourself?"

"That ain't any of your business, Carl Anderson. And you don't need to go spreading any tales about it neither. I got my reasons."

At that moment his two sons barged through the doors, almost dislodging the bell above it. Bart, the older and meaner of the two, stomped across the floor. "You about finished, Pa?"

"Yeah, if this man who calls himself a merchant can get my goods wrapped." He spat again into the brass pot.

At least he didn't spit on the floor. Luke realized why he didn't like Fowler. His anger and surly attitude made everyone uncomfortable. Two women who had been in the store when Fowler came in had left in a hurry when they saw him. Ma stood over by the fabrics. From the clenched tightness of her jaw, she wanted to hurl a few words of her own at the man.

When Pa pushed the bundle forward, Fowler grabbed it and glanced around the room. "I know you folks don't like me, but I tell you here and now, someday I'll be the wealthy one around here, and then we'll see who gets some respect." He flicked the brim of his hat and sauntered out of the store like he owned the place. His two boys followed him.

When the door closed and the bell jangled again. Ma hurried to the front window and gazed after them. "Oh, Carl, I do hope he's not going to start anything with the farmers or with Ben Haynes. We don't need that kind of trouble around here."

Pa shook his head. "Now, Bea, he's just spouting off. I don't think he wants trouble any more than we do."

Pa may say the words, but Luke recognized the tone. His pa didn't really believe what he said, and Luke didn't either. Men like Fowler had caused problems all over the plains. The same could happen even in this town.

Luke turned back to his work. What Fowler did or didn't do was no real concern of his until it affected him or his family.

Chapter 3

When the clock reached two forty-five, Luke untied his apron. "Pa, Martin wants to go fishing. Since we're not busy, I'm going down to the creek to meet him. I'll be back before closing to finish up."

"That's fine, son. Alice and your ma are here to help." He waved and then turned back to his customer.

Luke gathered up his pole and fishing basket from the back storeroom and headed out. He hadn't decided exactly what he would ask Martin about his interest in Dove, but he needed to be clear in that matter. Backing away might be the only solution. No sense in embarrassing himself with another situation like he'd had with Lucy.

Fifteen minutes later he joined Martin at the creek. His friend held up a string with six fish on it and grinned. "Beat you to it. They're biting good today."

"Won't take me long to catch up with you." Luke baited his hook then dropped it into the water. The words he wanted to say wouldn't come to his mouth, but they rolled around in his head like marbles. Finally, after he had five fish on his string, he laid his pole aside and turned to Martin.

"I've been meaning to ask you something."

Martin relaxed his grip on his pole and peered at Luke. "What's that, my friend?"

"Are you courting Dove Morris?"

Martin said nothing for a moment. "No, I'm not. We're good friends because she and her family are friends of my parents." Then a knowing grin spread across his face. "Do I detect an interest on your part?"

Heat rose in Luke's face. "Maybe. I wanted to see what your feelings were first."

Martin chuckled. "Dove's a fine young woman, but to tell the truth, I have my sights set on Sarah Perkins."

Luke bent one leg and encircled it with his hands. "Miss Perkins is pretty, but she talks more than any other girl I know." The few times he'd been near her at church, Sarah started chattering and didn't know when to stop. Most of the time he never paid any attention to her. Then he grinned. "I guess since you always complain that you don't know what to say to the girls, you can just sit back and listen to her."

Martin's cheeks turned red, but before he had a chance to reply, his line dipped into the water and he busied himself with bringing in one of the fish that lurked in the sandy bottoms of Barton Creek. With seven now on his line, Martin began packing away his gear. Luke secured the string he'd caught to his creel.

"So, do you think it's a good plan to call on Dove?"

"Yes." He shoved a straw hat on his head. "But your ma won't like that. I overheard her talking with your pa at Lucy and Jake's wedding. Dove's name was mentioned, and your ma wasn't happy at all."

"Ma has some painful memories from her past, and it will take a lot to overcome them. I wish she would try to get to know Dove and her mother better, but Ma's heart has a wall of bad memories surrounding it."

"Whatever I can do to help, let me know." He tipped back his straw hat and shouldered his fishing pole. "Gotta get these back and get 'em cleaned for supper."

Luke picked up his own string. He'd have to clean them since he'd taken the afternoon off to catch them, but he didn't mind that. He could almost taste the seasoned cornmeal coating Ma used to fry them. They'd be crisp and golden brown in no time.

He quickened his steps toward the store when he spotted the Morris wagon hitched nearby. At least now he knew Martin's interests lay elsewhere, so he could pursue his interest in Dove Morris.

He raced up the back steps to the kitchen, where he poured water over the fish until he could clean them. After washing his hands and combing his hair, he checked the front window to see if the wagon was still there. It was.

Two minutes later, Luke strolled into the store. His mother stood with her back to him, examining a shelf of canned goods. Mrs. Morris waited while Pa completed her transaction. He searched the room for Dove and found her standing by a display near the door. She wore a cream-colored dress that emphasized her complexion and dark eyes.

Luke sucked in his breath as her gaze locked with his. Her eyes opened wide, and she covered her mouth with her fingertips. He took a step toward her, but she bolted from the store as if she were afraid of his coming near to her. He took a step to follow her.

"Luke, come here. I need you."

His mother's voice stopped him in his tracks. He turned to face her. No wonder Dove had run. Disapproval glowed in his mother's eyes with a brightness that frightened even him. He glanced back toward the door. Mrs. Morris grabbed up her parcels, shook her head at him, and then followed her daughter.

Luke studied his mother's face. The vein along her chin throbbed from the tight clenching of her teeth. All thoughts of going after Dove disappeared at the sight of her disapproval.

Luke's breath swooshed out. He had no choice. If he defied Ma now, he'd never make any headway in changing her attitude. "Yes, I'm coming." With a glance back at the door, he headed to the shelves.

Tears stung Dove's eyes. She grasped the hitching post next to the wagon. The lead horse nickered and tossed his mane, and she reached up to stroke the horse's nose. She'd heard Mrs. Anderson calling Luke, and the anger in her voice sent darts of fear into Dove's heart even now.

She squeezed her eyes shut. *I am such a coward.* It wouldn't have hurt to stay and say a few words to him or at least say hello, but then she remembered his mother's face and shuddered. She didn't want to think about what might have happened had Luke actually talked to her.

Ma's hand touched her shoulder. "I'm so sorry." She then placed her packages in the wagon bed. "That woman makes me so angry."

Dove grabbed her mother around the waist and rested her head on Ma's chest. "Why did I have to fall in love with the only boy in town whose mother hates me?"

"I know, dear, but sometimes we can't control what our hearts want to do where love is concerned. God will help you through this. You must seek God's will in all of your relationships." She held Dove tightly then stepped back.

"Let's get those tears wiped away and hurry on home. We're late as it is, and Pa will start to worry."

Dove used her hands to swipe her cheeks. At least Luke hadn't seen her crying. Relationships with young men were hard to understand. She climbed aboard the wagon, glad to be heading home.

Bea Anderson's heartbeat had raced at the sight of Luke approaching Dove. It still pounded as she spoke with him. "Will you get a couple of cans of those peaches off the top shelf for me?"

Luke peered at her for a moment then pulled the ladder over and stepped up on it. The look on her son's face when he saw Dove told her more than words ever could say. Keeping her resolve to ignore the Morris women when they came into the store became more difficult each time they came to town. Today she'd almost lost it when she realized Lukc was attracted to Dove. The cans had been a ruse to keep him from going out the door after that girl, but it had been all she could think of at the moment.

He handed her the cans. "You could have reached these for yourself."

Heat rose in Bea's face. "I felt a little dizzy and didn't want to climb the ladder." Indeed, seeing Dove had made her dizzy.

Luke stepped around her and headed for the door. A few moments later he turned back. "They're gone, so you don't have to worry now, Ma." He strode to the stairs. "I'm going up to clean the fish for supper."

She set the cans on a box in the aisle and hurried after Luke. By the time she reached their living quarters, Luke had begun scaling the fish. Bea bit her lip. She didn't know how to help him understand something so devastating to her when she herself didn't understand why it still hurt so much. Common sense reasoned that Dove and her mother had nothing to do with the massacres in Nebraska all those years ago, but Bea's heart wouldn't accept it.

Bea closed her eyes. She couldn't stop the images that raced through her head. She'd prayed so many times for the fear and hatred to be lifted, but no forgiveness would come for the savages who slaughtered her family. Carl urged her to forgive them, but he had not seen the murderous looks in the eyes of the men who invaded her home, or seen the blood and dead bodies of her beloved family. A chill raced through her bones at the memory of a painted warrior holding a bloody knife in one hand and her pa's scalp in the other, his blood-curdling call filling her ears. The images and sounds of that dreadful day were stamped forever in her memory.

Luke scraped furiously with his knife. If he kept on like that, he'd surely cut his fingers. She placed her hand on his shoulder. "I'm sorry you're angry right now."

He threw the knife into the sink and turned to face her. "But you're not sorry Dove is gone, are you?"

She had to be honest, or he'd never understand, but even honesty wouldn't salve his feelings at the moment. Bea sighed and shook her head. "No, I'm not, Luke. Dove's mother comes from a heritage that only wants to kill whatever gets in the way of their life. They killed my parents and my brothers and took away my sister. They took away all that was precious to me—my family!"

"I know, Ma. You've told that story often enough." His shoulders sagged, and his eyes held a sadness that she could not remove. "I'm truly sorry for that time in your life, Ma. It should never have happened, but it did, and now it affects everything you do."

Her maternal instincts wanted to wrap her arms around him and make things right, but she couldn't make anything right for him until she made things right with herself or helped Luke see that her feelings were justified. "Dove will find someone who can love her and give her a good life."

"Ma, can't you see that Dove and her family are not like those savages who killed your family?" His green eyes glinted with his plea.

Bea's heart ached with the truth, and it hurt, but not enough to change her mind. *Dear God, I can't even help my son. What am I to do?* The answer was plain, but forgiveness would not come. She turned and went back downstairs.

His mother's words echoed in Luke's head. They cut through his heart like the knife in his hands cut the fish. She clearly wouldn't approve of his calling on Dove. If only she'd get to know the Morris family better, Ma would see that they were a loving Christian family just like their own. Until that day came, he'd have to do everything he could to keep Dove from being hurt even more.

"Those fish will be good for supper."

Luke jumped. His sister, Alice, stood beside him. "I didn't hear you come in."

"Well, I don't clomp my feet coming up the stairs like you do." She reached into the cabinet for the tin of cornmeal. "I'll start getting things ready for dinner. Pa and Ma will be closing up the store soon."

She grasped a mixing bowl. "What did you do to make Ma

so sad? She came back into the store a few minutes ago and looked like she might cry."

"She was lecturing me about Dove, and I tried to reason with her. I know I hurt her, but I had to say what I feel." He hadn't meant to be cruel or say anything in anger, but he'd done it just the same. Things were so mixed up in his head. His mother deserved an apology for his words, but the anger would still be there. If he didn't curtail that anger now, it would fester and then boil over into words that would do more damage. He loved his mother, but he couldn't begin to understand her reasoning.

How he disliked confrontations, whether it was with Ma, a customer, or anybody else. Arguments never seemed to settle things in a satisfactory manner. Somehow he'd have to come to a compromise with his mother, but at that moment nothing would make a difference.

Alice tied a clean apron around her middle. "Do you think she'll ever change? Eli Morris and I have been talking at church, but I know he can never come calling on me with Ma feeling the way she does."

Luke shook his head. "That's just the way it is for now."

She retrieved the black iron skillet and set it on the stove top. "I like to believe that maybe someday there will be a chance for you and Dove or Eli and me to be more than friends."

"I don't know, but if we pray about it, maybe her heart will change."

Alice hugged him. "Luke, I'm so glad you're my brother, even if you do tease me and make my life miserable sometimes."

Luke laughed. "I love you, little sister, and teasing you just shows it. Remember that." He stepped back. "Now let's get this fish ready to fry and those potatoes peeled. Ma will be happy to see we've started supper."

"And maybe she won't be so sad, especially if our little brother is up to his usual antics."

"Will should give us plenty of laughter to serve up with our fish and potatoes."

He washed his hands then rubbed them with salt to get rid of the fish smell. His thoughts returned to Dove. God's intervention was the only thing that could make a difference, and if God ordained them to be together, nothing could prevent it from happening.

Chapter 4

Dove mounted Lightning and headed for Lucy and Jake's new home. The cloudless June sky meant another hot summer day. The early morning sun warmed her shoulders, but in less than two hours, the rays would send the temperatures into the ninety-degree range. The barren landscape with its dying grasses attested to the fact that the grasslands needed rain badly. None had fallen since the tornado last spring.

Lucy and Jake had come back from their wedding trip and moved into their new home. How wonderful it must be to have as much love and devotion from a man as she had seen in Jake, but that was something she may never know. At the moment Dove hated her Cherokee heritage, and that frightened her. Always before, she'd been proud of how her ancestors had endured hardships to make a life for themselves.

Lightning's hooves kicked up dust as they trotted across the field. A group of steers lumbered down to the creek for water. Pa and her brothers had gone out early this morning to make sure the water troughs for their own herd were filled, but if the rains didn't come, even the creek would dry up.

The new log house came into view. The people of Barton Creek had helped Jake with the house before he and Lucy married, and now it stood as a testament of his love for his bride. Dove anticipated seeing it finished and urged her horse to go faster.

When she dismounted at the front porch, Lucy opened the door wide. "Good morning. I have cold tea and fresh cookies I baked this morning while waiting." She hugged Dove and led her inside.

Dove removed her hat and glanced around the room. "You've done so much with your home since you came back." Only a few days since the return from their wedding trip, and the house had everything in place. Dove ran her hand over the back of an upholstered chair.

"With plenty of help from my aunt and uncle. After we wired the list of things I wanted from the house in Boston, Uncle Ben had them delivered out here while Jake and I were gone. Aunt Mellie, Aunt Clara, and Becky unpacked them, and then they came over and helped me put it all in place."

"It looks beautiful."

"Thank you. We even had a few pieces sent up from Jake's home in Texas. His uncle had stored many of the items from his parents' house and left them for Jake." She led Dove down a short hallway. "Here are our bedrooms, and we even have a room for bathing and other necessities. Right now, though, we're being very careful with water in this drought."

Dove admired the curtains and the wedding ring quilt on the bed that must have come from Boston. The rich walnut and carving were not seen in most homes in Oklahoma Territory.

"It's really wonderful, but tell me about your honeymoon. Where did you go?"

Lucy led them back to the kitchen. "We traveled by train from Guthrie to Fort Worth, where Jake checked out the stockyards. He and Uncle Ben are considering taking the herd there instead of up to Kansas."

Dove sat down and reached for the glass of tea on the table. "That sounds like an interesting trip." But not very romantic.

Like Dove's father, Jake always tended to business when he had the chance.

Lucy chose the chair across from her. "It was, but that's enough talk about me. What has been happening in your life? Luke certainly seemed interested in you at the wedding. Have you seen him since?"

Dove sipped her tea. Her mind whirled with how she should answer. Nothing important had happened, yet everything with Luke had changed. Now that he had shown some interest in her, her own interest in him had increased. She set the glass on the table. "I saw him at the store a few days ago, and it looked like he wanted to talk to me, but then his mother looked so angry I just ran away. I...I've avoided him since then."

Lucy's eyes opened wide. "You mean you and Luke haven't even spoken to each other?"

Dove bit the corner of her lip and leaned forward. "Mrs. Anderson hates me and my family. Every time she sees us, it's as though she's seeing what happened all those years ago."

Lucy grasped Dove's hand. "I'm so sorry. I know how she feels about Indians, but what happened to her was so long ago. Surely she can see you and your family aren't anything like those men."

"But that's the problem. She can't—or won't—forget. Mr. Anderson waits on Ma when we go into town to buy supplies. Mrs. Anderson won't even speak to or look at us. It's like we have some disease that might infect her." Even now the memory of Mrs. Anderson's stiff back and pursed lips sent chills through her. "What those men did to her family was terrible, but I had nothing to do with that. Makes me wish I wasn't Indian."

"Oh, Dove, don't wish that. You have a wonderful heritage. I think time and patience is what is needed to even start a change in her heart." Lucy patted Dove's hand. "One of these days she'll see her mistake." She rose from the table. "I think it's time for a little chocolate." Lucy retrieved a plate of cookies from the counter. "Chocolate always makes me feel better. Mr. Anderson orders it from back east for me."

Dove smiled. "Thanks, but I'm not sure anything will help at the moment."

"Remember how bleak it looked when we learned Jake had killed a man in Texas, and he had to go back to face the judge? But God used it all for good, and Jake came back a free man."

Dove nodded. Those winter months without knowing whether Jake would be hung or set free had been hard on her friend, but Lucy's faith had held firm. If only Dove could have that kind of faith.

"I was almost as excited as you were when he came back." She made a face. "Poor Luke. He loved you as much as Jake."

Luke had recovered from his love for Lucy quickly. Maybe he was only interested in Dove because she was the only other girl near his age in town besides Sarah Perkins. The thought chilled her.

"Perhaps, but Jake had my heart, and I think Luke realized it even when we went to the box social. I'd like to think he's moved on." She leaned forward and held Dove's hands again. "If there's anything I can do to help you win Luke's heart, let me know, and I'll do it. And you don't need to say pray for you because I'll be doing that anyway."

Dove's throat tightened with gratitude for her friend's concern. She blinked her eyes to ward off tears. "Thank you. I'm so glad you came to Barton Creek." But even as the words left her mouth, she realized that Lucy's parents' deaths had been the reason for that. She covered her mouth with her hands. "I'm sorry; I didn't mean I was glad your parents died, but I'm happy God had a place for you to come and be with your family."

"I am too. It's been almost a year, and I still miss them, but God had a plan all along. He had Jake all picked out for me before I ever met him."

"Then I must believe the same will be true for Luke and me, and I should be patient and wait for His timing. Right now I must be satisfied with having Luke as a friend." But even being a friend would be most difficult if his mother continued with her prejudice toward the Morris family.

No customers waited in the store as Luke restocked shelves and swept the back room. Boredom and restlessness filled his bones. Finally he removed his apron and hung it by the counter. "Pa, I'm going over to the bank. Maybe Martin will be ready for a break. I've been meaning to try out that new restaurant down by the depot."

His father glanced up from the stack of receipts he counted. "That's fine. We're not busy and won't be for a while. Too hot to be riding in a wagon to come to town. I'll be closing the store and heading upstairs for lunch in a few minutes anyway. Enjoy your meal. If the food is good, maybe I'll take your ma there for supper one night."

Luke grinned at that. His ma's cooking skills were quite evident in Pa's rotund middle, but she might appreciate a night off one evening. He ambled outside and down toward the bank. Pa was right. The temperature must be near one hundred, and it was still June. Not many people were outside and those who were seemed to have a definite destination in mind. He entered the bank and waved at Martin.

"Be with you in a minute, Luke." He spoke to the customer

in front of his cage. "I hope things will get better for you, Mr. Dawson."

The farmer shook his head. "Nothin's goin' to be better iffen we don't get rain, and get it soon." He shoved a few coins and a bill into his pocket. "Thank you, Mr. Fleming." Mr. Dawson turned to leave and nodded at Luke. "You can tell your pa I'll be down to pay on my bill soon." He shoved his hat on his head and walked out.

Martin shook his head. "The farmers are having a hard time, and the crops are going to dry up without rain. I don't see how most of them are going to make it if the crops fail."

"I know. Pa still offers them credit. He doesn't want to see any family go hungry." He looked around at the empty foyer. "Can you take a break? Thought it might be nice to eat at that new place, Dinah's, down by the depot."

"Sure." Martin turned toward the office at the back. "Father, I'm going with Luke to eat at Dinah's. Should be back soon."

Mr. Fleming waved from the back office. The other teller, an older bald man, grinned.

"Dinah's a mighty fine cook if I say so myself."

Martin laughed. "Thanks, George." When they were on the street, Martin said, "I think George is sweet on Miss Dinah. She's only been open three weeks, and he's had dinner there about every night."

"Then the food must be good or he's got an iron stomach." Luke shook his head. Even George had someone to be interested in. Seemed like everyone in town but him had somebody.

Martin punched his arm. "You got that look. Thinking about Dove?"

Luke shrugged. "I might be."

"Thought so." His friend pushed open the door of the restaurant.

Heavenly odors of roast beef, fresh baked bread, and apple pie accosted Luke's senses and whetted his appetite. His stomach rumbled. If the food tasted half as good as it smelled, they'd be in for a treat. But the main reason for this meal was not about food, although that was a bonus. He needed Martin's help, and about now, Luke would be willing to listen to anything his friend might suggest.

Dinah greeted them, her brilliant red hair piled on her head in a heap of curls. A bright yellow apron covered a dark green dress. "Howdy, boys. I have a table over here for you."

She led them to a vacant place for two by the windows. The room hummed with conversation. More people sat at the tables than could be seen walking the streets. She handed them each a menu then headed for the kitchen.

After another woman took their orders, Martin sat back and sipped a glass of water. "Now tell me what you're going to do about Dove."

Luke fingered his napkin. "I have no idea. I thought maybe together we'd come up with something I could do to be near her. We only have a few minutes at church on Sundays, and she hurried away when I tried to talk with her."

Martin arched an eyebrow. "I noticed that." He leaned forward. "I'm willing to do whatever I can to help, but first tell me something. Do you like Dove because she's a wonderful, caring person, or because she's sorta like forbidden fruit?"

Luke jerked back. He'd never thought of that. "The times I've been around her, I've seen something different about her." His faced heated. "Of course I didn't pay much attention to her last spring when Lucy was around. But when I saw her at the wedding, something in me snapped, and I knew I had to get to know her."

"If you truly care for her, my friend, you'll do everything in your power to be near her and win her heart, even if it means angering your mother."

"I'm not sure I can do that." His heart wanted one thing, but his mind told him something else. When it came to standing against his ma, he was a coward.

"When the day arrives that you truly love Dove with all your heart, nothing will stand in your way, not even your mother."

"How can you be so sure?"

"Because when your heart wants something bad enough, and you've prayed and sought God's will, you have to follow through or you'll be miserable." He paused a moment while their food was placed before them. When the girl left, he resumed. "I'm going to be defying my father in a few weeks if I get the letter I'm expecting."

Luke gulped. Martin couldn't be going against his father. It wasn't in his character. "What in the world for?"

"I want to be a minister, but my parents expect me to go into banking and carry on with my father. I've sent off an application to a ministerial school to follow my dream."

Luke stared at his friend. The announcement didn't surprise him. Martin had the heart of a servant and a love for God that would make him a wonderful minister.

Martin bowed his head, and Luke followed suit. He sent a silent prayer toward heaven, thanking God for the food but also asking for the courage to face his mother's prejudices and the assurance he was on the right path.

As they ate, Martin told him more about the school and its courses. Luke listened, but at the same time his mind filled with images of Dove. If he didn't love Dove enough to defy his mother, then he had no business trying to be friends with her.

The food, although probably very good, lost its appeal. His appetite gone, he pushed the potatoes on his plate with his fork.

Either he wanted to know Dove because he cared about her, or he was simply attracted because she was out of reach. He must come to a decision soon.

Chapter 5

Sam reached up and assisted Emily from the carriage. She searched the groups of people in the churchyard until she spotted Mellie Haynes. She squeezed her husband's hand. "I'm going over to speak with Mellie. I need her advice."

He leaned down and kissed her cheek. "I'll meet you inside then."

She waved at her friend and hurried toward her. Only ten minutes until their Sunday school began, but that should be enough time to seek the advice needed.

Mellie grinned. "Good morning, Emily. It's good to see you today."

Emily grasped her arm and motioned toward the corner of the building. "I need your wisdom."

"Is this about Dove and Luke?"

When they were more secluded, Emily nodded. "Yes, but how did you know?"

"Lucy came for a visit yesterday and expressed her concern about them."

"I don't know what to do." That wasn't entirely true, but she needed the reinforcement and support her friend would give. Emily didn't trust her own judgments when her daughter was involved. "Dove really cares about him. She has for several years, but she's almost nineteen, and her heart yearns for his love. Now he's acting interested, but I just can't see Luke being able to pursue her as long as Bea holds such prejudice against us."

Mellie nodded. "I understand. My heart was so torn when Lucy fell in love with Jake. He wasn't a Christian, and we knew very little about his background."

"That's why I seek your wisdom. You handled that situation so well." Mellie's and Lucy's faith and strength during those days had made a lasting impression. Emily needed that kind of faith now. "I don't know how you stayed so strong. I would have fallen apart and given him up for dead. And you didn't let Bea Anderson's or Charlotte Frankston's words affect your belief in Jake."

Mellie smiled and wrapped an arm around Emily's shoulders. "Those words hurt more than you know, and you can truly understand how I felt. Aunt Clara has the wisdom in our family. I do believe God sent her here at just the right time for that exact purpose. She kept me on the right road of trust."

Emily did understand, but Charlotte and Bea had hurt her family more with their lack of words than with them. Words hurt, but their attitudes and behavior toward her family stung much more deeply. "Aunt Clara seems to care a lot about Dove. Perhaps we should ask her opinion. All I want to do is protect my daughter."

"Just like I did with Becky when Charlotte said her son could no longer be friends with her." She glanced over to where Becky talked and mingled with the younger folk.

Emily turned to observe for herself. Bobby stayed on the fringes, but his gaze followed Becky wherever she moved. "Do you see that? Bobby really cares about Becky. I wouldn't be surprised to see them together in the future."

Then she spotted Dove speaking with one of the other girls, Sarah Perkins. If only Dove could have the same adoration from an eligible young man that Bobby displayed for Becky, she wouldn't worry so.

Mellie hugged her. "Emily, our best plan for now is to hope that Bea Anderson's heart will be changed. Only God can do that, but we can help by showing love and setting an example for others. If Dove and Luke are meant to be together, nothing will keep them apart. Love will find a way. Just remember what God has done for Lucy and Jake."

Emily would never forget Lucy and Dove praying together, asking God to take care of Jake and bring him home. God did answer seemingly impossible prayers.

"Dove and Luke have a great deal to overcome, and the road is not going to be smooth. With the obstacles in their path, our only hope is in the Lord. Emily, I promise to pray for them every day, and I know Aunt Clara and Lucy will too. You're not going to fight this battle alone."

Mellie's words comforted Emily. No matter what might lie in the days ahead, with God and her friends behind her she could help her daughter through anything that came along. She tightened the strings of her bonnet. "Thank you. I appreciate it more than I can ever say. Now let's go to church. I need to hear some good preaching."

They headed toward the building, but out of the corner of her eye, Emily saw a flash of green. She turned in time to see Luke heading for the group of young people, but Dove dashed up the steps and inside before he reached them. Pain for her daughter squeezed her heart. *Please, Lord, don't let her be hurt today.*

Dove hurried into the classroom and sat near the window, staring at the floor. Luke followed her in, but she dared not look at him.

"Dove, may I sit here?"

The toes of his polished black shoes stood in her line of vision, and her heart beat so furiously that he surely must have heard it. She swallowed hard and nodded, her voice refusing to cooperate.

"Thank you. I've wanted to speak with you a number of times, but you are always in such a hurry." Luke tugged at the collar of his shirt. "I want to apologize for the way my mother treats you and your mother when you come into the store. You have to understand her history to know what makes her act like that."

Dove raised her eyes to look into his. This close she could see the golden flecks in his green eyes. The concern shown in them melted her insides, and she fought the urge to flee once again.

He reached out to touch her hand then pulled it back. "I'm not going to hurt you. I just want to get to know you better. All I know about you is that you are half Cherokee, a Christian, and a loyal friend to Lucy Starnes. But there's so much more."

A lump formed in her throat. If she were to ever have a relationship with Luke, she must trust him. "What is it you want to know?"

"Everything. What you like to do. What music you like. What are your favorite foods? If you have plans for your future, and all that kind of thing."

Some of those would be easy to answer, but the last one would take some thinking. She didn't really know herself what her plans might be, although she would like to be a teacher. The most she wanted was to be a regular citizen of Barton Creek without all the animosity she so often saw.

Before she had an opportunity to answer any of the questions, other young people came into the room. Lucy's cousin Matt came over and greeted Dove. Luke remained by her side, and the others filled the chairs around them. The only person who didn't speak to her directly was Caroline Frankston, but she smiled when Dove glanced her way.

A lively discussion of a passage from 1 Peter ensued as the teacher opened up for questions. Peter admonished believers to be vigilant because the devil was seeking those whom he could devour. Dove didn't contribute to the conversation but contemplated her own situation. Satan could certainly invade the hearts of Christians and cause them to do hurtful things to both themselves and others. She'd pray even harder for Mrs. Anderson in the days ahead. Satan kept those memories and images alive in her mind, and the Lord was the only one who could remove them.

As the class came to a close, talk began about the July Fourth celebration coming up soon. The church planned a big potluck dinner, and they also planned on having some games for the children. Since the holiday fell on Sunday, the church celebration would coincide with those planned for the town on Saturday.

Luke turned to Dove. "Can you think of any games we might include?"

For the first time she actually became a part of the group. "I think throwing a ball at those wooden bottles like we saw at that carnival over in Guthrie would be a lot of fun."

Luke grinned. "Then I'll have to work on my pitching so I can win a prize. And what about blind man's bluff or something like that for the younger children?"

They chattered on a few more minutes before dispersing to attend the worship service in the main building. From the corner of her eye, Dove spotted Caroline sitting all alone. Matt had spoken to her a few moments ago, but now he'd disappeared.

Caroline stood then started tentatively toward Dove. Luke

intercepted her. "What are you going to say to Dove? Another of your mother's rude remarks?"

Her face twisted to a frown. "I'm sorry I didn't speak earlier. Ma won't allow it."

"Then go on back to your mother and keep your hateful remarks to yourself." Dove's mouth dropped open, and Caroline's eyes blinked before she turned and ran from the room.

"Luke Anderson, how could you have been so rude? You hurt her feelings, and she was simply saying she's sorry. That was most uncalled for. You don't have to take your own anger out on her." Dove grabbed her Bible and ran after Caroline. Dove hoped she'd have a chance to speak with her before Mrs. Frankston saw them and made matters worse. Rudeness was a side of Luke she'd never seen before, and she didn't like it at all.

Luke groaned when Dove hastened through the door. He'd made a mess of that conversation. What was worse, Dove had been right. The remark was totally uncalled for. He'd never done anything like that before.

Martin stepped to his side. "What was that all about?"

"I probably just ruined any chance I have of being friends or anything else with Dove." He still couldn't believe his own stupidity. He'd acted no better than Caroline, her mother, or his mother for that matter.

"I must say Dove didn't look very happy with you."

"I know. Why can't Caroline do what she wants to do? Her mother has her reined in so tight I don't see how Matt Haynes ever gets a chance to be with her."

Martin shook his head. "Listen to yourself, Luke. Didn't you tell me you wouldn't go against your mother? That's all Caroline did. She respected her mother's wishes."

His friend's words fell like lead bullets in Luke's soul. Just as his words had hurt Caroline, his friend's words hurt now, but Martin spoke the truth. Luke sank into a chair, arms on his knees and his head in his hands. "You're right. I just wanted to protect Dove from any more hurt, and I ended up hurting a friend who's done nothing to me. Dove will probably never speak to me again."

Martin sat beside him. "Look, apologize to Caroline and to Dove. Let them know you're sorry for your actions. If Dove really cares about you, she'll forgive you."

Luke shook his head. "I hope so, but I wouldn't blame her for not speaking to me at all."

"Maybe I can do something about that. Sarah and I were talking about you and Dove. We think we have a way that the two of you can be together and get to know each other better."

"And how is that?" At the moment Luke wanted to try anything to earn Dove's forgiveness.

"We'll talk about it after the service. If we don't get in there, our parents are going to be hunting for us. Come on."

Luke followed Martin to the main building and scooted into his seat with his family just before the music began. His mother glared at him. He'd hear from her later, but at the moment nothing she said could be worse than the remorse he held in his soul. He sneaked a glance in Dove's direction, but she stared straight ahead, her mouth set in a firm line.

He was no better than his mother or Charlotte Frankston with their hurtful words. And he was guilty of the same behavior he accused Caroline of having. He breathed in deeply then exhaled. Seeking forgiveness from Dove and giving forgiveness to his mother were the only ways to make things right. But first he must ask the Lord's forgiveness and apologize to Caroline. He bowed his head in prayer. At least he could take the first step right now.

Chapter 6

After the service ended, Luke rushed to catch Caroline before her family left. He spotted her near her family's carriage. "Wait, Caroline. I must speak with you."

Caroline narrowed her eyes to slits. "I have nothing to say to you, Luke Anderson."

"Please, Caroline."

She glanced at her father, who nodded. She turned to Luke. "If you must, then let's step away from my parents."

Luke blew out his breath in relief and followed Caroline to a less-crowded spot.

She stopped and said, "Have your say, Mr. Anderson, and let's be done with it."

He rolled the brim of his hat in his hands. "I…I just want to say I'm sorry for what I said earlier. I had no call to be angry with you or say those things. Fact is, I was angry with myself."

Caroline shook her head. "You hurt my feelings, Luke, but if you're really sorry, I forgive you." She reached out and hugged him.

Luke removed her hands from around his waist and stepped back, heat rising in his face. "Thank you, Caroline, I think." She turned and ran back to her family. He glanced toward the Morris family, and Dove's beautiful smile sent his heart into somersaults. Doing something right felt good, and he hoped Dove would forgive him too.

Martin clamped a hand on Luke's shoulder. "Now that was a nice thing to see. I think it impressed Dove, and a hug from a pretty girl like Caroline was a nice reward."

"Oh, that. She's the same age as Alice. I hadn't really thought of her as more than Alice's friend. But now that you mention it, no wonder Matt Haynes is smitten with her." He grinned. "Anyway, Dove's opinion is the one that counts. And speaking of Dove, what's that plan you spoke of?"

Martin pursed his lips a moment. "Tell you what. Come by my home this afternoon, and I'll tell you all about it. Not enough time now."

Luke would rather hear it now, but with Sunday dinner ahead, it was best to wait. "All right, but it had better be a good idea. I'll come around three if that will work."

"Fine, my friend, and I think you'll be pleased." Martin's grin broadened, and he winked as he walked away.

Luke shook his head. No telling what Martin might come up with. He wanted to skip back home, but that didn't seem to be appropriate for a young man of nineteen, so he just walked a little faster but whistled while he did.

Bea listened for Luke to come up the back stairs. She heard his whistle before he came inside. Something at church must have made her son happy. If she hadn't left so soon to check on the pot roast of beef she had cooking, maybe she'd know. Perhaps he'd talk about it at the dinner table.

He kissed her cheek after he entered the kitchen. "Something smells wonderful, Ma."

She poked his side with the handle of her spoon. "You know what it is. Now get on with washing up. It's ready to serve."

After Carl said the blessings, Bea passed the basket of bread to Luke. "Something good must have happened to give you such a good mood today."

Alice giggled. "Caroline Frankston gave him a big hug after church."

Bea's eyes opened wide. "She did? Now what was that for? She's not one for public display like that."

Luke's cheeks reddened. "She was just thanking me for something I said. She's a sweet girl."

"And my best friend, so you be careful, big brother." Alice frowned and helped herself to the potatoes.

"Don't go jumping to any conclusions. She's like another little sister, and the one I have is getting to be a pest lately."

Alice glared at him. Before she could come up with a retort, Bea said, "Now, come, it's the Lord's day. Let's not be bickering." She handed Luke a bowl of peas. "Tell me what your group is planning for the July Fourth celebration."

"Oh, a few games for the children. Dove mentioned a game where you throw a baseball at some bottles. They had such a booth over at the fair in Guthrie last spring." Luke gazed at her, almost daring her to respond to the mention of Dove's name.

She kept her face unruffled. "I remember." So, Dove was the real reason for Luke's good mood. If only she didn't bring up such terrible memories, she might be a nice girl for her son, but for her own peace of mind, she needed to keep them apart. Someday he'd understand.

Her family talked while her mind went to work. That new university down at Stillwater might be just the place for Luke. He could earn a degree and still be close to home but far enough away to forget about Dove. That plan would be perfect.

Tomorrow she'd set it into motion by writing to the university and inquiring about admission. He'd be so surprised.

With her plan in place, the weight in her heart lifted.

After dinner Luke headed for Martin's home, walking along the hard-packed dirt of Main Street. He turned a corner and spotted the Fleming and Frankston homes, the largest on the block. Someday he'd build a house like theirs for his wife, one with scrolls and cutouts in the trimming and a porch that covered three sides of the house.

He turned a brass knob in the middle of the door and heard the ringing bell in the hallway.

Martin opened the door and greeted him. "Right on time, as usual. People could set their watches by you, Mr. Anderson."

"Maybe so, but I can't abide tardiness." Luke rocked on his heels. "So, what's the big plan?"

Martin nodded toward the porch swing. "Let's sit out here and talk. Mother will bring lemonade shortly as well as some cookies—that is, if those two brothers of mine haven't eaten them all."

Luke laughed. "That wouldn't surprise me." The twin boys, twelve years old, always stocked up on candy and sweets when they came into the store. "Can't understand why they're not fat except they have the energy of two more besides themselves."

"That they do. Sometimes they wear me out." Martin sat on the swing. A trellis of ivy provided a cool spot out of the sun.

"But we're not here to talk about your brothers. Tell me what you meant this morning about a plan." Luke plopped down beside Martin and set the swing to moving.

Martin gave it another shove with his foot and laughed.

"I believe you are a little too impatient, and that leads me to believe you're ready to court Miss Dove."

"Not court her, but to be a friend first. I don't believe her father would give permission for me to officially call on her." Not in a million years would Mr. Morris let Luke see Dove as long as his mother acted the way she did. This would have to be done in small steps, but he had no clue as to what the first one would be.

"That's true, and that's why my plan is such a good one." He sat back with a smirk on his lips. "I'm going to ask Dove to go for a ride with me, and then you'll show up. I'll go off a little ways, and you two will have a chance to talk and visit. That way you can see her and not have to deceive your mother. You can't help it if you run into us out riding, or if you go with me and we happen to meet her on the way."

Luke's eyes opened wide. That might work. Then again, Dove would need to agree to such an arrangement, and he didn't see that happening. "Sounds like a good idea, but I fear Dove may not be willing to cooperate."

"I'll talk to her, and we'll work it out. You'll see. This idea will be just the thing to give you a chance to talk without interfering adults around."

Mrs. Fleming stepped onto the porch carrying a tray laden with two glasses of yellow liquid and a plate of cookies. "And who's an interfering adult?" She set the refreshments on a wicker table near the swing.

"Not you, Mother. We're just two young men talking about our independence."

She pursed her lips. "I see. Well, enjoy yourself. I don't want to *interfere* with your conversation."

If not for the twinkle in her eye, she might have sounded

angry, but Mrs. Fleming was a kind woman with a mind of her own. He could see where Martin got his spark.

He sipped his lemonade then bit into a sugar cookie. If Martin's plan worked, he'd have a real chance to apologize to Dove, and then perhaps she'd talk with him.

Dove pulled on her boots. A ride on Lightning might clear her head. The incident with Luke didn't make sense. She'd never seen him so hurtful to anyone or anything. At least he'd apologized to Caroline after the service. He deserved some credit for that, and Caroline had hugged him. That must mean she was satisfied with his apology. Now the question remained whether he'd seek forgiveness from Dove.

She slipped her hat over her head and let it hang on her shoulders. Her hair, plaited in one long braid down her back, hung under the white hat. She found her parents in the parlor. Pa dozed over the open book in his lap, and Ma had her crochet. "I'm going to ride over to the creek."

Ma glanced up from her current project. "Don't you think it's too hot for riding?"

"No, I enjoy being outdoors. The heat doesn't bother me." Besides, she'd die of boredom if she had to stay here and sit around doing needlework or reading. Neither of those held any appeal for her at the moment.

Pa raised his head. "Then take a canteen of water with you."

Dove nodded and headed for the kitchen, where she filled the round container with water from the pump. She slung the belt of it over her shoulder. When she stepped outdoors, a rider approached. Martin Fleming waved to her. How unusual.

He'd never before come out for a visit this late on a Sunday afternoon.

"Hello, Dove. Were you going somewhere?" He stopped his horse nearby and pushed his hat back on his head.

"I'm going to ride Lightning. What brings you out here?"

"I wanted to talk with you. Do you mind if I go along with you?"

"No, but I have to saddle up." Maybe he wanted to ask her about Sarah Perkins. They would make a nice couple, and Sarah was sweet on Martin.

He followed her into the stable and helped her with the saddle. She tightened the cinch and checked the bridle and bit before leading the stallion from the building. She and Martin mounted their horses. "I was planning to ride to the creek. That all right with you?"

"Of course. Lead the way."

They rode in silence for a ways. Dove waited for him to explain what he wanted to talk about. Finally he tugged on his hat and cleared his throat.

"Dove, Luke Anderson would really like to speak with you and apologize for his behavior this morning, and he doesn't want to wait until next Sunday."

"I see. And how am I supposed to do that when his mother stands in the way every time I'm around or get near her son?" Luke should have come with Martin if he really wanted to apologize, but she'd listen to Martin just to see what he offered.

"I think we've come up with a plan." He pulled his horse aside. "Let's stop here in the shade, and I'll explain what I have in mind."

Dove reined in her horse and dismounted. She lightly secured the straps around the tree, and Martin did the same. She stared up at him. He must be as tall as Jake Starnes, and that was one reason she had never considered Martin as more than a friend. Her neck hurt from having to look up at him from her short stature.

He removed his hat and raked his hand through his dark hair. "Now here's the plan. I'm going to ask you to go for a ride with me."

She opened her mouth to speak, but he held up his hand. "No, wait until you hear me out. While we're out riding, Luke will happen along and meet up with us. I'll then go off and leave you two alone so you can talk."

Leave them alone? Dove furrowed her brow. Pa wouldn't like that at all. "But I can't be all alone with him when I'm supposed to be with you."

"I won't be out of sight, and you'll still be with me but talking to Luke. This way you can be together without angering your parents."

His plan did have merit, and she wouldn't have to deceive her parents. One other thing bothered her. "But what about Sarah Perkins? I thought you were sweet on her now and would be calling on her."

Martin laughed. "I am and I will, but she's in on the plan too and thinks it's a splendid idea. She even said she'd accompany Luke sometime, and then when we meet, we can switch."

Her mind weighed all the consequences if her parents or the Andersons found out, but they would only know that Luke was with Sarah and Dove with Martin, and both sets of parents would be satisfied with that. Common sense told her the plan was risky, and perhaps a bit less than honorable, but her heart told her that finally she'd have a chance to be near Luke. Her heart won the battle. "All right, I'll do it."

Chapter 7

Tuesday morning Luke checked the inventory list against what was on the shelf and marked off the items. Soon the telegraph and telephone would make replacing inventory much easier. They'd still have to go over to Guthrie to pick up shipments, but that didn't bother him. By the time he became a partner with his father, the mercantile business would be even bigger than now, and one train headed for central Oklahoma would come through Barton Creek.

His mother's voice sounded behind him. "I'm going up to fix our lunch now, and Alice will be helping me. If Will comes in this way, send him to wash up. Be sure to keep an eye out for customers and help your pa." She patted his back then proceeded up the stairs to their living quarters.

He shook his head and grinned. Such a creature of habit, his mother never failed to say the same words to him every time she left him in the store to help Pa. It was as though he'd never helped to take care of the place before. Luke continued with his counting and checking. If other customers entered, he'd hear the bell over the door in plenty of time to help Pa.

A few minutes later the bell jangled. Luke laid his pen and pad on the shelf and turned to assist whoever had come in. He sucked in his breath. Dove and her mother walked up to the counter. Mrs. Morris held a list in her hands, which she handed to Pa. Together they began to discuss some of the items.

Dove ambled over to the dress goods and fingered some of the material.

Now was the chance to speak with Dove and apologize. With Ma upstairs and Pa busy with Mrs. Morris, they'd have some privacy. Quickly he crossed the room and spoke to her in a low voice.

"Good morning, Dove. It's nice to see you again."

No welcoming smile returned his greeting, but he plunged ahead. "I want to apologize for my behavior this past Sunday. I allowed my anger toward Mrs. Frankston to spill over to Caroline. In doing so I embarrassed you, and for that I'm deeply sorry. Will you forgive me?"

Her eyes, black as the night sky, locked with his for a moment. She held her head high. "I forgive you, Luke. This time."

His breath escaped in a swoosh. "Thank you. It won't happen again; I promise." And that was a promise he intended to keep.

This time a smile graced her lips. "I believe you."

"Thank you again." He hesitated then said, "Martin Fleming came out to see you Sunday. He said you'd agreed to his idea."

"Yes, I did, but I've had second thoughts. You must realize that I will never deceive my parents."

"Of course not, and I understand that. Martin and I have a plan for Friday evening. He'll tell you about it, but it's essentially what he told you we'd do. I'll meet you two wherever you plan to go, and then you and I will have a chance to talk."

She crossed her arms at her waist. "I said I would go the first time. We'll have to see how it works out. I cannot and will not lie to my parents."

"And I don't expect you to do so." But then, he'd be lying to his parents. No, he wouldn't, he just wouldn't be telling them everything. His conscience pricked, but he brushed it away. At this point he'd do anything to spend time with Dove.

"Dove, I want to know you better. That can never happen if we don't have the chance to be with each other."

"I don't know, Luke. With your mother so opposed to me and my family, I can't see how this will ever work."

He had to do something to convince her to at least let him spend some time with her. "I understand, Dove, and I admire you for not wanting to deceive your mother, but I believe that we can overcome any obstacles if we really want to be together."

Her eyes narrowed. "Including your mother?"

Luke gulped. "Yes, including my mother." As much doubt as he had about that happening, he had to believe it would. It might take a miracle, but then God was in the miracle business. He wanted to reach out for Dove's hand but restrained the impulse. After all, he wasn't exactly courting her.

"Dove, let me visit with you this one time on Friday. If you still have doubts, I will step away and wait until you're ready." It would be difficult, but he would do it just to gain her trust.

She nodded. "All right. This one time. We'll see about others." She glanced over his shoulder. "My mother is ready to leave. Good-bye."

Mrs. Morris's scrutiny didn't encourage Luke at all. Her eyes pierced through him as though she knew what he thought. They left, and he turned from the door to find his father watching with a thoughtful expression on his face. "Son, don't do anything you might come to regret later on."

"I won't." And that was a promise.

Bea had seen the Morris wagon out front, and she waited until she knew they were gone before heading downstairs.

"Lunch is ready," she called as she stepped into the store.

Luke turned with such a guilty look on his face that Bea's stomach lurched. She should have been a few minutes sooner so she could have seen what had transpired to give that expression to Luke. Only one way to find out.

She nodded at him. "The meal is on the table. Go up and join Alice and Will. I want to speak with your father."

"Yes, ma'am." He untied his apron, laid it across the counter, and trudged up the stairs.

She waited until he'd closed the door to the living quarters before turning to her husband. "Carl, what happened when the Morrises were here?"

"Nothing. Luke spoke with Dove for a few minutes, but that's all. He was just being courteous. Don't go reading into it more than there is."

"I don't have to read anything into anything. I have eyes, and I can see for myself that Luke is interested in her. It's a good thing I sent off for that information about the university. That's the place for Luke now. It'll do him good to be in another town where he'll meet more people."

Carl removed his apron then placed his arm around Bea's shoulders. "The university would be good for him for more than your reason, but it should be Luke's decision to go. What if he doesn't want to leave Barton Creek?"

Bea thought of that but pushed it from her mind. He'd have to agree, but she didn't know what to do if he didn't. She sighed. "We'll take care of that when the time comes." She patted his hand. "Now, my meal is getting cold. We can discuss this later."

Together they climbed the stairs to join their family.

Dove rode silently beside her mother while one of the ranch hands handled the team of horses. Her mother's expression did relay the idea that they would discuss the incident in the store once they were home. At least Ma respected her privacy and didn't question her in front of the driver.

As much as she wanted to see Luke, she would not get her hopes up until it actually happened. Mrs. Anderson could still find out and put a stop to it some way. Dove bit her lip. One of her dreams coming true lay before her, but she couldn't squelch the fear that rose with every thought of it.

Maybe she needed to visit with Lucy again and find out more about what was going on in the heart when one was in love. Dove's own heart wanted to be with Luke as much as possible, but her common sense told her to beware.

The wagon rolled into the ranch yard, and the driver pulled to a stop. He helped Dove down from the back then turned his attention to her mother.

Dove picked up a few parcels and headed for the house. "Ma, after we eat, I would like to ride over and visit with Lucy."

Ma grabbed up the few remaining packages. "I think that would be fine, dear. You must invite her and Jake over for dinner some evening soon."

Dove hurried to finish her meal, light today because the men were out rounding up strays and checking feeding water levels. As soon as she helped clean up, she scurried outside to keep her mother from asking questions. She would be glad to answer them later, but not now. Dove mounted her horse and headed for the Starnes spread.

Drop-in visits such as this were not encouraged, but Lucy was her best friend, and they had always enjoyed visiting each other. Lucy had not been married then, and her time might not be as free as Dove's. Still, her friend could provide much-needed advice.

Lucy welcomed her with a delighted smile. "Oh, I'm so glad you came to see me. Jake is off with Uncle Ben and the others working on the range. It does get lonely without another person around to talk to."

Dove followed her into the spacious parlor. Its high ceiling and enormous oil-lit chandelier never ceased to amaze her. She stared at it now. "How in the world do you light that thing at night?"

Lucy laughed. "It's like the ones back home but made of oak instead of glass crystals." She strolled over to the wall and unwound a rope that let the wagon-wheel-shaped light down to a level where all the lamps could be lighted then raised back to the ceiling.

"How clever. Pa must see this."

Lucy returned the light to its original position and wound the rope around the hook on the back wall. "I have fresh lemonade made, and Jake chipped some ice chunks for me this morning. Come on into the kitchen, and I'll pour us each a glass."

After they were seated with the drink before them, Lucy leaned forward. "I don't believe this is just a casual visit. More trouble with Luke and his mother?"

Dove gripped her glass, the icy cold numbing her hands. Lucy knew her too well. "Yes and no. Luke and Martin have devised a plan for us to be together. Luke says he wants to know me better."

"That's not a bad thing. What does Martin propose doing?"

"He is going to call on me, and then while we are riding, we'll run into Luke. Martin will then leave us alone—well, not really alone, but he'll give Luke and me a chance to talk."

"That will work as long as his parents don't know about it."

Dove leaned forward and grabbed her friend's hand. "I don't want to lie to Ma or Pa. It's a sin to lie. Perhaps they shouldn't have told me what they planned." If that had been the case, she would have thought Luke's appearance a true coincidence. Things were getting too complicated.

"That's true. Forget the circumstances, and tell me how you feel about seeing Luke. Do you want to spend time with him?"

"Oh, yes, I do. My heart beats faster just talking about him."

"Then you should go and see what develops. Up front, if you say you are going on a picnic or a ride with Martin and you do just that, you are not lying. But I do believe you should let your mother know whenever Luke does show up at these outings. As long as you are honest like that, you will gain more trust."

"Oh, Lucy, I knew you would have the best solution." Her heart filled with happiness. On Friday she would be spending time with Luke with no worry about anyone around frowning upon it.

Lucy reached over and grasped Dove's hands. "Aunt Mellie and your mother talked with each other after your last visit. She and Aunt Clara would like to see the two of you together. Don't hesitate to seek our help. We care a great deal about you, and we want to see you happy."

"Thank you. You always make me see things in a better light." Dove stood. "I really must leave and get back to help Ma with supper preparations, but knowing her, she'll have everything done by the time I get there."

Lucy walked with her to the door. "Just remember, praying for Mrs. Anderson to have a change of heart isn't a selfish prayer. Until she resolves the memories of her past and faces them, she can never be truly happy. I learned that with Jake. We could have run away together, but the killing back in Texas would have forever hung over our lives. Then he did go back to face his past, and prayer brought him back to me. I believe prayer will bring Mrs. Anderson to a new understanding of herself."

Dove hugged her friend. "Oh, I do pray so. You are such a comfort to me." She stepped back. "Thank you again, and tell Jake I said hello."

She went out and mounted Lightning, then turned to wave before riding homeward. A cool breeze stirred the grasses. The sun hung lower in the sky, but her heart rose higher in the realization that Luke cared for her and was willing to risk his mother's wrath to be with her. "Thank You, God." Her voice rang out across the prairie as she spurred her horse into a run. Friday couldn't come soon enough.

Friday finally arrived, and Dove prepared for Martin's visit. She chose her split skirt and a yellow blouse for riding. Her nerves had calmed considerably since this morning when it seemed she dropped everything she handled. Now, the joy in her heart at seeing Luke overrode the few ripples of anxiety rolling in her stomach.

She braided her thick black hair into one long plait down her back and tied it with a yellow bow to match her shirt. What if something happened and Luke couldn't come? What if his mother made him stay and help in the store? What if… She stopped and remembered her mother's words—that what-ifs were the things we worry about that usually never happen.

A deep breath sent the thoughts scurrying as horse's hooves sounded in the yard. She pulled back the lace curtain and spotted Martin below dismounting. Dove pinched her cheeks, smoothed her hair, and hurried downstairs to meet him.

Martin stood talking with her brothers Hawk and Eli, who, by the looks of their clothes, had just come in from the range. They could have at least cleaned up a little before coming into the house. But they did that only when Ma caught them first.

She scowled at them, and Hawk shrugged and grinned. He knew what caused her frown. Hawk shook Martin's hand. "You and Dove have a good ride. I saw that picnic basket, so I suppose we won't have the pleasure of your company at dinner."

He reached out to hug Dove, but she sidestepped his embrace. She didn't want his dusty, smelly arms around her clean shirt. "No, you don't." She grinned up at Martin. "I'm ready to go if you are."

"Quite ready." He nodded toward her brothers. "I'll take good care of her and have her back before sundown."

Dove grabbed her hat from the rack by the door and hurried outside. She'd saddled her own mount earlier and left him in the corral. Together they rode off toward the part of the creek running through Morris property. Although he didn't ride all the time like her brothers, Martin sat tall in his saddle and rolled with the gait of the horse. He wore Levi pants like her brothers and a solid blue shirt that enhanced his blue eyes. He was tall and thin and needed some meat on his bones. He reminded her of the character Ichabod Crane, although Martin was by far more handsome than Irving's schoolteacher.

"Thank you for setting this up, Martin. I had my doubts about the plan, but Lucy Starnes helped me sort it out."

"I'm glad she did. I think you'll enjoy getting to know Luke."

Dove laughed. "And you're sure Sarah Perkins is OK with what we're doing?"

"As I told you before, it's quite all right with her. In fact, she helped me come up with this idea. She had planned to come with Luke, but her mother had something else for her to do."

"Hmm, I'll have to thank her on Sunday. She's a dear, sweet girl." Sarah was among those who befriended her and chatted with her before their Bible class each week. In school, Sarah had sat in the desk across from Dove, and they had studied together. Sarah and Martin would make an ideal couple.

Martin slowed the horses as they neared the creek banks. "People say Sarah talks too much, but when a person never knows what to say around girls, she makes it quite easy. All I have to do is listen and answer in the appropriate spots."

This brought more laughter from Dove. "That's true, but you never have trouble talking with me." She'd never felt uncomfortable or at a loss for words around him either, but that's what made a true friendship.

Martin echoed her thoughts. "You are a friend. I know whatever I say won't be misunderstood or laughed at." He dismounted then helped her down.

"I understand. I get completely mindless around Luke and never know what to talk about. I hope it's not like that today." She'd listen to him first and answer questions, but she hoped he wouldn't expect her to choose their topics. If he did, it would be a very quiet visit.

Martin spread the cloth his mother packed in the basket and nodded for Dove to have a seat. She sat and leaned back with her hands behind her. The day so far had been beautiful, and when Luke arrived, it would be even better.

The basket contained fried chicken, home-canned pickles, homemade bread, and slices of Mrs. Fleming's popular chocolate cake. Dove and her mother had decided the secret ingredient for the unusual flavor of the cake to be cinnamon and some of that new chocolate powder the store carried. She could taste the thick chocolate icing even now.

When it was spread, she realized he had three plates and three sets of utensils. That must mean Luke would join them soon. At that moment Lightning's nickering caught her attention. She looked backward to see Luke riding up.

He swung down from the saddle. "Just in time, I see." Luke grinned broadly and plopped down beside Dove. "Hmm, that chicken looks good enough to eat." He reached for a piece.

Martin caught his hand. "Not before we bless it, Mr. Anderson."

Luke grinned and drew back his hand. "Yes, sir, Preacher Martin."

Heat rose in Dove's cheeks. If she moved even slightly, her arm would brush against Luke's. Surely he must hear the *thump-bump* of her heart. She bowed her head as Martin prayed for their meal.

As soon as Martin said "Amen," Luke grabbed a chicken leg. Then, as though remembering his manners and Dove beside him, he held the plate toward her. "Would you like a piece?"

Dove selected one then reached for the pickles. Her hand shook, and she let go of the jar, afraid she'd drop it if she picked it up. She clasped her hands together in her lap. If she didn't get her nerves under control, she'd spoil the entire evening. She inhaled deeply and counted to three before exhaling. That was better.

She smiled at Luke, who had started on his second piece of meat. "Mrs. Fleming included some of her famous cake, so be sure to save room for it."

Luke picked up his napkin and wiped his mouth. "Now that is worth the trip out here."

Dove bit into a piece of thigh. Looked like food was more important to Luke than being here with her. Just like her brothers. Always thinking about food.

What a dumb statement to make. Dove would think he cared more about the food than her. He swallowed the bite of chicken that seemed to grow larger by the moment. Dove must think him a pig. He had to get control of himself before he spoiled everything.

He gulped again to make sure the lump of meat had gone down. "Thank you for meeting me like this. I apologize for my mother's behavior."

"I understand it, Luke. She went through a terrifying experience as a child. We can't fault her for that. I only wish she didn't blame every one of us for what those men did back then."

"So do I; so do I." All things he'd wanted to say and talk about with Dove had disappeared as quickly as fresh-baked cookies from his mother's oven. How could this tiny young woman have such an effect on him?

Martin stood. "I'm going to walk a ways down the creek. It looks like it's getting pretty low. I'll be back for cake in a while." He grinned then strolled away.

Now Luke's tongue grew thicker than a slab of beef ready to fry. He gazed into Dove's dark eyes. "You're very beautiful, you know." His hand jerked. Had he just voiced his thoughts? Of course he had, for a blush now covered Dove's cheeks.

"I'm sorry, I didn't mean to…I…uh…I didn't mean to embarrass you." He groaned. How utterly stupid.

"I hope you meant it as a compliment, and if so, I thank you. I only wish I were not so short."

Luke grinned. "I did mean it as a compliment, and you're the perfect height." Indeed, he remembered how her head had just reached his shoulder level as they danced at Lucy and Jake's wedding. He pictured his arms around her with her head against his chest. He shook himself. Too soon for such fantasies.

"It would be nice to be as tall as Lucy is. She reaches the top shelves with no effort, and I have to climb on a stool each time." She leaned forward. "I went to visit Lucy, and you wouldn't believe the things they have in their new home. She has a wooden box lined with some kind of metal that keeps ice cold. Pa has talked of getting us one, but that's the first one I've seen."

"Oh, yes, Pa ordered that for them. We have one at the store. I imagine more and more people will be ordering them when the new icehouse is finished. Ben Haynes did." The last thing he wanted to talk about was iceboxes and icehouses. He searched his mind for something else. Horses would be good. Dove rode horses.

"What is your horse's name?" Well, not such a good question, but a start.

"Lightning. I named him that because he was born during a great storm. And when I ride him, his hooves pounding the ground remind me of the thunder, and his swiftness is like lightning."

"It suits him just like your name does you."

Again her cheeks turned red. "We all have birds' names because Ma loves birds. Her Indian name is White Feather, and my brother Hawk is John Hawk. I called him that growing up, but when he reached fifteen, he chose to be Hawk. Eli's middle name is Eagle, but he thinks Eli Eagle sounds silly, so he just goes by Eli." She stopped and put her fingers over her mouth. "Oh, I'm sorry. I'm babbling."

Luke chewed the end of a grass stalk. "I don't mind a bit. Tell me about where you lived before moving here."

"Pa lived in Missouri. He was in the cattle business there too. He came down to Oklahoma to sell some cattle to the army. That was when he met Ma at an army post. They fell in love, and he married her. They went back to Missouri and lived there until the land down here opened up."

"I'm surprised he didn't get a parcel of land closer to Guthrie.

That place grew up overnight. It's twice the size of Barton Creek." He often wished his pa had chosen to live there.

"I know, but Pa says the land he claimed was much better for cattle grazing. I'd rather be here too. I don't think I'd like Guthrie that much. Too many people." She straightened her split skirt and moved her legs to sit cross-legged next to him. "What do you plan to do with your life, Luke Anderson?"

He jerked back. "Hmm, well, I guess I'm going to help Pa run the store. He plans on expanding it and adding more merchandise. I heard him talking about having two stores in one. One part would be devoted to food and produce, and the other half would carry clothing, supplies, and household items. He also has a piece of land picked out for a house." He stopped. Dove wasn't interested in the business, and once he got started talking about future plans for it, he couldn't quit.

"Your father sounds like a man with a vision for the future. Pa is planning to expand our ranch to include horses like Jake has. He, Pa, and my brothers are going up to Wyoming in the fall to round some up to bring back here. I certainly like horses more than I do cows."

Luke laughed. "I imagine they're a lot easier to handle."

Martin ambled up. "I know you two are having quite a conversation, but the sun will be setting in an hour, and if you want to eat your cake, we best do it now then head back."

Dove grinned and reached into the basket for the slices sent by Mrs. Fleming. She handed a piece to Luke. He bit into the dark, rich dessert and let the chocolate icing melt on his tongue. "Your mother makes the best chocolate cake in the territory."

Martin said, "I'll be sure to tell her. By the way, the next time we plan an outing like this, Sarah is expecting you to ask her so she can join us."

Luke wiped chocolate from his fingers with a napkin. "I plan to do that. I'm sorry she couldn't come with me today." He turned to Dove. "Does that meet with your approval?"

She smiled and reached for the napkin to put it back in the basket. Their fingers touched, and he moved his to wrap around them. The strangest sort of shock streaked up his arm. He didn't want to ever let go. "Does it? Will you be here?"

She glanced at his hand then back at his face. Her eyes shone and bored straight into his soul. Dove nodded then slipped her hand from his.

A little understanding of what Martin had meant a few days earlier dawned on him. Love had taken its hold on his heart.

Chapter 9

Dove rode between Luke and Martin. She drank in every moment to lock them in her memory. This evening's picnic had marked a turning point in her relationship with Luke. Whenever they met in the store now, she would not run like a coward as in the past. They cut across the pasture and headed for the main road.

Martin pointed toward a fence. "I didn't know your father had fenced in any of this land."

Dove peered at the barbed wire in front of them. "This isn't his fence. It's sloppy. Pa would never allow such slipshod work. Besides, he believes the cattle should have free range. He and Mr. Haynes agreed to that." She gazed around at the surroundings. She'd need to be able to tell Pa exactly where this fence was located on their property.

Luke dismounted and inspected the wire and posts. "This might belong to one of the farmers. We sold some supplies like this to that farmer Dawson recently."

"Then we must tell Pa as soon as we get back." She turned her horse toward the ranch. Pa would be angry, but her brothers were the ones who would insist on tearing it down and confronting whoever had put it up in the wrong place.

Luke reined in his horse and turned away. "This is where I have to leave you and head back to town." Then he rode up to Dove.

He reached over and covered her hand on the saddle horn. “This has been a day I'll never forget. I hope it's the beginning of more like it.” He squeezed her fingers then rode off.

Dove shivered despite the heat and the warmth of his hand lingering on hers. She stared after him until he turned and waved before taking the road to Barton Creek.

“Thank you, Martin.”

He grinned and tipped his hat. “You're quite welcome. I'll do anything to help two friends.”

She glanced back over her shoulder. “We have to tell Pa about the fence. It'll be dark soon, so I doubt he'll do anything tonight.”

Martin nodded then nudged his horse into a trot. Dove followed close behind. Her prayers would be even stronger now for Mrs. Anderson. Except for that one blind spot toward Dove and her family, Luke's mother was a wonderful Christian woman who did so much to help people in town. Luke had shown the same characteristics, and now her hopes grew that their relationship would become more than friendship.

Dusk was upon them as Dove dismounted. “Thank you again, Martin. I had a wonderful time with you both. I hate that it will be dark before you get back to town.”

“Oh, don't worry about me.” He patted his horse's neck. “We know the way by heart, and besides, without a cloud in the sky, we'll have light from the moon.”

Dove's parents stepped through the door. Her father greeted them. “Good evening, Martin. Thank you for seeing our daughter home safely.”

“You're welcome, Mr. Morris. Good-bye, Mrs. Morris, Dove. I hope to see you again soon.” He tipped his hat and then rode off toward the road to town.

Dove twisted her hands in Lightning's reins. "Pa, we found fences in the west pasture. You didn't put any up, did you?"

His face clouded. "No, I didn't, and the boys didn't either." He glanced up toward the sky. "It's too late to do anything tonight. We'll go out in the morning and see what we have."

Ma embraced Dove. "Come, and tell me about your evening." She turned to Pa. "Will you take care of her horse so we can talk?"

"Of course. You two go on in and visit." He leaned down and planted a kiss on Ma's cheek.

Inside, Ma sat on the sofa and patted the seat beside her. "Now come and tell me all about your outing with Martin."

Dove swallowed hard. If she were to be completely honest, she'd risk Ma's anger, but if she said nothing, her conscience would make her guilt even greater. "Mrs. Fleming prepared a wonderful picnic supper for us. She even included some of her chocolate cake."

"Now that was a treat. I've often thought of asking for the recipe, but then if everyone made it, the cake would no longer be her specialty, so I haven't asked." She grasped Dove's hands. "Now tell me about Martin."

"He's a nice young man, very courteous and sensitive." But he wasn't Luke.

Her mother peered at her. "I sense there's more. Will you be seeing him again?"

"Yes." She breathed deeply, then the truth burst forth. "Ma, Luke was there too. Martin had arranged it. We talked, and it was wonderful. He's so kind and thoughtful."

Ma leaned back and tilted her head. "Did you know about the arrangement in advance?"

Dove bowed her head. "Yes, I did, and I'm sorry I didn't tell you."

"I see." Ma said nothing for a moment then shook her head. "My dear sweet child, this is a dangerous game you're playing. I don't object, but if Mrs. Anderson finds out, I fear Luke will be in serious trouble."

She reached over and wrapped her arms around Dove's shoulders. "I just don't want you to be hurt. I see love in your eyes, and I will continue to pray that all will end well for you and Luke. Until then, please be very careful."

Tears clouded Dove's eyes. Her mother understood and wasn't angry, only concerned. Love for her mother swelled in her heart. She would never do anything to deceive or hurt Ma, who loved and cared for her family more than life itself.

Back in town, Luke guided his horse to the stables and unsaddled him. As he cared for the animal, his thoughts filled with Dove. Although she lived in a fine home and had a wonderful family, her life wasn't as easy as others might think. He couldn't imagine living with so much prejudice. True, most families accepted the Morris family, but too many didn't and shunned them whenever they came to town. Some even said mean, ugly things to Mrs. Morris, Dove, and her brothers, especially Mrs. Frankston and her circle. At least Ma kept silent and spoke against them in the privacy of her home.

It seemed that no matter how much people talked about equality and freedom, there were those who didn't think it included everybody.

With his horse cared for, Luke managed to go upstairs and to his room without engaging in conversation with his parents. His little brother lay sprawled across his bed in the room they shared. Luke straightened the covers that would be all over the floor by morning and leaned down to kiss the boy's cheek. At seven years of age, Will still had the innocence of childhood, but his form was filling out. Someday he'd be too big for Luke to tease and toss around. If only that innocence could stay, but too soon he would learn about the things of the world.

Luke undressed then lay down with his hands under his head. He stared at the ceiling. Muffled sounds of conversation and wagon wheels from the street flowed through the open window, but his mind filled only with the images of a young woman with eyes as dark as the night surrounding him now.

The next morning, Dove led her father and brothers out to the site where she found the fences the day before.

When her father inspected them, he yanked at the wire. "This is my land, and no farmer is going to get any of it." His face turned red, and he pulled wire cutters from his saddlebags.

Hawk and Eli helped him tear down the fences' lines. Dove bit her lip. She'd never seen her father in such a state of anger. When the posts lay in shambles and the wire cut, he turned to his sons. "I'm going into town to see who has the deed to that property. You boys check out the rest of the area and see if more fences are up."

He mounted his horse and galloped away. Dove turned to her brothers. "I'm going with you." Before they could protest, she dug in her heels and raced off. Hawk and Eli followed her and yelled for her to slow down.

When she finally did, Hawk grabbed her reins. "You can go with us, but don't ride off like that again."

She shook her head and swung her long braid over her shoulder to hang down her back. "I won't." She jerked the reins away from him and moved ahead at a slow trot. If more fences were found, Pa would be outraged. No telling what he'd do in such a state. The only one who could calm him down was Ma, but even she might not be able to handle the anger he showed this morning.

Hawk touched her elbow. "Look. It's another fence."

She peered ahead and spotted the barbed wire and post several yards ahead. They rode for a closer inspection. Hawk and Eli dismounted. Hawk ran his gloved hands over the posts and leaned in to look at the connections.

He straightened. "This isn't a farmer's work." He gazed off in the distance. "That's Chester Fowler's land up that way. That's odd. He hates fences. Pa needs to know about this."

Hawk hitched his leg over his saddle. "Dove, you go back and get Ma. We're going into town. You bring her. Maybe she can keep Pa from doing something he'll regret."

"All right. I'll saddle up Dusty for her. It'll be faster than the wagon."

At that moment three other men rode up. The foreman, Walt Sanders, pulled his horse to a stop. "Where's your pa? We've found some of our herd behind a fence on Fowler's land up north of here. Looks like Fowler is trying to take what ain't his."

Hawk nodded toward the fence behind them. "I don't understand this. Why would Fowler put up any fences? Eli and I are riding into town. Pa went in earlier to check who owns that land to the west. He's not gonna like this news."

"Like I said, Fowler is greedy. Maybe he thinks he can put some of your pa's herd in with his. Best your pa knows so he can nip it now. We'll keep checking and making sure the herd is all right." Walt waved at his men. "Let's get busy." They rode off in a cloud of dust.

Dove raced back to the ranch, and her brothers rode toward

town. She prayed no fights would break out. The last thing they needed with this drought was a range war over cattle and fences.

Luke glanced out the window of the store and spotted Mr. Morris entering the land office down the street. Luke untied his apron. This would be as good a time as any to speak with him about Dove.

"Pa, I'm running an errand. I'll be back in a few minutes." His father waved at him and tended to the customer at the counter. Luke made his way down the street to the land office where Mr. Morris spoke with the clerk.

Luke stopped, not wanting to interrupt. Mr. Morris's voice carried to the street. "I don't care how many fences he has as long as they're on his land. He can't be putting a fence on mine. I'm going to take care of this and make sure it doesn't happen again."

He slapped his hat on his head and turned to see Luke. "What do you want?"

Luke gulped. This didn't look like a good time, but the man expected an answer. "Um, I…I was just going to ask how Miss Morris is. She didn't come into town with you, did she?"

"No." He narrowed his eyes and glared at Luke. "I've seen your spark of interest in my daughter. I'll tell you this, Luke Anderson, and you listen good. You stay away from Dove. I don't want you anywhere near her until your mother can act like the Christian woman she's supposed to be. When she can accept my family for who they are, I'll consider giving you opportunity to call on my daughter."

"Yes, sir." Luke's heart sank to his toes. He couldn't defy Mr. Morris.

"I can't help what happens when I'm not around. But if you so much as look at her wrong or cause her pain at church or at your store, or wherever, you'll answer to me." With that he stomped off the boardwalk and mounted his horse.

Luke's hands clenched at his sides. He had no intention of ever hurting Dove by his actions or his words, but he had no control over what his mother might do. Then a glimmer of hope began to shine. Mr. Morris had said he couldn't help what happened when he wasn't around. That meant he wasn't completely opposed to Luke at least being friendly with Dove.

Clattering hooves and a shout caused him to turn around. Eli and Hawk rode up to their father. "Pa, we found more fences. We think they belong to Chester Fowler."

Mr. Morris's face turned red. "What's wrong with that man? He told me he hated me because I let the farmers protect their crops with the fences on their property, and now he does this."

Luke bit his lip. When someone got this angry, violence was likely to result. He prayed that wouldn't happen now. He understood the anger because fences were so hated by most cattlemen who preferred open range for grazing their herds. Luke remembered Chester Fowler's threats in the store, but those were against the farmers. This didn't make any sense at all.

Luke stepped around the horses and hurried back to the store. This wasn't his concern, but it could concern the town. Men like Fowler were greedy and gave the territory a bad name.

He reached the store just as Mr. Morris and his boys passed by. He glanced over at Luke. "You remember what I told you, boy." The man spurred his horse, heading back to his ranch, leaving dust to settle around Luke.

Chapter 10

After the noon meal, Luke swept the area in front of the store. He must talk with Martin as to what their next step would be. In light of Mr. Morris's warning, he would have to be careful. Luke didn't plan on hurting Dove or causing her any pain, but he couldn't speak for anyone else in his family, except perhaps Alice, who still showed more than a casual interest in Eli Morris.

His instincts were to protect his sister and warn her to stay away from Eli. At sixteen, she should be fully aware of the problems that could arise. If he couldn't stop his feelings for Dove, though, he couldn't ask her to do the same with Eli. She'd be much better off with someone like Matt Haynes, but, then, he had eyes only for Caroline Frankston. Love made everything so complicated.

The sound of horses down the street caused Luke to turn in that direction. Mr. Morris had returned with Eli and Hawk. This time Mrs. Morris and Dove followed on their horses. They stopped in front of the store. Mr. Morris stared with hard eyes at Luke, the warning clearly written there.

He turned to his wife. "We'll meet you back here. If you need any supplies, get them now. We're going to speak with the sheriff." He stared once again at Luke before riding away to take care of his business.

Mrs. Morris's face twisted with concern. She blinked her eyes then swung down from her horse.

Luke moved forward to assist Mrs. Morris when she stepped down, and by the time she turned to thank him, Dove had already jumped down from Lightning. After a quick smile, she hurried through the door.

Mrs. Morris patted his hand. "Dove told me everything you and Martin planned. Please be careful."

Luke nodded. Dove had told her mother, and Mrs. Morris hadn't told him not to see Dove again. A glimmer of hope filled his heart.

He followed Mrs. Morris into the store and glanced around. His mother must still be upstairs with Will, who wasn't feeling well. Dove stood near her mother in the piece goods section. Luke hurried to assist them. "May I help you find something?"

Mrs. Morris smiled. "No, if we decide to buy anything, we'll bring our selections to the front counter when we've finished." She handed him a sheet of paper. "However, here is a list of a few staple items I'll need this week. If you could gather those for me, I'd appreciate it."

"Yes, ma'am. I'll be glad to do that." He headed toward the shelves where they kept sugar, flour, and meal. He glanced out the window and spotted Chester Fowler and his sons on the street. From the looks on their faces, they were not here to just pick up supplies. He debated with himself as to whether he should warn Mr. Morris. After a quick look at Dove, he made his decision.

"Pa, here's Mrs. Morris's list. I have an errand to run. Be back in a minute." He tossed his apron onto the counter and raced outside and down to the jail. He skidded to a stop then peered back over his shoulder. The Fowler family had stopped in front of the bank. Luke opened the door and stepped inside the room.

Mr. Morris leaned on the desk with both hands. "Look, Claymore, Dawson's fence was a misunderstanding of his property lines. We straightened that out, but Fowler is just crazy enough to try this way to encroach on my land and take cattle from my herd. He knows the boundaries as well as I do. That's why I came back to town."

"That may be, but I can't do anything about it until I get the plat map from the land office and go with you to check it out."

Mr. Morris shook his head and glowered. "Ever since you were named as our sheriff, you've used these delay tactics." He leaned on the desk. "My men and my boys found Fowler's fences while I was in town this morning. When I confronted him, he just laughed. Said he was protecting what was his like Dawson protected his crops, and he had no intentions of removing them. And if I did, he'd see to it that I regretted it, but my men had already done cut them down."

He balled his hands into fists. "You are the law, and it's up to you to take care of this and keep a range war from happening. And a range war is what we'll have if Fowler keeps putting up fences on my land. I don't care what he does on his own property, but he's not taking mine."

Claymore stood. "I know that, Sam. Get the maps from the land office, and we'll go to Fowler's ranch now." He reached for his hat.

Luke cleared his throat. "Sir, I don't mean to interrupt, but I came to tell you that the Fowlers are in town now. They're over by the bank."

Anger flashed across Mr. Morris's face. He pounded one fist into the palm of his hand. "We're going to make sure whatever Fowler intends doesn't go any further." He strode from the office with his two sons and the sheriff following.

Luke hurried after them. He crossed to the other side of the street and made a dash for the store but stopped when Fowler exited the bank and called out to Mr. Morris.

"There you are, you no good scum. I told you you'd be sorry if you took down my fence." His two boys stood behind him.

Mr. Morris faced him, his hand on the butt of the gun in his belt. "Hold on, Fowler. That fence was on my land. You had no right or cause to put it up."

Fowler spat on the ground. "All you care about is grabbing up all the land you can get. You and Ben Haynes are just alike. Greedy polecats. You let Dawson put one up, but you don't want me doing it. Now you know how I feel."

Mr. Morris narrowed his eyes and glared at Fowler. "That doesn't even make sense. Your land is on the other side of mine, and I'm only helping Dawson to protect his crops from my cattle."

Luke listened but noticed movement and turned to find Bart with Eli. Luke cringed. If Bart started something, he'd beat Eli senseless. Hawk was a more likely opponent for Bart, but Zeb had Hawk's attention in front of the bank.

Before Luke could react, Bart hit Eli, and then everything broke loose. Fowler swung at Mr. Morris, and Hawk went after Zeb. People shouted, and a crowd gathered like vultures over a dead cow. Luke backed himself against the wall and inched his way along to the store. The group in front of him parted as Eli and Bart hurtled their way toward him.

Luke pressed his fist to his mouth, and his heart pounded in his chest. The sight of blood on Eli's face sickened Luke. One of Eli's eyes was already swelling shut. The boy fell not far from Luke's feet, and Bart stomped on Eli's side. As much as he wanted to help, fear glued Luke to his spot. Finally two men grabbed Bart and pulled him away from Eli. Luke sank against the wall, his knees too weak to hold him.

Claymore shouted at the crowd to move away. Doc Carter appeared and knelt beside Eli, who lay still. Mr. Morris pushed Fowler toward the jail, and Hawk held Zeb in a death grip. Claymore took Fowler from Mr. Morris, who raced to Eli's side.

A woman screamed, and Luke turned to find Mrs. Morris rushing to her son. Dove stood frozen in place, her eyes wide open in shock. Luke pushed to his feet and hurried to her side. He reached for her hand, but she jerked it away from his and ran to be near her brother.

"Should have known something like this would happen with those Morris boys in town."

His mother's voice chilled Luke. He turned to her. "It wasn't their fault, Ma. Mr. Morris came to town to get the sheriff. Mr. Fowler and his sons came for trouble."

She shrugged her shoulders and grunted. He turned back to the street. Hawk and Doc Carter carried Eli over to the Doc's office. Sheriff Claymore told everyone to go on about their business. He escorted Chester Fowler and his sons into the jail.

When his parents returned to the store, Luke hurried around to the back stairs to go up and tell Alice about Eli. When he reached her room, she stood staring out the window. Her hand gripped the curtain. Tears streamed down her ashen cheeks.

Luke touched her shoulder. "Alice."

She turned and hugged him. "Oh, Luke, I saw the whole thing. Bart hit Eli, and then everyone was fighting. I saw Eli fall just before those men broke it up." She sobbed onto his chest.

He patted her back. "I think Eli is going to be all right. I'll check on him if you want me to."

She gazed up at him with tear-filled eyes. "Please, I have

to know how he is. He must be hurt bad if they took him to Doc's."

"You stay here until I get back." He kissed the top of her head then left.

Halfway down the stairway, his parents' angry voices reached him.

"Bea, please calm down. You don't know the whole story. Chester Fowler's been looking for trouble for weeks."

"I don't care what you say, Carl Anderson. Indians are savages, and those two boys are half Indian. They don't think anything of fighting and brawling to get their way."

Luke's throat filled with bile at his mother's words. He didn't want to hear any more of her anger. After using the back outside stairway, he rushed to the doctor's office. He hesitated at the door then pushed it open. The family stood around Doc Carter. Mrs. Morris and Dove saw him first.

Dove came to him. "He's going to be all right."

Relief flooded his soul. At least he'd have a good report for Alice. "That's good news." He stepped toward Mr. and Mrs. Morris. "I'm so sorry this happened. I'll get your supplies together, and you can pick them up when you leave." The words had just popped from his mouth. They sounded rather dumb at the moment.

Mrs. Morris patted his arm. "Thank you, Luke. That will be fine."

He gulped then backed from the room. Once again on the street, he breathed deeply to calm his nerves. Rumors and talk of gunfights in other towns had reached Barton Creek, but never had such a thing happened here. Violence rarely solved problems, and he hated anything to do with it. Still, remorse ate at him because he should have done something to help Eli.

What that would have been he didn't know, only that he had been rooted in place and had done nothing.

Luke's shoulders drooped as he returned to his home using the back stairs once again. At the moment he didn't care to see his parents, but he did have good news for Alice.

Alice pushed open the door. "I saw you coming. Is he going to be all right?"

He brushed her damp cheek with his finger. "Yes, he is. I guess it wasn't a serious wound."

She hugged him. "Thank you." When she leaned back, she tilted her head. "I have a favor to ask. Please take me over to Doc Carter's so I can see for myself."

Luke hesitated. Ma would be angry. And they'd probably be in big trouble if caught, but seeing Dove again would be worth the chance. "Where's Will?"

"He's downstairs helping Pa stack cans."

"Then let's go. We can't stay but a few minutes, and I'm not sure you'll even get to see him, but we'll try."

He led her down the back stairway and across to the doctor's office. Mr. Morris and Hawk were gone, probably to report to the sheriff on Eli's condition. "Mrs. Morris, Alice wanted to have a word with Eli."

She peered at Alice then over at Eli, who lay on a bed behind a slightly drawn curtain. At his nod, Mrs. Morris turned back to Luke. "For just a moment or two; that's all. We'll be taking him home shortly."

"Thank you, Mrs. Morris." Alice hurried to Eli's side. She leaned over to speak to him.

With their voices too low to hear, Luke directed his attention to Dove. "I repeat what I said earlier. I'm sorry about Eli. Bart had no right to attack him like that."

"I can't believe Bart would actually start a fight with someone younger and smaller than he is. Mr. Fowler has about as much land as Pa, but it's hemmed in by ours and the Kansas border. I guess he thinks it's all right to take some of ours so he can add to his. I don't understand how some people can be so greedy."

"It's been happening all over the West as the frontier has opened. Pa hears all kinds of stories, and we read about them in the papers from Guthrie and Oklahoma City. But I'd always hoped Barton Creek would be spared that kind of thing."

He glanced around and saw that Mrs. Morris stood near the curtain talking with Doc Carter. "Dove, I spoke with your father. He won't allow us to see each other officially, but he said he couldn't control what happens at church or in town. So, we'll have to continue our chance meetings for now."

"Luke, I don't want to disobey my father, but he hasn't told me I can't be friends with you." She peered over his shoulder. "I think you should leave with Alice. Pa will be back in a few minutes, and it might not be a good idea for him to find you here with her."

"I agree." No need to give Mr. Morris cause to be upset with Alice. Besides, if Alice and he were gone too long, Ma and Pa would be angry too. He called to his sister.

She stepped away from the bed. "Good-bye, Eli."

The boy on the bed smiled. "Good-bye, Alice, and thank you for coming."

Her cheeks turned pink, and when she turned to Luke, her eyes sparkled. "I'm ready to go."

He grasped her arm, and they headed back to the store and up to their home. Luke checked the clock; they'd been away only a little more than five minutes. At least his parents wouldn't notice them being gone.

Alice hugged him. "I'm so glad you took me over to see Eli. He said his ribs are cracked from that last kick from Bart. That was what hurt the most and why he didn't move at the end. Doc Carter sewed up the cut on his head and wrapped his ribs, so he's going to be fine."

"That's good." He frowned. "Alice, please be careful with your feelings about Eli. You know what Ma thinks."

"I do, but then you have them for Dove. I see it in your face every time she comes into the store, and I noticed how you were talking with her in the doctor's office."

"You're right. We'll both have to hope Ma will change her ideas about the Morris family. Until that happens, we'll have to be careful. I'm old enough that I can stand up to her, but I don't think now is the best time to do that."

"I agree." She hugged him again. "You're a smart big brother. Thank you." She turned and went downstairs to help their parents.

When he returned to the store, his father helped a customer, and Alice led Will up to their rooms to get him a snack. Ma stood with her back to him, but the set of her shoulders said she was still upset over the afternoon's brawl. Luke tied on his apron and picked up a carton ready to be unpacked and shelved. If only people were as easy to sort out as canned goods, life would be a lot simpler.

Chapter 11

Emily stood in the background near Eli's bed as her husband spoke with the doctor. He'd returned from talking to the sheriff, but anger still spotted his cheeks with red. She had seen his temper before, but nothing ever like now. Her own fury lay squelched beneath years of hiding the hurt inflicted by rude and uncaring people.

As she waited, she thought of Alice and Eli. Every time Emily saw Alice, she felt as though she knew the girl from somewhere beyond Barton Creek. The girl's hair and eyes and the way she moved her hands when talking were so familiar, but that wasn't possible, as Emily hadn't met the Andersons until moving to this town. Such a pretty girl, and a sweet one, and she'd be good for Eli. Emily sighed. Now she had two of her children to worry about being hurt by Bea Anderson.

Dove held Eli's hand. He grinned up at her and then at Emily. Emily reached over to kiss his cheek. Her baby had become a strong young man. She smoothed back his hair. "Soon as we get you home, you're going straight to bed and stay there as long as the doctor thinks it's necessary."

He frowned. "Ma, I'm not that hurt. I'm fine." He moved then winced. "Well, maybe not so fine." He turned to Dove. "Thank Luke for me for bringing Alice here. She made me feel better just by coming."

Dove grinned. "I will do that. Is something brewing there?"

Eli's cheeks turned pink. "I've been careful. She told me about her ma, but then you know all about that seeing as how Luke is sweet on you, my sister."

This time Dove blushed and ducked her head. Emily stepped closer and placed her arm across Dove's shoulders and frowned at Eli. "Even though you didn't start it, fighting in the streets like you did will only add fuel to what Mrs. Anderson already believes. I love you both, and I don't want to see either of you get hurt."

Eli tried to sit up but grimaced in pain. He spoke through clenched lips. "I don't care what that woman thinks."

Emily sighed. If he meant that, then he and Alice would face more troubled days than Dove and Luke. Her son had been no match for Bart Fowler, and she didn't see how he could be much of a match for Mrs. Anderson either, but then her youngest wasn't one to follow conventions.

Sam turned away from the doctor. He strode to the bedside and placed a hand on Emily's shoulder. Nodding toward Eli, he said, "Let's get our boy home. Doc Carter gave me some salve to make sure the wound he stitched up doesn't get infected. You and Dove can see to that. I got a wagon from the livery since he's in no condition to ride his horse."

He motioned for Hawk to join him. "I want to get home and make sure we take care of any fences Fowler may have put up." He slipped his arm under Eli's shoulders and lifted his son to a standing position with Hawk's help. Emily stepped back to allow them to pass. She grabbed Dove's hand and followed the two men outside.

Out on the street, people went about their daily business. Only a few stopped to watch them help Eli into the wagon. True to his word, Luke had secured their purchases to her horse. Relief flowed through Emily. At least people were going on about their business now, although a few did cast hostile glances their way.

When Sam turned to assist her up in mounting Dusty, she stopped him and grasped his arm. "I'm going to drive the wagon. Tie Dusty to the back." She hesitated then squeezed his arm. "I see anger in your eyes, and it worries me. Don't do anything foolish. We've already had enough trouble."

He patted her hand. "Fowler overstepped his bounds, and he knows it. I won't seek revenge since Eli's not badly hurt, but I will press charges so Bart will stay in jail. I won't let Fowler get away with thinking he can intrude on our land. I'll fight to the death to protect what belongs to us. If he wants a range war, then that's what he'll get."

"That's what concerns me. Chester Fowler is a dangerous man. I tried to speak to his wife one time in the store. She smiled and said hello then glanced at him. He yanked her arm and dragged her out to the wagon, cursing at her all the way. It frightened me, Sam. If he does that to his wife, what will he do to you or any of our family?"

Sam wrapped his arms around her. "Nothing. I won't let him." He kissed her cheek. "Let's take Eli home and tend to him there."

"I know you'll do the right thing, but I'll still worry about you." She settled herself on the bench seat after he boosted her up.

Dove climbed up beside her. "I'll go with you. Hawk can bring Lightning. He put all our packages in the wagon too."

Hawk may be her oldest and strongest and sometimes the most impulsive, but he always knew what needed to be done. Emily wove the straps through her fingers. She checked behind to make sure the horses were secure. When Sam waved, she flipped the reins.

A mile or two out of town, Emily said, "Tell me about Alice and Eli. I was surprised when Luke brought her to the doctor's office."

Dove glanced back at Eli before answering. "I think he and Alice are sweet on each other. They sit together during Sunday school, and they've been with each other on different occasions."

Emily frowned. Just as she feared, another one of her children involved with an Anderson, and that could only lead to more trouble with Bea. "I see." Her daughter and youngest son had grown up overnight. How she wanted to protect them from a world of prejudice and hate, but she couldn't keep them locked up at home. Dove's beauty and Eli's kind heart would take them down a path of sorrow and disappointment if things didn't change with Mrs. Anderson.

Dove wanted to tell her mother about the next meeting Martin had planned for her and Luke, but couldn't find the words after what had happened today. Everyone in town would blame her father and brothers for the incident simply because of who or what they were. Now adding Alice to the picture brought on more complications.

Her mother's silence bothered her. Dove couldn't decide if it was because of what she had said about Alice and Eli, or the trouble with Mr. Fowler. She had never seen her father as angry as he was today.

When they rolled up to the ranch house, her father dismounted and came to assist Eli inside. She and Ma climbed down from the wagon.

Hawk grabbed the reins from the seat box. "I'll take care of this and the horses. You and Dove go on in and see to Eli. I'll bring in the rest of the supplies." He led all of the horses toward the stables.

Dove followed her mother to the house and then to Eli's room. He had slept some on the way home, but it had still been a rough ride, and his fatigue was evident in his face.

"He needs rest. Take care of him, and I'll go out to help Hawk." Pa strode from the room.

Eli winced when he moved, but when he settled, he grinned up at them. "I feel much better now, and I sure am hungry."

Ma laughed. "You could be dying and still want something to eat. Let me check your wound first." She inspected the bandage on his side. "Well, I don't see any blood seeping through, so I don't have to change it now." She turned to Dove. "Come, let's find something to fix for this starved young man."

In the kitchen, Dove retrieved leftover chicken and some fruit from the counter. Now would be a good time to tell her mother about Martin. She reached up into the cabinet for a plate. "Ma, I spoke with Martin this morning at the store."

"Yes, I saw him come in right after we did. What has he planned for you this time?"

Dove blinked and swallowed hard. She couldn't keep secrets from Ma any more than she could change the seasons. "Another picnic, but this time Sarah is joining us. Martin likes her, so this will give them a chance to be together even though she'll be with Luke."

"And what does Sarah think about this arrangement?"

Dove sliced and washed the greens from the garden. "It was her idea for the picnic. She's a nice girl and speaks with me on Sundays and whenever we see each other."

Ma arranged the chicken and apple slices on a plate. "Yes, she is, and her mother, Dinah, is friendly also. I'm glad you have friends like Sarah and Lucy." She covered the plate with a napkin. "Now, let's get this into your brother."

A knock sounded on the door. "I'll get it, Ma. You take care of Eli."

Ma nodded, and Dove headed for the door. When she opened it, her eyes opened wide. "Aunt Clara, Mrs. Haynes. What a nice surprise!" She stepped back so they could enter.

Aunt Clara removed her bonnet. "We heard about the ruckus in town and came to offer our help."

Dove smiled. "Ma will be glad to see you both. She's in with Eli now." She led them to her brother's room. "Look who just arrived on our doorstep."

Ma clasped her hands to her chest. "Clara, Mellie. How good of you to come."

Aunt Clara stepped to the bedside. "I understand you engaged in a little fisticuffs while you were in town."

Eli nodded. "I did, but I only busted a rib or two. See." He pulled back his shirt to show the bandage.

"Not what I heard. Let me have a look-see at that place on your cheek." She proceeded to loosen the bandage to inspect the wound. Ma and Mrs. Haynes stood back and let the older woman examine Eli. Dove remained at the foot of the bed. Eli winced when Aunt Clara pulled the gauze away.

"Hmm. Just a nick? I say this gash is bigger than that. Looks like Doc Carter did a fine job of tending it." She replaced the bandage and examined his swollen eye. "This will take a few days to heal, and it'll turn some pretty colors, believe me."

She stepped back. "I think you're in good hands here, but I had to see for myself. I've treated lots of fight wounds in my days on the frontier with my brother and his family." She stood. "We'll go and let you get some food in your belly. Then you get some rest." She grinned and stepped back. "That's an order."

"Yes, ma'am." He grabbed his plate and stabbed a chunk of chicken with the fork.

Ma laughed. "Nothing wrong with his appetite." She nodded at Mellie and turned toward the door. "Now come and tell me the latest news in your family."

Dove followed the three women into the front parlor. Ma headed to the kitchen for lemonade and cookies. Aunt Clara pulled Dove aside. "Lucy told me a little about you and Luke. How is that progressing?"

"I'm not sure. Martin Fleming is arranging for us to be together at times. In fact, he has a picnic planned for next week."

"Does your mother know about this?" At Dove's nod, she continued. "That's good. But I would imagine Bea Anderson knows nothing of Martin's scheme."

Using the word scheme made the meeting sound more like a plot to hurt someone than a pleasant afternoon outing. Still, the meaning implied trickery, and that's exactly what she, Martin, and Luke were doing—tricking Mrs. Anderson. She hung her head. "No, ma'am, she doesn't."

"I only hope Luke understands the implications of what he's planning because I don't like the idea of deception. Bea is a kind woman in most ways, but she can't let go of her past and look to the future." She hugged Dove. "I'll pray for you and your relationship with Luke, and for God to soften Bea Anderson's heart."

The elderly woman's kind words soothed Dove's doubts. No matter what the outcome might be, she would enjoy whatever time she could have with Luke. He wasn't really lying to his mother, but he wasn't telling her the full truth either. The thought made her uneasy.

The bell jangled over the doorway, and Luke glanced up from his inventory. Martin strode toward him. "Good afternoon, Luke. Quite a bit of excitement around town today."

Luke laid aside his tablet and pen. "Yes, there was. I saw you in here earlier, but then you were gone before I had a chance to speak with you. Do you have anything planned?"

Martin grinned and glanced around the room. Ma and Pa were busy with customers, but Luke pulled his friend to the corner, out of earshot of both. "Did you speak with Dove?"

"Yes, I did, and I told her what Sarah and I came up with last night."

"And?"

"You are to invite Sarah to go on a picnic one afternoon after we get off work. Ask your ma to fix up a basket for you. Dove's going to take care of ours. Then you'll go by for Sarah and bring her out to the edge of town and the clearing down by the creek. We'll meet you there."

Luke's heart thumped in his chest at the thought of being near Dove again. Then he remembered Alice. "Would it be all right to bring Alice and then have you and Dove bring Eli?"

At Martin's startled look, Luke explained. "I took her in to see Eli after he was beaten. She has feelings for him just like I have for Dove. Well, maybe not as serious, but I could tell from the way they looked at each other that something's going on there."

Martin didn't answer for a moment. If he didn't want to include them, no harm would be done since Luke hadn't mentioned it to Alice. If Martin agreed, then Luke would have to come up with an excuse for Alice to accompany him on Saturday afternoon.

"I don't see a problem on my side, but we must be careful. Are you sure you want to involve your sister in our cover-up?"

Doubt crept in. Luke wanted his sister to be happy, but that wouldn't happen if she were caught up in the deception. "You're right. I don't want to get her into trouble. When I get things worked out with Dove, then she and Eli will have no problem with their relationship."

Martin looked askance at Luke. "You said when. Does that mean you're going to stand up to your parents anytime soon, or has there been a change in your mother?"

"No," he admitted glumly. In fact, the afternoon's events had only made things worse.

A sudden commotion behind him caught his attention. He turned to find his mother cradling Pa in her arms. "Go get Doc Carter! Something's wrong with your pa."

Chapter 12

Luke raced to his mother's side, and Alice ran out the door to fetch the doctor. His father's pale face sent shivers of anxiety through him. "Pa, Pa, what's the matter?" When he didn't answer, Luke grabbed his father's shoulders. "Ma, clear that bench. Martin, help me get Pa on the bench."

Martin grasped his feet, and Luke tucked his arms under Pa's. Together, the two of them laid his father out flat. Luke grabbed several aprons and rolled them up to place under his father's head.

"Ma, tell me what happened."

"I don't know." She squeezed her hands together. "The Shipleys had just left, and he said he felt light-headed and weak. Then he just fell right there by the counter."

Doc Carter rushed through the door and to Pa's side. He opened his bag and pulled out a stethoscope then held it to Pa's chest. After a moment, he said, "His heartbeat is strong, but a little fast. Let's get him to my office, where I can examine him properly."

Luke and Martin lifted Pa and carried him across the street. Once again Luke found himself in the doctor's office. This time it was his father in need of help. He and Martin settled Pa on the examination table then stepped back. He draped an arm around his mother's shoulders.

"Doc Carter will take care of him, Ma. He's strong. He'll be all right." If only he could believe those words. But his mother needed reassurance at this point. Barely into his midforties, his father had too much life ahead of him to be seriously ill.

They waited quietly until Doc finished his examination behind the curtain. When he appeared, he pulled back the curtain. Pa smiled then winced.

Ma rushed forward and grabbed Pa's hand. "Carl Anderson, you gave me such a fright." She turned to Doc Carter. "What's the matter with him?"

"Well, I can't say for sure, but I'm pretty sure it has to do with his heart and blood pressure. I measured his blood pressure with this instrument I put on his wrist."

Luke bent forward to examine the unusual apparatus. It fit like a small belt and had a boxlike contraption on it along with a little metal needle sticking up. "What's this thing called?"

Doc Carter grinned. "It's a Dudgeon wrist sphygmograph. Only one like it around these parts. I asked a doctor friend of mine to send me one when I heard about them. It measures how his blood is pumping through his arteries."

Luke's mother and father looked at each other then back to the doctor. Ma wrapped her other hand around Pa's. "What does that mean? How serious is it?"

"He'll be all right if he takes care of himself. I worked with cases like this back in Philadelphia a few years back. Right now he needs a few days' rest from heavy work, and it wouldn't hurt to lose a little weight either."

Pa frowned and patted his rather rotund middle. Ma covered his hand. "Don't worry. You'll have good food to eat, just not as much." She turned to Luke. "This means you'll have to take over running the store for the next several days."

Luke nodded. Of course he would, but he'd never be able to take off and keep a picnic date. By the time he closed the store and helped Ma, it would be too late. As much as he wanted to see Dove, his father's health was more important at the moment. Such were the responsibilities of an eldest son.

"Don't worry, Pa. Alice and I can handle everything at the store so Ma can take care of you."

"Thank you, son." Pa tried to sit up. "When can I go home?" He winced again and lay back on the table. "I guess I'm still a little dizzy."

Luke leaned over to reassure his father. "Martin and I will go back to the store now and take care of things. Alice is there with Will. Ma can stay with you until you feel better."

He nodded to Martin and then left the office. Outside he turned to his friend. "I can't go on a picnic with Pa sick. I'll have to be at the store. Will you explain to Sarah and Dove?"

Martin clapped Luke on the shoulder. "Of course I will. We can postpone the meeting until you can take time off. The ladies will understand."

Yes, they would, but he had no idea at the moment how long this extra responsibility might last. If his father didn't improve quickly, he may be in for a longer convalescence. And with the Fourth of July bearing down, the store would be busier than usual.

They walked in silence across the street. Several people stopped to inquire about his father. Luke briefed them and continued on to the store. At the door, Martin stopped him.

"I have an idea. The store is closed on Saturday for the celebration, right? So, we can get together then and have dinner."

Luke nodded. Saturday would work. Ma would be helping the church ladies, and Will would be with friends. "Sounds like it might be a good plan."

Martin clapped his shoulder again. "Good. I'll let Sarah

know of the change. You go take care of business." He grinned then sauntered down the street.

Luke's heart grew heavy. Pa would be all right, but it would be days before he'd be able to take over at the store. At least he'd worked with Pa long enough to know the routine, but he'd need help, and Ma needed Alice to keep up with Will. His brother could get into more mischief than a puppy. Perhaps Alice and Will could both help him in the store since Will liked to stack things.

He sighed and pushed open the door. The bell rang above him, jangling his nerves. In just a few hours life had grown even more complicated.

By suppertime, Dove sensed her pa had settled down and didn't appear so angry. Ma always had a calming effect on him. After the blessing for the meal, he and Hawk discussed what to do about Mr. Fowler, but Dove didn't care to listen to them. Her mind filled with thoughts of Luke instead.

He'd been as concerned about Eli as her family had been. It had been kind of him to bring Alice to see her brother. At least Pa hadn't been there then. He'd made it plain that he didn't approve of her being friends with Luke, although he hadn't forbidden it.

She pushed food around her plate, her appetite having lessened as she remembered Martin's information. A picnic would be fun, especially if Sarah joined them. Sarah had been friendly, and having another girl around would help with conversation. Dove laughed inside. That is, if anyone else got a word in edgewise. Sarah did like to talk.

"Dear, you're not eating. Is there a problem?" Ma's voice broke her reverie.

"No. I was thinking about all that happened today." Which was partly the truth because Luke had been there today.

She picked up her plate and took it to the counter by the sink. The busier she stayed, the less she thought about Luke or worried about Eli. If she and Luke could work things out, then there would be a possible chance for Eli and Alice.

Her mother carried the remaining plates to the counter. Dove reached for the pump handle to get water for the dishes. The water came out less strong than it had last month, but Pa had reassured them that the well had plenty of water and not to worry. She gazed out the window at the gathering dusk. The purple and gold hues of the sunset usually gave her peace and satisfaction that all was right, but a day like this one troubled her soul.

God had been good to the Morris family in providing this fine home and everything she needed, but sometimes longings filled her that material possessions couldn't satisfy. Ever since she'd admitted to herself and to her mother that she cared about Luke, the restlessness in her heart grew.

Pa's chair scraped the floor. "I'm going out to the stables to see to the horses and talk to the men." He grabbed his hat and shoved it on his head. He opened the door, and a clattering of hooves filled the air. "It's Fowler and his boys. They're supposed to be in jail." Pa reached for his rifle.

He stepped onto the porch. Dove and her mother hurried to the door. Mr. Fowler and his sons sat astride their horses.

"Come to talk to you, Morris. The sheriff let us go since Eli is OK. It was just a little fist fight over a difference of opinion, and he said he couldn't hold us for that."

Pa's shoulders tensed. "That may change when I go back in

to see him. Eli will be OK, no thanks to you. What's your business now?"

Mr. Fowler glanced at his sons. "I did put up that fence to spite you because you let those farmers put up some around their crops. Looks like Dawson was trying to take advantage of that."

"He just had the property borders wrong." Pa hesitated a moment. "We settled peaceably this afternoon."

"What's to keep more of them from puttin' up other fences and cuttin' us off from the water?" Mr. Fowler spat a stream of dark brown juice to the ground.

Ma cringed beside Dove and whispered, "What a nasty habit."

Dove agreed, but almost everything about the Fowler men was nasty. They smelled bad, and their clothes looked like they'd worn them for days. His wife didn't take very good care of her men. Ma made Eli and Hawk bathe at least twice a week. She wished they'd leave before Pa's anger returned.

Pa stepped off the porch. "I don't think that will happen, and if it does, I'll handle it with the land office."

"I got a better idea of how we can get rid of them once and for all."

His words sent chills down Dove's back. Men like Mr. Fowler had no conscience. She bit her lip when her father's hands tightened on his rifle. He turned and motioned for Dove and her mother to go back inside.

Dove obeyed but stayed close to the door. She had to know what Mr. Fowler wanted to do. Ma stayed nearby and wrapped her arm around Dove's shoulders. Concern filled Ma's face, and her lips trembled.

Fowler's voice rang out. "I say we burn them out. Their fields are so dry they can't grow crops, so let's burn it all and end it for them."

"Are you crazy? Trying to burn their crops in a drought like this could set off a prairie fire that would hurt us all."

"Not if it's done right."

"I want no part of such a scheme, Fowler. It's far too dangerous. Somebody could die in such a fire."

"Have it your way then, but you'll be sorry you didn't go in with me. I aim to keep this land for cattle and horses, not some corn and beans somebody wants to grow. I'm warning you, though. I don't want your men on my land. Any cattle that come up that way will go into my herd. That goes for Ben Haynes's herd too."

"Don't worry. We'll take care of our own. Now get off my property."

Ma gasped beside her. Pa's anger had returned, and it worried Dove. With no fences and free range, how could he be sure his steer wouldn't stray onto the Fowler land? Dove trembled, and a chill shook her body. With Mr. Fowler so determined to take what wasn't his, Pa would be in danger. Perhaps even her entire family might bear the brunt of his evil ways.

She needed to see Luke and Martin right away, but with dark coming, she had no way of going into town to tell them what she'd overheard. Luke had a clear head as did Martin, and they would think of some way to stop Mr. Fowler before anyone got hurt.

All that could be done was to wait for morning. Surely they would be at church.

Chapter 13

Reluctant to leave Eli behind, the Morris family missed church on Sunday, so Dove had no one to talk to about the weekend's events. Not only had she not been able to see Luke, but her thoughts had conjured up even more evil things that could happen if somebody didn't stop Mr. Fowler. Of course she should let Pa handle it, but if Luke and Martin could tell Sheriff Claymore, then maybe he could head off trouble.

She hurried through her chores now on Monday morning and tried to think of a reason for another trip to town. The confrontation with Mr. Fowler still weighed heavily on Dove's mind. When approached, Ma hadn't wanted to talk about it, and Dove didn't dare speak to Pa with the mood he was in. That left Luke and Martin as the only two with whom she could discuss the matter.

Finally she came up with an idea and approached her mother. "Ma, I spotted a bolt of red gingham fabric that would make up a wonderful dress. With all the trouble, I completely forgot to mention it when we were there. Could we go back now and get it?"

Ma studied her for a moment with narrowed eyes. "All right. I need to stop by Doc Carter's and check with him about Eli anyway."

Dove suppressed a retort. Her brother had insisted on riding out this morning with the others but had come back in a hurry and was now in his room resting like he should have done in the first place. He was a stubborn one, but the pain in his rib cage would keep him down.

Dove saddled her horse and Dusty for her mother. Ma stopped at the door, shaking her head. "I've changed my mind. Someone needs to stay here with Eli. Dove, you go ahead and ride into town. Hawk can go with you. You'll be safe with him."

Her brother moaned. "Ma, can't this wait? Pa needs me out on the range. I was supposed to be back by now."

Ma crossed her arms over her chest and tapped her foot. Hawk may be six feet tall and twenty-two years old, but he didn't cross his mother. He turned on his heel and led her horse back to the stable. A few minutes later he returned and mounted his.

"This trip better be important." He snapped the reins.

The scowl remained on his face the entire trip. Dove rode beside him, thankful he was accompanying her. Her mind raced with all that she wanted to say. She didn't know exactly what Martin and Luke could accomplish, but they would think of something. If they spoke with Sheriff Claymore, he would listen to them and realize there might be trouble in the days ahead. He certainly wouldn't believe her. She lifted silent words toward heaven. *Oh, Lord God, please protect my family from any harm. Help Pa keep Mr. Fowler from burning the fields.*

Hawk rode faster than Ma, so the trip seemed much shorter today, but then with so much on her mind, Dove hadn't really paid attention to the time. Hawk stopped the team in front of Anderson Mercantile. He dismounted and secured his horse.

When Dove stood beside him, he leaned his head down to hers. "Be careful about who you talk to and what you say."

Dove's eyes opened wide. Her brother knew her too well. She

nodded. "I will." He hadn't said not to tell, just be careful, and she planned to be.

Inside the store, she found only Luke and Alice. Mr. and Mrs. Anderson were nowhere in sight. That was a good sign, and there were no other customers in the store. That meant she could talk with Luke alone. Luke hurried to Dove's side. "There's so much I have to tell you."

"Oh, me too, Luke, but where are your mother and father?"

"That's one of the things to tell you. Pa had an episode Saturday after you left, and we had to rush him to the doctor's office. He needs lots of rest, so Ma is up taking care of him, and I'm in charge of the store."

"Oh, Luke, I'm so sorry to hear that." First Eli was injured, and then Mr. Anderson took ill. What a day Saturday had been. "Will he be all right?"

"Yes, but he must stay in bed for several days and rest. Ma has her hands full keeping him down. He wants to be here in the store of course." Luke glanced over her shoulder. "Will, stay out of the candy jars. You can't have any until after you eat."

The little boy scowled then ambled over to Dove. "Hello, my name is Will. What's yours?"

Dove bent down and shook his hand. "Good morning, Mr. Will. My name is Dove."

A grin spread across Will's face. "Dove? That's a bird. You're not a bird."

"No, but that's what my ma and pa named me." She resisted the urge to reach out and run her hand through the boy's blond curls."

"Oh, that's funny. I'm seven. How old are you?" His grin revealed a missing tooth.

Alice stepped up. "That's quite enough with the questions. Go find a game to play." She took his hand and led him away.

Dove grinned. "He's a cute little boy."

"Yes, and Ma and Pa spoil him. I had a brother who died of rheumatic fever when he was about four years old, so when Will was born, my parents thought of him as a gift from God to fill the gap left by Tom's death."

"Oh, I'm sorry about your brother, but I can understand your parents wanting to spoil him." The death of her child must have only added to Mrs. Anderson's bitterness. She had suffered so much in her life, but she had let her distress color her attitude in such a way that she hurt others. There was so much to understand about other people and their problems and how they affected one's behavior.

Luke touched her hand, and needles of delight shot up her arm. "Dove, we won't be able to have our picnic this week because I'll have to stay here and take care of the store. With the Fourth of July coming up, we'll be extra busy with everyone coming in to stock up for the holiday."

Her heart plummeted. She had so looked forward to that time together, but of course he couldn't leave the store unattended. She nodded, but then he smiled, and hope returned.

"Martin has an alternate idea. Since we'll be closed for the town's observance of July Fourth on Saturday the third, we're going to meet up for dinner that day. I'll take Sarah as originally planned, and you'll be with Martin."

"That will be wonderful." Her spirits soared again. Trust Martin and Luke to have a solution. That brought to mind the excuse for her trip to town. She headed back to where bolts of fabric filled the shelves. "I want to buy this red gingham."

When he reached up to pull it down, she lowered her voice. "I must talk with you and Martin about something that happened Saturday evening out at the ranch."

His green eyes darkened. "Did you have more trouble with Chester Fowler?"

"Yes. He came to seek Pa's help. He wanted Pa and my brothers to join him in burning out the farmers. Pa said no because it's too dangerous."

"Of course it is. What was Chester Fowler thinking? Stupid question. That man never thinks. He acts then waits to see the damage before he does anything like apologize."

Luke knew Mr. Fowler for sure. His impression was the same as hers. "What can we do about it?"

"I'm not sure, but the sheriff needs to know." He carried the fabric to the front and placed it on the counter.

"He won't listen to me, but maybe he'd listen to you and Martin." The sheriff had to believe Luke and do something before tragedy struck.

"I'll speak with Martin when I close for the noon hour." He wrote up the purchase. "Is there anything else you need to go with this? Buttons, thread, trim?"

She wanted to hug him for being so understanding and willing to help her, but she simply grinned. "Thank you. I knew I could count on you, and I do need a few sewing notions to go along with this."

Another customer entered, so Dove sorted through the sewing supplies and picked out red and white buttons and white thread for her dress. A piece of eyelet caught her attention, and she added it to her purchase. It would make a nice collar or trim for the bodice.

She waited until the other customer had left to put her things together. Luke added them up and then wrote the amount on her father's account. Dove savored these few minutes alone with Luke and wished she could stay longer.

He wrapped the purchases, but before handing them to

her, he grasped her hand. The warmth from the touch flooded through every part of her. She wanted this moment to never end.

Alice cleared her throat, and Dove jumped. Heat rose in her face, and she pulled her hand from Luke's. "It's best I get back home."

Dove picked up her package and turned to Alice. "I'm truly sorry about your father. He's always been nice to me, and I pray he will be up and about in good health soon."

Alice's eyes cast a knowing look at Dove, as if to say she'd keep what she had seen a secret. "Thank you. Doc Carter seems to think a few days' rest will be just what he needs."

Luke walked with her to the door and smiled. "I'll take care of that little matter we discussed."

Dove's soul sang a happy tune. Luke was kind and tender-hearted like Eli, yet brave and strong like Hawk. He was everything she could hope for in the man she longed to marry.

"Tell your father and mother I'm praying for them." She heard steps on the stairway and hurried out the door to avoid meeting Mrs. Anderson.

Ma appeared at the bottom of the stairs. "Luke, you can close up now. I have lunch ready upstairs."

Will came running around from the back of the store. Ma grabbed him by his shirt. "No running, young man. Go upstairs quietly and get washed for lunch. Pa is resting." She followed him back up the steps.

Luke turned the sign on the door to indicate they were closed for the noon hour. Alice stood by the counter.

"Dove is a very nice girl."

"I know. If only Ma could see that." The memory of Dove's soft hand filled his heart with happiness.

"She will someday."

Luke hugged her. "Keep believing that. It's our only hope." He stepped back. "Go and tell Ma I'll be back in a few minutes. I must go and speak to Martin."

She nodded then bounded upstairs. Luke chuckled. Alice may want to be treated more grown-up, but she still acted like a child in many ways. He didn't mind. She'd be grown and gone too soon, and he liked having his little sister around. His stomach growled its hunger, but he had another matter to see to at the moment.

A few minutes later he entered the bank lobby. Martin stood in one of the teller cages. "Do you have time for a few minutes' conversation?"

Martin grinned. "It's time for a break. Just a minute." He turned away and then reappeared as he came through the door from the offices. "What's on your mind?"

"Dove and her brother were just in the store. I told her about Pa and the picnic idea you and Sarah had. You'll need to see her before she leaves town. I saw her go into Mrs. Weems's dress shop, so you can find her there. I'll let Sarah know our plans."

His eyebrows arched. "That's good. You actually talked with Dove?"

"Yes. Ma was upstairs with Pa, so I had a few minutes with her. But that's not the only thing we discussed." He pulled Martin to the side as a customer entered the bank.

"What's the problem? You look worried."

"I am. Mr. Fowler went to the Morris ranch Saturday night."

"What in the world for? Didn't he cause enough problems already?"

"Dove said he wanted to explain what he'd done."

Martin snorted. "I just bet he did."

"Well, he did, but then he tried to get Mr. Morris involved in a scheme to burn the farmers' fields." Even as he said the words, Luke had difficulty wrapping his mind around such a threat. Still, with Mr. Fowler, anything was possible.

"Say what? That's dangerous."

"I know that, and so does everyone with a sane head on their shoulders. But we need to do something. I told Dove we'd help." Now that he'd actually proposed it, he had no idea what or how he and Martin could do anything.

Martin stroked his chin. "It probably wouldn't hurt to tell the sheriff about it."

"That's what I thought. Let's see him now." He turned and strode through the door with Martin following. If the sheriff took over, then he and Martin wouldn't have to get any more involved with the situation. He had enough problems of his own without inviting them in from somewhere else.

They crossed the street and headed down the boardwalk to the jail. Hawk met them coming out the door from the sheriff's office.

Luke gulped. As tall as he was, Hawk stood taller and broader. Not someone he wanted to cross. Hawk eyed them both but didn't say anything. Luke finally found his voice. "Good day, Hawk. Dove told me about Mr. Fowler's visit on Saturday."

"She did? I'll speak to her about that. It's no concern of yours."

Luke swallowed hard. Now he'd done it. Dove would be in trouble with her brother, and then her father would find out. He should have kept his mouth shut.

Hawk pulled on his gloves. "I've taken care of it. Claymore

knows it all. Now I suggest you boys get back to your work and leave this problem to the men who are involved."

Heat rose in Luke's face, and his hands clenched at his sides. He was no match for Hawk, but the man had no cause to be rude. He worked his jaw but kept quiet as Martin grabbed his arm. Hawk sauntered away toward the stables.

"I wanted to hit him. You hear him call us 'boys'?" Luke relaxed his jaw but not his fists.

"Yes, and I saw your anger. That's why I grabbed you. We don't want to mess with Hawk Morris."

Luke strode back across the street and to the bank. "He may be older than we are, but he had no reason to call us that. We're men as much as he is." His anger simmered, but deep inside thankfulness filled him that there had been no further confrontation. Hawk had always been bigger and stronger than any of the other boys in town. At least he'd been in the last few years of his schooling when the family moved here, but he had never posed a threat to Luke or Martin. He'd kept his promise to Dove to talk with Martin, and that's all he planned to do for the time being. Let the Morris, Fowler, and Haynes men take care of their own problems.

Chapter 14

Luke stepped outside the store. The street filled with people ready to celebrate the birth of their country. Red, white, and blue bunting, flags, and banners decorated the buildings and the bandstand that had been erected in what was to be the first city park. He loved the holiday that marked the summer events.

His hopes of seeing Dove today rose when he spotted her family's carriage down by the church. It had been a long week for Luke as he took over the duties of storekeeper for his father, and he looked forward to being closed today. He strode toward the church where many of his friends gathered and passed two new buildings that stood near completion as the town kept growing and expanding. Today they would celebrate the coming of the telegraph and a newspaper to their town. Getting the news sooner through both the telegraph and the paper would be a welcome change for Barton Creek.

Martin waved and hurried to him. "Good to see you, friend. Sarah has talked with Dove, and they've made some arrangements for us to eat together at noon. Mr. Morris and Mr. Haynes are already cooking up the beef they'll serve."

Luke laughed. Food and Sarah, the two things Martin appreciated the most, were foremost on his mind. "Sounds good to me. Let's see what else is going on."

They strolled back up Main Street. Businesses had closed for the day, and a spirit of celebration filled the air. Alice ran out to join them.

"Isn't this the most exciting day? There's so much more going on this year." She hugged herself and spun around.

Luke grinned and tweaked her hair when she stopped. "Yes, it is a fine day, but that isn't all that has you in a merry mood. Planning to meet someone today?"

A deep pink rose in her cheeks. "Maybe," she said hopefully. "Ma said I didn't have to keep an eye on Will all afternoon and keep him out of mischief. He's going to be with Mrs. Porter and her family. Ma will be down in a little bit. She's anxious to get to the park and see what desserts the ladies are bringing." She spotted a friend and waved. "See you boys later." Alice laughed and ran a few steps then slowed to a more sedate walk before glancing back at them and giving them a big grin.

"Your little sister is growing up. She's become a very pretty young lady."

Luke grinned. "That she is." If he could find a way to make it possible for her and Eli as well as for himself and Dove to be together with his mother's approval, then both of them could have reason to celebrate.

They turned and headed back to the church. Both he and Martin greeted many of the people who bustled about getting ready for the major events of the day. As a storekeeper and a banker, he and Martin knew almost all of the citizens of their town. Today, every rancher and farmer for miles around had come to celebrate not only the holiday but also milestones for the town.

He'd be glad when the train spur made its way from Guthrie to Barton Creek. That would save several hours every few weeks when supplies could come straight to their town. Luke's head filled with ideas of what he and Pa could do to make Anderson Mercantile the premier merchandise center of the area.

As they passed land marked off for the new park, Ma waved at Luke. He waved back then stopped short when he spotted Mrs. Morris setting pies and pastries on the table not far down the line from where Ma oversaw the cakes and cookies. *Please, Lord, let Ma be civil and not make a scene today.*

Dove searched the crowds for Luke and Martin. Sarah had said to be at the park to meet them for the noon meal. The dedication of the park and the official opening of the telegraph were to be the highlights of the day just before the meal line would open. It had been five days since they talked, and that occasion was far too brief.

Sarah grabbed her arm. "There they are. I see them over by the bandstand." She pulled Dove along. "Come, let's join them. The festivities will begin soon. I hope they're not too long. I can smell that meat cooking from here, and my stomach is calling to be fed. If Mayor Frankston gets to talking, no telling how long he'll be."

She talked so fast, Dove had a hard time keeping up. Luke was right about Sarah, but her heart was as big as all outdoors, and that counted a lot for Dove. She shaded her eyes and finally spotted Luke and Martin where Sarah indicated. The two young men waved and met them at the edge of the park where a crowd had gathered to hear the speeches.

When Luke smiled at her, Dove's knees weakened and her heart thumped against her ribs, and she grasped Sarah's arm to keep from falling. She gathered her wits about her and stepped to Martin's side.

Martin bowed. "How nice to see you lovely ladies this morning. You'll join us as we enjoy the program?"

Sarah batted her eyelashes at Martin. "It will be our pleasure." She placed her hand in the crook of Luke's elbow as he offered it to her. Dove did the same with Martin. If she could be more open with her feelings like Sarah, perhaps Luke would be more attracted to her. But being what Aunt Clara called a coquette didn't fit in with the way Dove had been taught.

At that moment, Aunt Clara strolled by on the arm of Doc Carter. Dove hid her smile. Doc Carter was one of the more eligible older men in Barton Creek, and he couldn't have found a more charming companion than Ben Haynes's aunt. Aunt Clara spotted Dove and gave her a broad smile as well as a knowing wink. Heat rose in Dove's cheeks. Nothing got by Aunt Clara.

Dove gazed around at her surroundings. So many changes since she had come to live in Oklahoma Territory. Most of them she liked, but some didn't add anything to the town. The saloon that had opened in the middle of town offered a good example of that. It stood about halfway between the jail at one end and the church at the other. Somewhat like halfway between heaven and hell.

Luke stood beside Sarah, but he stared at Dove. "Let's stay here for the speeches. There's some shade here, but then you ladies have your parasols, so that may not matter."

"Oh, this will be perfect. We can see the stage quite well, and I'm sure we'll be able to hear without a problem. This is so exciting. Just think, we can send messages on that wire they put up over there. Pa says he bets the first one to use it will be the bank. Is that right, Martin?" Sarah's words gushed forth like the water from the pump in a kitchen.

Luke stepped closer to Dove and bent close to her ear. "My

pa already has an order ready to send out for merchandise for the store. I'm to take it over soon as the office opens Monday morning."

Dove giggled. "I wish I could be there to watch it. Pa is planning to wire down to Ft. Worth and inquire about the cattle market there. He and Mr. Haynes may take the herd to Texas instead of Kansas this year."

Martin touched her arm. "Here's Mayor Frankston and his wife. The program should start soon."

Luke stepped over to stand beside Sarah, and Martin chose to stand on her other side. Dove peered around them at Luke. He winked at her and mouthed the word, "Later." Joy filled her so that even her toes tingled with the anticipation of that "later."

She looked forward to the afternoon, when she and Luke would take their turns manning the booths with games for the children. The one with tin cans to knock over and the grab-bag ones were her favorites.

Bea covered the plates on the table with a cloth and noticed Emily Morris down the way with her part of the desserts. Bea clenched her teeth. This was a day for celebration, and she refused to let her feelings get in the way of a good time. Emily may have a right to be here, but Bea would not seek the woman out. If their paths happened to cross, she'd speak, but that was all. She planned to keep her promise to never say a word against the Morris family in public, although most of the townsfolk did know her feelings.

Making that decision, she turned her attention to the crowd, seeking to find Luke. Lily Porter stopped at the table. "Looks like we have plenty of desserts to sell, and that meat smells delicious. I hope the mayor isn't long-winded today."

"I do too, and I do want to thank you for keeping an eye on Will for me. Alice and Luke have been so helpful in the store this past week that I wanted to be sure they had a holiday."

"I'm glad to do it, Bea. Will is the perfect playmate for Jimmy. They've been having fun down at the games, and I'm on my way to get them now. I'll send him to you when we get ready to eat."

The woman hurried away to get her charges. The generosity and love of the citizens during Carl's illness amazed Bea. Every night this past week someone had brought dinner. So many times she'd taken care of others, and now being a recipient of such care from folks warmed her heart.

Bea craned her neck and spotted Martin and Luke. Dove and Sarah were with them, but Dove was obviously with Martin and Sarah with Luke. Sarah was a nice girl. Maybe Luke would turn his attentions to her and give up on the idea of Dove.

"What are you thinking, my dear?"

Bea jumped and whirled around. "Carl, you scared me to death. What are you doing out in this heat?"

"I came to hear the mayor's speech and to see the ribbon cutting for the new park. This is a great day for Barton Creek. And I feel fine."

She kissed his cheek. "I've been so worried about you, but today you do look much better. You have some color in your face. The rest that Doc Carter suggested must be working."

"It's been only a week, but I do feel almost like a new man, even if I can't stand lying around." He peered over her shoulder. "I see Luke and Martin with Dove and Sarah."

"Yes. Don't Sarah and Luke make a nice-looking couple?

She'd be the perfect wife for him when he returns from the university."

"Now dear, be careful about making plans for your boy. He may have entirely different ideas."

"And what could be better than what we want for him? He'll learn more about business and be a better helper when he returns from college." Anything she could do to get him away from Dove would be best for him.

"That may be true, but it must be what he wants to do." He turned her around. "Look, the mayor's ready to start. Let's move closer so we can hear."

She walked with Carl to a place nearer the stage, but she never let Luke out of her sight. Mayor Frankston held his hands up for quiet and began to expound on the convenience of having the telegraph service. When she saw Luke glance over to Dove, her heart lurched in her chest. She'd seen that look before. Her boy was still interested in the Indian girl. Getting him out of town was even more important now.

Luke's stomach rumbled and reminded him of his hunger. He glanced at his pocket watch; the time showed half past noon. The smells of the meat cooking over a wood fire tempted the taste buds. He just might buy two plates of the beef Mr. Haynes and Mr. Morris cooked.

Finally Mr. Frankston completed his speech and acknowledged the editor of the newspaper and the man who would send the telegraph messages. He then cut the ribbon for the new park. A cheer went up from the crowd, which soon scattered around the grassy area.

Luke grabbed Sarah's hand. "Let's get over there and get our plates of food now before the line gets too long."

Sarah reached for Dove. "Let us find a place to eat, and you boys bring our plates to us. Whatever they have will be fine with me. I'd like for us to have a place under one of the trees. Come, Dove, let's go find a good spot."

Dove glanced back at Luke and shrugged but followed Sarah across to the park. Luke headed for the concession stand, where the men set up the serving line for the meat and beans with a hunk of homemade bread. He'd never seen meat cooked like this until Becky Haynes's birthday last winter. Mr. Haynes had told him that was the way they prepared meat on a cattle drive. It had been cooking since early morning, and the aroma filled the air.

After they had purchased the plates, Luke led Martin to the park area, where he spotted Dove and Sarah. Luke sat in the space Sarah had left between her and Dove, and Martin sat across from him. Sarah winked at Luke then turned her attention to Martin.

Luke had to admit, the town had done a fine job with the park. The gazebo structure in the middle was the perfect size for a small band, and a concert had been planned for this evening before the fireworks. He looked forward to hearing the rousing patriotic tunes of John Philip Sousa.

He handed a plate to Dove. Her cheeks glowed with color as her hand touched his. That same spark traveled up his arm as when he'd held her hand before. He searched his brain for a topic of conversation but came up against a blank wall. Martin had no such problem as Sarah launched into one of her long-winded exhortations.

Dove finally opened the door for their own conversation. "How is your father getting along? I saw him a little while ago, and he looks like he feels better."

"Yes, Doc Carter put him on bed rest, and it seems to have

helped. He told Pa about some diet he'd learned about in the hospital in Philadelphia, where he was before he came west, and Pa is beginning to look much better."

His father looked as healthy as he had before his illness, a good sign that he'd be able to be back in the store soon. However, Luke had enjoyed being in charge, and now he looked forward to the day when he could take over more of the responsibilities. This week should prove that he had the capabilities to run the place as much as his father.

As though reading his mind, Dove said, "I know you've been running the store while he rested. How do you like it?"

"I enjoy it. Pa plans to buy the space next door when the post office moves to its new building, and I'm to become a partner with him. We're planning to expand the type of merchandise we carry and separate the food supplies from the hard goods like tools and equipment and even have a section just for soft goods like clothing. He's even purchased land to build us a house so that we can use our second-floor dwelling as part of the store." There he went, rambling on again, and most of it he'd already told her before. He sounded worse than Sarah. Dove must think him to be the most self-centered person alive.

"That sounds like you have your life ahead well-planned. Ma thinks I should go to school and learn to be a teacher. I like that idea, but leaving Barton Creek would be difficult."

Luke's heart sank. If Dove left town, he'd never get to see her. So much could happen if she went away. She might even find someone else and fall in love. He shoved that idea aside in a hurry. That was one possibility he didn't even want to consider on such a fine day.

Conversation buzzed around them like flies. Excitement filled the air. He and Dove had the whole summer ahead to make plans and be together, or at least he hoped they would with Sarah and Martin's help. He cleared his throat. "I'd miss you if you had to leave, but teaching is a fine profession. I heard Mr. Fleming say that the school would be divided into two groups in the next year or so because they needed to separate the older students from the younger ones. I suppose teachers are needed everywhere."

Dove pushed the food around her plate. "I'd miss Barton Creek and seeing you, Luke, but it may be the best opportunity I'll have to be of service, and a teaching position may even have to be away from here."

Luke could think of no answer to that thought. With the way so many people in town viewed her and her brothers, she was right in saying she may have to teach in another town.

Luke grabbed Dove's empty plate and carried the dishes for all four of them to the clean-up area. He was glad he hadn't pulled that committee. His work would come later with the booths and games for the children and young people. He turned and headed back, eager to rejoin the group. The sound of music from the town hall carried outside. Luke didn't want to think anymore about the possibility of Dove leaving Barton Creek, and a round of dancing sounded like a good alternative.

He held Sarah's arm as they crossed over to the town hall. He spotted his mother standing near Emily Morris. She appeared to be talking, and her face was pleasant, not twisted with hatred. Hope sprang in his chest. Perhaps his prayers were being answered and his mother was beginning to soften.

When he and Sarah entered the hall, several couples already swirled and turned on the floor. One of them was Eli and Alice. The look of pure joy on Alice's face reinforced the hope that things could be different in the future.

A finger poked his arm. He jumped. "Aunt Clara, I didn't see you come up."

"I didn't think so. You're following Dove around with your eyes like she was a prize piece of beef."

Heat burned Luke's cheeks, and his chest tightened. If Aunt Clara had been so observant, probably his mother had too. He'd have to be more careful.

The elderly woman patted his arm. "Of course I know all about your little scheme with Martin and Sarah. I only wish you didn't have to go to such tactics to be with Dove."

Luke's eyes opened wide. She nodded her head. "Yes, I know all about your plans."

"How...how did you know?"

"A little Lucy bird told me." Then she grinned. "Your secret's safe with me. I admire Emily Morris and that precious girl. I'd never do anything to hurt her. Besides, we have a little something cooked up for you. Are you doing anything right now?"

Luke raised his eyebrows. "Just the dancing. Just what are you planning?"

She smiled, and he detected a hint of conspiracy as she leaned closer. "You'll see. Just go over to the park and stand near the gazebo, and I'll be back soon."

The plump little woman walked away, her skirts swaying with each movement. He hid a smile as she headed straight for Doc Carter. Those two would make a fine pair.

The tension between Luke's shoulders relaxed. If Aunt Clara had anything to do with it, he and Dove would be together despite his mother's opposition.

"Watch out. Aunt Clara has something up her sleeve," Luke reported when he rejoined their group. "She wants us to wait here for her."

"What do you think it is?" Dove tingled with anticipation.

"She said to meet her by the gazebo."

"I think I can guess," Martin said.

They stepped outside, and Martin pointed down the street. There was Aunt Clara seated beside Doc Carter in the Haynes's three-seated surrey. The doctor slapped the reins on the team, driving the surrey toward them.

Aunt Clara waved them over. "Come on!" she called. "We're going to take you two young couples for a ride."

Dove gasped. "For a ride? All six of us?"

Sarah grabbed her hand. "Come on; it'll be fun!" They ran together to the surrey.

Aunt Clara greeted them. "As you can see, I've borrowed the Haynes's three-seater, so we can all fit at once. When we're out of sight of town, you two couples will switch partners and have your time together."

Dove blushed, but Sarah only giggled. Aunt Clara clapped her hands. "Now hop aboard. I've already told Mellie and Ben what we're doing. Doc and I will be the proper escorts or chaperones or whatever for the four of you."

She shooed them to hurry up and get aboard. Luke shook his head and helped Sarah into the middle seat then climbed up to join her. Dove let Martin lift her up to the back row. How Aunt Clara managed to do the things she did to make others happy always came as a surprise. This time Dove was grateful to be on the receiving end.

Once away from town, Doc stopped the carriage. Aunt Clara glanced over her shoulder. "Now, switch."

Luke traded places with Martin and settled beside Dove. She grinned at him, and his answering one bode well for the afternoon. At the moment she didn't care whose idea the ride had been, only that it worked.

He reached for her hand. "Isn't Aunt Clara crazy?" He grinned.

"Crazy like a fox," she agreed.

She glanced back at Sarah and Martin. They sat with their heads close together, and he clasped her hands in his. How nice it would be to have that ease around a boy. Her cheeks flushed warm. That behavior was not fitting for her and Luke, at least not yet, but she could dream.

Luke swiped his right hand down his trouser legs, his left one still holding hers. "I've been wondering about what you said awhile ago. What if something happened and you didn't go off to school?"

She smiled and ducked her head. "Like what?" she said. "The only reason I'd stay here would be if I were to marry. Then I'd have no cause to leave Barton Creek. I could stay here and teach my own children." Dove jerked back. Her thoughts had become words, and those words had slipped out without any warning. What must Luke think of such brazen talk?

He laughed. "Now that's as good a reason as any I've heard." Then he covered her hand with both of his, his expression now very serious.

"How I wish to be the one to marry you and keep you here. I can only pray that when you're finished, you will come back."

Words now failed her. His desire was the same as hers. Joy filled her heart at the realization that he did care for her, much more than she had imagined. But until Mrs. Anderson changed her attitude, it would be a long time before Luke could ask to court her with the intention of marriage.

Chapter 15

Luke opened a box of canned goods that had arrived yesterday from Guthrie. The days since the Fourth of July celebration had been filled with work and listing new inventory. He enjoyed unpacking the merchandise and arranging it on the shelves. He had a plan to make this section much more organized, and this Wednesday morning would be a good time to implement it.

He had only removed a few items to be rearranged when the bell over the door clattered to signal someone's entrance. Martin sauntered in, and Luke stood to greet him. "Wish I had banker's hours. I've been here for nearly an hour already."

His friend laughed. "I do like not having to start until nine, but I'm not here to laud time over you." Martin's eyes sparkled with glee.

"And what might your reason be?" He hoped it had to do with Dove because he had missed her this week. He'd enjoyed being with her last Saturday more than he ever thought he would. After the ride with Aunt Clara, they had danced and had a good time. And at Sunday school the following day he'd sat next to her, and they'd talked before and after the lesson.

"Sarah and I have another idea to get you and Dove together. She's planning a dinner at her home for us on Sunday. She will invite Dove, who will ask me to escort her, and Sarah will invite you. What do you think about that, my friend?"

"It's a great idea. How can I ever thank Sarah enough for all she's doing for us?"

Martin laughed again. "Just give us plenty of time to be together. Soon as we get this all worked out with Dove and your parents, I intend to ask Sarah to marry me."

"What? I didn't know it had gone that far."

"Oh, we've been heading toward that goal for a while, but she's such a matchmaker. She's determined to get you and Dove together. I hear women in love are like that. They want everyone else to be in love too."

"I hope her efforts pay off this time." If they did, then perhaps he could make Dove his bride by year's end. He stopped short in his musings. No sense in thinking that far ahead when he didn't even have Mr. Morris's permission to call on Dove.

Martin turned to leave, but footsteps from behind Luke stopped him. "Good morning, Mr. and Mrs. Anderson."

Luke pivoted to see his parents at the foot of the stairs. "Pa, are you planning to work today?"

"Yes, I am, son. Doc seems to think I'm good enough to take care of business." He grinned at Martin. "Tell your father I'm sorry he was disappointed not to be the first to use the telegraph."

"That's OK, sir. He decided that buying goods for a store was more important than sending a message to a friend. Now if you'll excuse me, I must get on with my day. The bank opens in ten minutes." He left, the bell jangling behind him.

Ma tied an apron over her flower-sprigged dress. "That Martin is a fine fellow. I'm glad you two are friends." She headed for the fabric section with a box of sewing supplies.

Pa went to the counter and pulled out his ledger books, and Luke returned to his chore with the canned goods. Ma had been most pleasant since the Fourth of July. The grim look whenever someone mentioned the Morris family had disappeared. Whether it was his father's illness or the Lord softening her heart, Luke didn't know, but he welcomed the change.

One family had been noticeably missing at the festivities, however. The Fowler clan had not made an appearance at all. If the man wanted to cause any trouble, the Fourth would have been a perfect time to do it. Everyone else from the farms and ranches had been in town.

Even the girls from the saloon down the street had exchanged their fancy dresses for more sedate ones and joined the throngs celebrating. He chuckled to himself at the memory of Charlotte Frankston's face when the girls made their appearance. That lady didn't like anyone who wasn't in her social class or belonged to the church. People like her gave Christians a bad name.

He gulped. His own mother had been exactly like that. First with Jake and the story of his killing someone in Texas and then with Dove and her family. He'd never understand how two people could claim to love the Lord like they did and then show distaste and even hatred for someone else.

Sheriff Claymore entered the store and said he needed some shells for his shotgun and coffee for the jail. After he made his purchase, Luke spoke to him. "Have you heard any more from the Fowlers or any news about what they said they'd do?"

"No, and don't you go getting involved. It may be that Fowler just made idle threats since there's been no more trouble. Just in case, I don't want you getting hurt. Understand?"

Luke swallowed hard. "Yes, sir, I do." But if anything happened involving Dove, he'd be right in the middle of it. He wouldn't let anyone or anything harm her.

His mother tapped his shoulder. "You listen to his advice, son. The law will take care of anything Fowler might do." She stepped back. "I'm going up to give Will a bath before lunch. He came in looking like a street urchin. Alice will come down and help you." She turned to Pa. "Carl, you come on back up and rest awhile before we eat."

Pa nodded. "I will." He waited until Ma was out of sight then asked, "What is this about the Fowlers and the sheriff?"

"After the big fight, Chester Fowler went out to see Mr. Morris. He wanted Mr. Morris and Mr. Haynes to join with him in getting rid of the farmers and their fences. When Mr. Morris wouldn't agree, Mr. Fowler threatened him and said he'd be sorry he didn't take care of those sod busters."

"And how did you come to know about all of this?"

His father's stern look and piercing eyes didn't leave any room for half-truths. Luke cleared his throat. "Dove told me about it one day when she came in for supplies. I went to report it to the sheriff but Hawk was already there. He told me to let him and his pa handle things."

"I see." He stared at Luke a moment and then as if satisfied with the answer, a twinkle appeared in his eye. "I noticed you on the Fourth. I thought you were to escort Sarah, but it looked to me like she had eyes only for Martin, and you paid much more attention to Dove."

Luke sighed. They hadn't been as discreet as they thought. If Pa had seen it, then Ma must have too. But if she had, she would have said something to warn him away. Ma was hiding something, and whatever it was probably wouldn't bode well for him.

Dove picked up a book Lucy had loaned her and settled herself to read. She loved the large room Pa called a "great room" after the great halls in medieval castles, but Ma called it a living room because that's what they did there. A massive staircase leading to the bedrooms separated it from the dining room. She chose a chair near a window and opened her book.

Ma walked into the room pulling on a pair of gloves. "I have a surprise for you. Remember last year when we sent off applications for you to go to school?" She handed Dove a letter. "We heard from Baylor University down in Texas, and they have accepted you into their program for the fall semester."

Dove read the letter and tried to take it all in while her mind raced with what this would mean. She'd told Luke about her plans for college, but it had always seemed so distant and far away. Now the reality of it was staring her in the face. "When...when did this come?"

"In yesterday's mail. Hawk brought it back from town. Are you surprised? Of course you are. Your father and I talked it over and think it's a wonderful idea, and your grades were excellent in school, so you should have no problem picking right back up. Now you can be a teacher like you've always dreamed of being."

Her heart fell. That had been her dream last spring when she had no hopes of attracting any young men. All she had seen then was a summer of heat and dull church socials. Now she couldn't bear the idea of moving away and not seeing Luke. She had to figure out some way to change her parents' minds without being disrespectful.

Ma must have taken silence to mean happiness and acceptance because she now put on her bonnet. "Come, we're going into town to purchase some fabric so we can make you some new clothes to take with you. I saw some patterns in a Godey's book that would be perfect for skirts and shirtwaists for college.

Since we won't have time to do it all ourselves, we can take them to Mrs. Weems and have her make them for you."

Dove's mind whirled with all the images rushing through. She had to tell Luke, and she had to think of a way to stay in Barton Creek. She followed her mother to the carriage, her mind mulling over how she could tell Luke about this new development.

Ma chattered all the way to town, but Dove didn't see a need to respond as no questions were asked. The summer heat bore down on them, and she questioned once again why her mother chose midday to travel, but her heart quickened at the thought of seeing Luke soon.

When they finally arrived in town, it was near the noon hour. Ma climbed down from the carriage and tethered the horses to the post in front of the store. "We'll go in for a few minutes now so I can check that book. Then we'll eat at Dinah's and do our shopping after."

Dove nodded and followed her mother into Anderson's Mercantile. Martin leaned on the counter talking with Luke, and the elder Andersons were nowhere in sight.

Luke greeted them. "Good day, Mrs. Morris, Dove. How can I help you ladies?" His eyes locked with hers.

Ma glanced from him to Dove. "I just want to take a look at those pattern books in the back." She headed that way. "When I find something, I'll call you, dear."

Ma was giving her the chance to tell Luke now. Bless her. Maybe Ma did understand her feelings. She turned to Luke and Martin. "I have something to tell you. Where are your parents, Luke?"

"Upstairs. Ma's getting lunch ready for us."

Martin said, "Yes, I was just inviting him to have lunch with me at Dinah's, but he'd rather eat his ma's cooking. Can't say as I blame him though." He grinned. "Now what's your news?"

Luke stood up straighter. "It's not about the Fowlers, is it?"

"Oh no, nothing like that." She hesitated then plunged ahead. "I've been accepted into Baylor University in Texas."

Luke's face paled. "What are you saying?"

"I'm going to school this fall and become a teacher like we talked about last week."

Luke's face told her all she needed to know. He did care about her, and the thought of being apart from him for months at a time caused her stomach to churn. She had to think of some excuse for staying in Barton Creek.

Luke's heart sank to the pit of his stomach. Dove couldn't leave and go to Texas. He still had too much to tell her, especially how much he cared about her. His mind whirled with things he wanted to say, but before he could utter a word, Mrs. Morris returned.

"We'll be back after we eat to look at fabrics. Come, Dove, let's go."

Martin bowed and offered his elbow to Mrs. Morris. "May I be so honored as to accompany you ladies to the diner? I was just heading there myself."

"That would be a pleasure, young man." She grasped his arm, and they walked away. Dove sent one last look his way. "We must talk later, and I'll explain more." Then she was out the door.

This time the jangling set his teeth on edge. Sadness engulfed his soul. Texas was far away, too far for a casual visit. If she were going nearby, he could manage to get away and see her.

With a heavy heart he turned to trudge up the stairs, his appetite completely gone.

At the sound of anger in his parents' voices, he stopped. He started to back down but then heard his name. He stood still for fear of causing a creak in the step. Their voices carried to him.

"Bea, I say we must give Luke the choice. He'll be twenty years old this fall, and he's been out of school for four years."

"But he had good grades and is a smart boy. It'll all come back to him when he gets into his studies. Besides, just think what an asset a degree will be when the business grows."

Luke's throat tightened. They were talking about sending him away to school too. That was the reason for his mother's attitude in the past week. She had plans to get him away from Dove. He couldn't let that happen. He moved up a step. His father's voice stopped him again.

"I planned to speak to Luke about making him a partner. He has more ideas and common sense than any young man I've seen. He loves this store, and when I expand next year, I want him with me."

Luke swelled with pride. Pa trusted him and wanted him to be a partner now rather than later. He stepped into the room. "And I want to be with you, Pa."

Ma whirled around. "Have you been eavesdropping?" Her eyes narrowed at him.

"Sorry, but I couldn't help but overhear when I came upstairs to eat. I don't want to go away to school to learn what Pa can teach me right here. All I want is to be his partner and turn this store into the best mercantile in the Territory."

"But what about your future? It would be so much better for you to have a college degree." His mother clasped her hands together at her waist.

He stepped over and kissed her cheek. "Don't worry. I'll have the best education money can't buy. Pa has already taught me what it takes to be a merchant, and that's what I want to be. We can use the money I'd spend on school to help expand the store. Besides, I want to be here to help with our new house."

When he bent to hug her, he whispered in her ear, "Dove is going away to school in Texas. You don't have to worry about her anymore."

Ma jerked back and stared up at him. Slowly understanding dawned in her eyes, and a smile formed on her lips. "How nice for her." She stepped back and wiped her hands on her apron. "Now that that's settled, I guess we should eat. I must admit my heart was a little sad at the thought of your not being here to help."

Pa nodded at Luke and grasped his shoulder. Ma's attitude had made a complete turn at the news of Dove's leaving. She hadn't changed at all in her feelings toward the Morris family. The further away Dove was, the happier his mother would be. No matter what Ma said or how she tried to separate them, Luke's heart would be with the girl he loved, and he'd wait for her no matter how long it took her to come back to Barton Creek.

Chapter 16

Luke raised the shades and opened the door to let people know the store was now open for the day. Another wonderful Sunday had come and gone. Again he'd sat next to Dove in Sunday school. Better yet, Sarah's plans had worked out, and they'd enjoyed a wonderful Sunday dinner at her home. Sarah's family proved to be just as talkative as she was, so he hadn't had any time alone with Dove. But he'd enjoyed the laughter and chatter of the group, and Dove's smiling face told him she did as well.

Luke went outside to sweep the walkway. Even with the dirt hard packed from no rain, the dust was still bad and covered the entrance to the store every morning. The noise from the construction across the way no longer bothered him as it had when they first began. As soon as the town business building was complete, the post office would move and the land next door would belong to the Anderson family to expand the mercantile.

With his head swimming with ideas on how to organize the new space, he put away the broom and went to look over the ledger book.

"You're certainly buried in your work early in the day."

Luke jumped. "Martin. I didn't hear you come in."

"You have the door open, so the bell didn't sound." He leaned on the counter. "Those your records for the month?"

"Yes, and something bothers me. Our farmers are having a hard time paying their accounts, but Pa doesn't want to deny them food. Their debt just keeps growing."

"I know. Same thing is happening at the bank. My father is afraid he'll have to foreclose on many of them before fall. Usually he'd wait until after the harvest, but it doesn't appear that there will be much, if any, harvest this year."

Luke understood. His father held to the same practice, but a summer without rain didn't bode well for crops. "Wish there was some way we could help. I haven't seen it go this long without substantial rain since we've been here. A few showers now and then, but we need a steady downpour to soak the ground."

"It has been a strange summer; I will say that. But I think we may have a solution to help the farmers with their bills. I heard Ma, Mrs. Haynes, and Aunt Clara talking about it yesterday. They want to hold some kind of big party or such and raise money to put toward their debts."

Sounded like a good idea, but Luke had seen firsthand how stubborn some of those men could be with pride and not wanting any handouts. "What if the farmers don't want the money?"

Martin laughed. "Aunt Clara thought of that. She said if we put it all in two funds, one at the store and one at the bank, your pa and my father could divide the money up among the accounts and help pay the bills."

Luke stroked his chin. "That might work. That way they wouldn't have any money to give back. It'd just be done. When do they want to do it?"

"I don't know about that. I only overheard that bit of their conversation, but I think the ladies are planning a meeting of the Women's Mission Society to discuss it."

"I hope it's soon. Don't know how much longer we can carry

these bills." The figures on the page before him told the grim story of the hardships for the homesteaders. "At least Fowler hasn't been up to any of his tricks lately. I've worried that he may act on the threat he made."

"That's the last thing those farmers need about now, but Sheriff Claymore should be able to handle it." He turned to leave. "I've got to get on to the bank. Just wanted to let you know what I heard."

Luke stored the ledger book under the counter. If the ladies did have a social, perhaps he could convince Pa to donate some of the supplies. That could be their part in helping out.

His mother entered the store pulling on her gloves. He'd never understand why women wore hats and gloves in this heat. Her skirt swished as she walked to the door.

"I'll be at the church for the Women's Mission Society. Marie Fleming has called a special meeting this morning. Pa is resting. Alice will be down shortly to help you. She's making sure Will is dressed in his old clothes before he goes out to play."

She stepped outside at the same time the first customer of the day entered. Luke smiled and welcomed his patron. At least the ladies of Barton Creek didn't let any grass grow under their feet when they had a project in mind. The results of the meeting should be very interesting.

Bea made her way down the aisle of the church. A number of the other members were already gathered, including Emily Morris. Bea hesitated then turned and sat on the opposite side of the aisle. If she kept her distance, there would be no need to have conversation with Emily.

A few minutes later, Charlotte Frankston called the group

to order. "Ladies, we've called a meeting this morning because Marie Fleming and Mellie Haynes have come up with a wonderful idea for a town social sponsored by the church. Marie, you have the floor."

Marie stood and nodded to Charlotte. "Thank you." She turned to the group. "We all know what a horrible summer this has been with the heat and no rain. Well, the thought of those families, especially the children going hungry, hurts me deeply. Mellie Haynes, along with Aunt Clara, and I have come up with a plan we think will help them and not take away their pride."

Heads turned, and women around Bea murmured. Marie raised her hand. "Let me elaborate. We are going to have an ice cream social where we will sell bowls of ice cream along with cookies, cakes, and pie donated by our townspeople. The money will then be put into a fund at the bank then distributed in equal amounts to each account at the Anderson's and each loan at the bank."

Bea's mouth gaped open. Those past-due accounts had worried both her and Carl this past month, but they didn't know what to do about it except to keep giving them credit. This plan would help not only the homesteaders but also their own store. She raised her hand, and Marie recognized her to speak.

"I think this plan is wonderful. We won't be giving the money to them directly, so no one of them will know exactly who gave it. In fact, Carl and I will donate ingredients and supplies for the ice cream. We also have several freezers on order, and they should be here in time."

The ladies clapped and nodded their approval. Bea's heart swelled with satisfaction. This was a way to show their goodwill from the store as well as return some of the care the people had shown her and Carl the past few weeks.

Marie asked for quiet again. "Now, ladies, since Mellie Haynes and I had the idea, we've come up with a committee we think will do a wonderful job of organizing it all. Of course Mellie and I will be on it with her as chairman. We will also include Clara Haynes and Emily Morris. To spark the interest of the young people we chose Lucy Starnes, Dove Morris, and Sarah Perkins."

A moment of silence followed the announcement. Bea fought to control her feelings. She'd have to work with Emily and Dove. She swallowed hard. *Lord, what are You doing to me?*

At that moment, Charlotte Frankston stood and puffed out her chest. "I don't know why as the mayor's wife I was not consulted as to the purpose of this social you ladies proposed. The farmers have brought this on themselves. Why should we spend our hard-earned money to pay their debts? And I'm even more insulted to think you'd choose those two women over me." She pointed at Dove and her mother. Charlotte's cheeks burned with anger, and she marched from the meeting.

Bea's eyes opened wide. To feel that way was one thing, but to voice it in public like this was something else. Bea glanced over at Dove and Emily. Several others had gathered around them and offered their sympathy. She didn't feel led to do the same, but public criticism like that was uncalled for. If Charlotte's husband wasn't such a good mayor, she'd have ruined his chances for reelection for certain.

Marie Fleming stood at the front with disbelief written across her face. Bea hastened to her side. "I'll stand by what I promised earlier and take care of all the ingredients we might need for the ice cream."

"Oh, thank you, Bea. I had no idea Charlotte would cause such a scene."

"I'm sure your committee will do a wonderful job." Bea

almost bit her tongue. She could say the words, but she didn't mean them. "Now I need to get back to the store. Let me know what date you decide on." She really didn't need to go, but she had no desire to finish out the meeting with Dove and Emily there.

When she arrived back at the store, several customers waited for Luke to handle their orders. Bea removed her hat and gloves and then tied an apron around her waist. She patted Luke's shoulder. "You finish totaling up, and I'll package these for our customers."

Luke expelled a relieved breath. "Glad you're back. We've been busy. Alice had to take Will upstairs to keep him out of trouble. He wouldn't stay out of the candy jar."

"I'll have to speak with him about that. He knows better." Bea turned to talk with each customer as she handed them their parcels, but her mind continued to return to this morning's meeting. Charlotte Frankston had been outright rude, making a scene like that.

Then a swell of realization overcame her. Rudeness didn't always take the form of unkind words. She'd been just as rude as Charlotte with her silence.

She took out a rag and began to polish the counter. She didn't want to think about that right now.

Dove walked out of the meeting with Lucy and Sarah. Charlotte Frankston's words had hurt, but the fun of working with Sarah and Lucy dulled the pain. As the other two girls discussed how they might organize everything, Dove's mind rested on Mrs. Anderson. Today she had not sided with Mrs. Frankston, and she had not gone back on her promise to help supply the cream and eggs needed for the ice cream. That was a small miracle in itself.

Luke and Martin would probably be enlisted to help crank out the ice cream. They'd be a good choice too. These days, Luke was never far from her thoughts, and the idea of working with him at the ice cream fund-raiser filled her with anticipation.

Lucy grabbed her arm. "Dove Morris, you haven't heard a word we've said. You have that dreamy look in your eyes again. Are you thinking about Luke?"

Dove grinned and nodded. "Yes, I am. Sunday's dinner was so much fun. I can't thank you enough, Sarah."

Sarah winked. "My pleasure."

Dove glanced up and realized they were on the walk in front of the store. Dove stepped back as Sarah and Lucy walked through the door.

For a moment she paused. Then Dove squared her shoulders and marched in behind her friends. She had just as much right to be here as anyone else.

Mrs. Anderson was greeting Sarah and Lucy, but her smile disappeared when her gaze rested on Dove. "How can I help you ladies today?"

Lucy said, "We want to thank you for volunteering all the supplies for the ice cream. That will go a long way to help us have more money for the farmers."

"You did that, Ma?" Luke wrapped an arm around his mother's shoulders.

Butterflies danced in Dove's stomach when he turned to lock gazes with her.

This time Mrs. Anderson's eyes were not as cold as earlier. She beamed under the compliments of her son and the thanks from Lucy and Sarah.

"It will be our pleasure to help, and I'm sure you three young ladies will do a very fine job on the committee. Mrs. Haynes and Mrs. Fleming are bound to have wonderful ideas."

This time Mrs. Anderson included Dove in her statement. Dove swallowed hard. Perhaps just a tiny, tiny crack had penetrated that wall built around Mrs. Anderson's heart.

Chapter 17

Dove stepped down from the family carriage. Two weeks of planning had paid off, and the ice cream social had finally arrived. So far the plans had gone well. Merchants had decorated the streets, but not as lavishly as they had done on July Fourth. Still, everyone wanted to participate, and that gladdened Dove's heart.

She helped her mother carry the cakes they had baked for the desserts to go along with the ice cream. Long tables covered with white cloths were set up in the town hall to receive the sweet goods.

All the young men of the town had been enlisted to turn the cranks on the freezers. Dove joined Sarah, where women poured their homemade ice cream recipes into the tin cans to be placed in the wooden buckets. Every ice cream freezer in town now sat lined up on the boardwalk outside the hall.

Dove counted them. "Do you think we'll have enough for everyone?"

Sarah began cutting slices of cake. "I hope so. Father had plenty of ice brought in to fill the freezer buckets, and Mrs. Anderson is keeping more mixture cool in her icebox at the store."

Lucy Starnes joined them. "I haven't quite mastered the art of cake baking yet, so I brought my sugar cookies with cinnamon." She set a platter on the table.

Dove laughed. "At least you learned to bake the most delicious cookies. They are sure to go fast." She remembered the tales Mellie and Lucy related about her friend's first attempts at cooking. They laughed about them now, but then Lucy's cousins had teased her without mercy.

More women gathered to submit their goods for the bake sale. Dove joined Lucy and Sarah in cutting cakes then covering them with parchment paper and damp cloths until the ice cream was frozen and cured.

The young men gathered and took their places at the freezers. Younger boys were enlisted to sit atop the freezers as the older ones cranked. Luke manned one of the machines with Will sitting on top. She strolled over to speak to the boy.

"Hello, Will. I see you're helping your big brother make ice cream."

A big grin spread across the boy's face. "I am, but it's cold." He peered at her. "You're that girl with the bird name."

Dove laughed. "Yes, that's right. I'm Dove. You are a smart boy to remember."

His little chest puffed out. "I'm the smartest boy in the second grade."

Luke tweaked the boy's hair. "But there are only two boys in the second grade."

Will nodded his head. "And I'm the smartest one."

Dove patted his arm. "I'm sure you are." She turned to Martin, who manned the freezer next to Luke. "Sarah has some plan for getting together this afternoon, but she hasn't said what they are. Do you know?"

Martin shrugged. "Haven't a clue, but I'm sure she'll tell us soon."

Luke turned the crank on his machine. "All that matters

to me is that you'll be there, right?" He smiled at her with joy spilling out of his face.

Martin's laughter rang out. "My friend, this is going to be a splendid afternoon."

Heat rose in her cheeks, but her heart sang with happiness. Then she spotted Mrs. Anderson across the street, and the singing stopped. "I'll let you two make your ice cream. I must get back to helping with the desserts."

Of course all the cakes and cookies were ready for purchase, but Dove didn't want to have an encounter with Mrs. Anderson. The woman's back had been toward them, and she hadn't seen Dove talking with her boys. There would be time enough to talk with Luke later at whatever Sarah had planned for them today. Anticipation set her nerves to tingling.

She spotted her mother with a group of women from the church. They were smiling and talking in a friendly way, and her mother looked so happy. It seemed now that Charlotte Frankston and Bea Anderson were the only two women who ignored Ma. Dove cared nothing about Mrs. Frankston or what she thought, but she did wish that somehow Ma and Mrs. Anderson could become friends.

Dove bit her lip. She had not yet revealed to her parents her wishes about not going to school. She hated to disappoint them, but the closer she came to the time she would have to leave, the harder it would be to tell them. Right now she needed a good dose of courage before confronting them.

Lucy spoke at her side. "I saw you talking with Luke and Will. How are things with him?"

Dove turned her gaze back to Luke and his little brother. "He always seems so glad to see me, and we have a wonderful time when we're together, but the issue of his mother is always just below the surface. Nothing serious can happen until his mother gives her blessing, and I don't think that will be any time in the near future."

Noise from the street interrupted their conversation. Dove stepped outside with Lucy, who gasped. "It's Mrs. Frankston."

The mayor's wife stood with her hands on her hips, her lips set in a firm line. Mellie Haynes looked almost as angry. Lucy grabbed Dove's hand, and they stepped closer to hear.

Although red spotted her cheeks, Mellie Haynes spoke with even tones. "Charlotte, if you can't speak civilly to Emily, then it's best that you be on your way. I will not let you stand here and demean her in front of these people."

"Well, I never..." She whirled around and marched over to the mercantile, where Mrs. Anderson stood on the boardwalk. Mrs. Frankston stopped as though to speak, but Mrs. Anderson whipped around and went inside. Mrs. Frankston frowned then turned back to stare at Mrs. Haynes.

Dove sucked in her breath. The woman's face filled with hatred. She turned and marched down toward the bank. At least Mrs. Anderson had not stayed and talked with her. *Please, Lord, don't let those ladies spoil this day for Ma.*

Cranking the ice cream handle, Luke watched the confrontation on the street. They were at a distance where he could not hear their words, only the anger expressed by the two women.

When Mrs. Frankston joined his mother outside the store, his heart sank. Then when she went inside without speaking to Mrs. Frankston, his hopes rose. He wasn't sure what it meant, but he'd take it as a good sign.

He leaned forward and cranked harder. His freezer needed more ice and salt. "Will, hand me the bucket of ice."

By the number of people now milling about the streets and in the town hall, just about everyone from around Barton Creek was in attendance. He hadn't spotted the Fowlers yet, but they'd most likely make their appearance sometime since all the family was now back together. Luke loved this town, and it grieved him when people like the Fowlers got greedy and wanted more than their fair share.

Martin leaned back and rolled his shoulders. "This is hard work, but I think mine's finished. How about yours?"

Luke gave one more push on the crank and met more resistance. "Think this is ready too." He lifted Will. "OK, little brother, you can go play now. Thank you for your help."

The boy grinned. "My seat is cold, but I love ice cream. Bye." Off he raced to join his friends.

Luke checked the ice level, added a little more rock salt, then covered his freezer with towels to keep it cold while it hardened even more. "You say Sarah didn't give you any idea what she has planned for us today? She wouldn't give me a hint earlier." Just knowing he'd have time with Dove later gave added sparkle to the day.

Martin secured the ends of the towel on his freezer. "The only thing said was to watch you and her when she headed toward the church."

"I suppose she means that when you see us headed that way, you and Dove are to follow."

"I believe that's the plan." A huge grin spread across Martin's face. "I have some grand news. The letter came yesterday, and I've been accepted into the seminary program I applied for."

Luke grasped Martin's shoulder. "That's wonderful news. Congratulations."

"And the best part is that my father is delighted. He thinks being a preacher is as good as being a banker, if not better. I plan to tell Sarah this afternoon." Martin patted his stomach. "Now let's go check out some of those desserts the ladies have been bringing in. I can tell you more about the school while we eat some of Mother's chocolate cake."

Luke's heart filled with joy for his friend. Both had worried about Mr. Fleming's reaction, but he had been delighted. If only Ma would have such an attitude about Dove.

When they stepped into the main meeting hall, the women were lined up behind the tables, ready to assist in serving the cookies and cakes. Luke even spotted a few pies added to the display. A sign stated no set prices, but a minimum donation of ten cents would be appreciated for each selection of a dessert.

Martin and Luke headed for the cake table. Mrs. Fleming's was easiest to spot as it was darker and richer looking than the others. They each added a huge dip of vanilla ice cream from the freezers brought inside. Luke plunked down a quarter, and Martin did the same. They strolled out to the streets where the mayor stood at a podium on the gazebo speaking to the citizens of the town. It'd been only four weeks since his last public appearance, and here he was again telling the good citizens of Barton Creek what things he planned for the future. Even if he carried through with only half of them, Barton Creek would be a better place.

Luke shook his head. Martin appeared to be listening closely. Why anyone would want to get mixed up in politics Luke didn't understand. As a career, it had no appeal at all for him. He turned to look down Main Street. In less than a year it had almost doubled in size, exploding with buildings and citizens.

He noticed a crowd gathered on a corner across the way. A voice shouted out from a group of men, and Chester Fowler raised his hand to shake it at the men gathered around.

"This is a big waste of time and good money. Farmers have

no place in this territory. This land's no good for crops and fences. I say we run them off and save that money to build up our town."

Several men nodded, appearing to support Fowler. Luke scowled and clenched his free hand into a fist. "That man brings nothing but trouble everywhere he goes. Why can't he leave well enough alone?"

Martin frowned then shook his head. "I thought he'd learned his lesson and would stay out of trouble. Apparently not."

At that moment, the mayor shouted out to calm the men. "Come now, good citizens of Barton Creek. There's enough room for everyone here. Nature has chosen to keep rain from our land, and that has hurt the crops the farmers planted. The least we can do as Christians is to help them stay in their homes."

Murmurs arose among the crowd. Most were nodding in agreement, but Mr. Fowler had a few supporters himself. Luke spotted his father with those who sided with the mayor. At least Pa wanted what was best for everyone, and he didn't care if there wasn't enough money for the farmers to pay their store bills.

Most of the crowd dispersed, but a small group still stood around Chester Fowler, listening to his complaints. Luke yearned to step closer just to hear what the man said, but he didn't want to appear to be a part of that group of men. He ate the last bit of his cake and ice cream then threw the piece of parchment that held it in the trash bins provided along the street.

Martin did the same. "I don't think Chester Fowler is through for the day. A few more men, mostly ranchers, are gathering around him."

"Oh, I think Sheriff Claymore can handle them." A broad grin spread across Luke's face. "Look who's coming this way."

Dove and Sarah headed toward them twirling their parasols. Sarah's yellow curls bounced on her shoulders as she turned her head toward the small group of men. "Was that Mr. Fowler I heard shouting a few minutes ago?"

Luke offered his arm to her but glanced over at Dove. Her brown eyes held a mixture of merriment and concern. He could understand her worry. "Yes, it was. He's saying this social is a waste of time and money. He's ready to run the farmers out of the territory."

Dove spun around to Martin. "Do you think he'll carry through with his threats?"

Martin scowled. "He very well could." He turned toward the church. "Let's walk down the other way where it's quieter."

Sarah sniffed and shook her head. "I wish those men would all go back to their ranches or whatever and leave everyone else alone. They might do something really terrible if they get riled up enough."

Dove said nothing but continued to glance over her shoulder at the group gathered around Chester Fowler. Luke wanted to do nothing more than to calm her fears, but he could do nothing until they were together and alone.

Sarah slipped her hand around Luke's arm. "Let's go down to the church then take a walk behind the building. There we can change partners and continue on our way down to the creek."

Luke exchanged looks with Martin, who nodded. Luke scanned the streets, but his mother was not in sight. He relaxed and turned his attention to Sarah and her prattle as she complained once again about the men with Fowler. In less than five minutes he'd be with Dove.

When they stopped behind the church, Martin grabbed

Sarah's hand and waved good-bye. "We'll see you back here in half an hour or so."

Luke bent his arm and held it out to Dove. "Shall we take a walk?"

Her smile filled her eyes with happiness as she placed her hand in the crook of his elbow. "I'd like that."

After a few minutes she spoke. "It's such a lovely day. I hope we make enough money to pay the bills of the farmers and their families."

Luke considered the amounts owed to the store by the three men. Pa had told Mr. Fleming that the money should go toward the loans first and then to his store. "I think there should be what they need to pay what they owe." He glanced toward the sky. "If the rains had come like normal, their crops wouldn't be drying up. They'd have a bountiful harvest, but as it is, the drought has ruined it all."

"That's why Pa's glad he's a rancher. The cattle live on grass, which doesn't need as much rain. Still, if it doesn't rain soon, the ranchers could suffer too."

Although Luke's knowledge of ranching and cows was limited, he did understand how the drought would affect them too. If the grasses all dried up, the cattle would have no feed themselves. But he didn't want to talk about cattle and crops; his interests lay elsewhere. He couldn't get to know Dove better and he certainly couldn't persuade her not to go off to college if he didn't mention it.

A branch cracked behind them. Luke turned to investigate but saw nothing. He placed his hand over Dove's, still on his arm. How small her hand was in comparison to his. He hadn't truly noticed that before. It lay there, light as a feather but warm as the summer day. So much to learn about her and so little time to do it.

Then the noise came again, and Luke jerked around to see somebody hiding in the bushes.

Zeb Fowler stepped forward. "Well, lookee here. If it ain't the boy from the store and the Injun girl. You plannin' to keep her all to yourself, boy?"

He hooked his thumbs into his waistband and rocked back on his heels.

The evil grin on the man's face sent a chill through Luke's bones. The last person he wanted to tangle with today was one of the Fowler boys. "We're just out for a stroll with our friends." His hand tightened over Dove's. The fear in her eyes filled him with anger toward Zeb and increased Luke's courage to stand his ground against the man.

Zeb glanced all around. "I don't see any friends." He chuckled. "All I see is a purty little girl." He lunged forward and grabbed Dove. Her hand slipped away from Luke, and Zeb pulled her against him and held her against his body.

Dove screamed and kicked, but he covered her mouth with his hand. Luke froze in place, just like he had when Eli had been attacked. Dove's eyes opened wide in terror and pleaded with Luke to save her. The string of curse words and other foul language spouting from Zeb's mouth spurred him into action. This time he'd do something. He couldn't let Zeb hurt Dove. He searched the ground for a weapon as Zeb carried Dove toward the trees.

Luke went down to his knees and grabbed a large rock. He stood and held it high before lunging at Zeb's back. Luke brought the rock down hard on the man's head, and Zeb grunted before falling to the ground. Blood oozed from the gash, and he didn't move.

Luke grabbed for Dove's hand and pulled her to safety. He wrapped his arms around her. "Are you all right?"

She nodded then sobbed against his chest. At the moment he wished the man to be dead, but the rock had only knocked him unconscious. "Come on. We have to get back and tell the sheriff what happened."

Martin and Sarah crashed through the trees. Luke saw them and gasped in relief. "Martin, Zeb tried to attack us."

"We heard the scream and got here quick as we could." Martin nodded at the body on the ground. "Is he dead?"

"No, only knocked out. We've got to get the girls back to safety before he wakes up."

As much as he hated to let go of Dove, he did so when Martin grabbed her hand. Luke reached for Sarah's. He turned to Martin. "You take Dove to the sheriff. I'll go find her father." With that he ran around to the front of the church with Sarah stumbling along behind him.

Chapter 18

Luke searched the crowd for Mr. Morris and spotted him down near the jail. "Martin," he called. Martin turned. "Dove's father is headed for the sheriff's office. We're going there too." Dove shot him a look of terrified relief, and he sent her what he hoped was one filled with reassurance.

On the boardwalk in front of the jail, loud voices sounded from inside. Luke recognized Mr. Morris's and Chester Fowler's. Luke edged up to the door and peeked into the office. Sam Morris, Hawk Morris, Jake Starnes, and Chester Fowler still argued about the farmers and fences.

The sheriff raised his hands. "Look, no crime has been committed here. All I hear is accusation and anger. I suggest everyone calm down and go get some ice cream. If you don't like it, Chester, then go on home and let the others enjoy the day." He pointed a finger at the man. "But I'm warning you. If you or your sons do anything to spoil this event or to hurt the farmers and their families, you will hear from me."

Luke's breath caught in his throat and he almost choked. That had already happened. Not to the farmers, but to Dove. He grabbed Martin's arm. "You're the one who was supposed to be with Dove. Go in there and tell him what Zeb did."

Martin swallowed hard, twice, before he stepped through the door. Sarah and Luke followed him, and for once Sarah had nothing to say.

Martin's voice cracked as he said, "Sheriff, I wish to report that Dove was attacked by one Zeb Fowler just a few minutes ago."

Sam Morris reached out and gathered Dove to his chest. His face contorted with an anger that exploded in a torrent of words. "I warned you about hurting my children. First Eli, now Dove. I want your filthy hide in jail along with those no-good sons of yours." He stopped for breath and turned to Martin. "Tell me exactly what happened."

"The four of us had gone walking down toward the creek. Zeb Fowler jumped from a clump of bushes and grabbed Dove before we knew what was happening. Luke picked up a rock and hit him over the head. We left him down there."

Hawk's face turned thunderous, and he disappeared from the office.

Fowler raised his fist. "My boy didn't do that, and even if he did, she's just an Indian girl."

At that Sam Morris released Dove and lunged for Fowler. He knocked him to the ground and hit him once on the jaw before Claymore grabbed his arm and, with Jake Starnes's help, pulled him off Fowler.

"Let me at him. No man is going to talk about my daughter that way or think it's OK for his son to lay his hands on her. I'll kill him."

Jake held his arm. "Sam, let the sheriff handle this. He'll find Zeb and arrest him."

"Then you'd better put this foul-mouthed man in jail so he can't go warn his boy and help him escape."

Claymore reached for a pair of handcuffs. "That I can do."

Fowler swung his fist toward the sheriff. "Ain't nobody gonna arrest me."

Jake and Sam grabbed Fowler and managed to subdue him

for the sheriff. Claymore shoved him into one of the cells and locked it. "That should keep you out of trouble until we find your sons."

The whole scene left Luke weak in his knees. He turned around to find Martin had taken Sarah and Dove back outside. Luke groaned. He should have thought of that. He remembered Hawk leaving and ran outside in time to see him disappear at the end of the street riding his horse like the devil himself chased him.

At that moment Bea ran from the town hall. "The money's gone! All the money's gone!" Bea rushed to the sheriff then pointed a finger at Sam Morris. "It was your boy Hawk that took it. He was in the town hall just a little while ago." She glanced around at the men. "I see he's not anywhere around now either."

Sam Morris clenched his jaw. "Wasn't my boy that took your money. He's been right here with us."

Claymore spoke up. "He's right. Hawk was here until just a moment ago. I'll get someone to look into that, but we have a more important attack to investigate."

Mr. Morris glared at Bea. "We have to catch Zeb Fowler. He attacked Dove."

Bea didn't say anything at that, but she looked at Dove with a frown on her face that sent flames of anger straight at Luke's heart. She turned and marched back to the town hall.

Luke clenched his fists to his side. At the moment he wanted to hit her and kill Zeb Fowler. He had never been so angry in his life.

Claymore took charge. "Sam, you and I are going to the place where Dove was attacked to see if we can find Zeb. Jake, if Bart's not in town, you take Luke and Martin out to the Fowler place.

If we don't find Zeb, Hawk will be out there. Find him and talk sense into him. No telling what he'll do if he gets hold of Zeb."

"What do you want us to do if the Fowler boys are there?" Jake asked.

"Just stand guard and make sure nobody leaves. We'll join you out there if Zeb is gone."

Luke turned to Dove. "You need to find your mother." He reached out and took her hand. "We'll find Zeb and arrest him. Tell your ma not to worry."

Dove blinked back tears, holding on to his hand for dear life. "Thank you for being so brave."

He didn't feel like any hero. Fear for her had spurred him to act, not heroics. All he wanted to do at this moment was to gather her into his arms and comfort her. Instead, he squeezed her hand reassuringly. "I'd do it all over again to keep you safe."

"I'm scared. What if Hawk went after Zeb? He could get hurt."

Luke pictured Hawk's size up against Zeb. "You don't need to worry about Hawk. He's much stronger than Zeb, and he knows how to use his gun if he has to."

Sarah wrapped her arm around Dove's shoulder. "Come with me, Dove. Let's go find our mothers."

Luke peered over their shoulders and sighed with relief. Both mothers were already headed their way.

Mrs. Morris grabbed Dove and hugged her. "Mrs. Anderson told us Zeb attacked you. Are you all right?"

Tears finally streamed from Dove's eyes. She explained to her mother what had happened. "Zeb didn't hurt me," she finished. "Luke hit him in the head, and we all ran back here."

Mrs. Perkins wrapped her arms around Sarah. "What an awful ordeal. Thank God you girls are all right." She stretched her hand toward Luke and grasped his arm. "Thank you for taking care of my Sarah."

Heat rose in Luke's face. He hadn't done anything for Sarah, but he couldn't tell her mother that. This deception was leading to complications, and he didn't like the consequences that could result if his mother learned the truth.

Jake Starnes stepped up to Mrs. Morris. "Have you seen Bart Fowler anywhere around?"

Mrs. Morris shook her head. "No. He was in the town hall the last time I saw him."

Jake frowned. "Then we're heading out to the Fowler place. The sheriff and your husband have gone down to the creek to see if Zeb is still there. I'm taking Luke and Martin with me to find Bart."

He motioned for Luke and Martin to come with him. Dove was in good hands now, so he followed Jake to get their horses. He prayed they could find Hawk before he took revenge on Zeb or Bart. More violence wouldn't solve anything and would likely make things worse.

Now that the attack was behind her, Dove experienced a new fear for her brother. "Ma, what if Hawk finds Zeb? I'm afraid of what he'll do to him."

"I've raised Hawk to be better than that. I have to believe he'll do the right thing and bring Zeb in to face justice." Yet her mother's worried face belied her words.

Ma guided her into the town hall where a few people still gathered to buy ice cream and desserts. Mrs. Fleming beckoned to them.

Ma went over to the table. "What is it, Marie?"

"Mrs. Anderson has people saying your son Hawk took the money box, but I'm sure he didn't."

"What are you saying? Did you see who took the box?"

"Not exactly, but Hawk was nowhere around. It's my fault really because I'm in charge of it. I stepped away for only a moment, and the next thing I knew the money was gone. I did see one of the Fowler boys in the building before that."

Dove frowned. "Sheriff Claymore said Hawk was with them when Mrs. Anderson came out and accused him. It must have been Bart because Zeb was down behind the church at the creek scaring me half to death." She explained what had happened.

Mrs. Fleming's fingers touched her lips. "Oh dear, I'm so thankful you two girls are all right. What a dreadful experience."

Dove's heart still pounded when she thought about what could have happened. She hoped nothing like it would ever happen again.

Ma and Mrs. Fleming busied themselves with putting out more cake and cookies. Now that the excitement had died down, people were ready to get out of the heat and eat ice cream. As they made choices and paid, Dove heard snatches of conversation, and they all involved the robbery. Several cast glances in her direction. The account of her attack had made the rounds quickly. She blinked back tears and wished she could go home, but then she wouldn't know what happened with Luke.

Sarah leaned toward Dove and whispered, "Let's get out of here. We can go to my house where it's quiet and wait until the boys come home and tell us what they find."

"That sounds like a good idea." She turned to her mother. "Ma, I'm going to Sarah's house with her."

Ma hugged her. "Go; we'll take care of things here. You girls need to recover after the morning you've had. I'll be there soon as I finish up."

Dove followed Sarah, but even as they walked through the doors and outside, her name and that of her brothers dotted the conversation of those around her. Dove ducked her head but then raised it again. She had no cause to be embarrassed.

Sarah grabbed her hand. "I see Mrs. Frankston and Mrs. Anderson across the street. Let's hurry before they see us. No telling what Mrs. Anderson might say about your brother."

Those two women were the last ones Dove wanted to meet. Ma might be able to stand her ground and not be intimidated, but Mrs. Anderson's silence cut through Dove's heart and soul like one of Pa's knives slicing open a steer.

On the outskirts of town, Luke heard hooves pounding behind them and turned.

"Eli, what are you doing here?" Jake pulled on his reins as Dove's brother raced to join them.

"I want to help. Dove's my sister too. Those Fowlers can't just get away with this."

Jake leaned on his saddle horn. "Do you think Hawk went after Zeb?"

"Of course! Where else would he go?" Eli swung his fist. "I just hope he beats the stuffing out of him when he finds him."

Jake frowned. "Believe me, Eli, fights don't solve anything. They just lead to more trouble. You don't want your brother to end up in jail for murder, do you?"

To Luke's relief, Eli sobered up fast. Only Jake, with his history, could talk sense into the Morris boys, but he didn't believe it would work with Zeb and Bart.

Jake scrutinized Eli to make sure his words had been heard then nodded. "All right. You can come as long as you promise to keep a cool head. Our job is to find Hawk and watch the Fowler ranch. If the Fowler boys are home, we keep an eye on them until Claymore arrives. And absolutely no fights except in self-defense." He turned his horse to the northeast, and Luke followed with Martin and Eli.

Luke unbuttoned his shirt, thankful he hadn't worn a tie or jacket for the social today. The brim of his hat did shade his eyes, but the rays of the sun from a cloudless sky created a glaring brightness on the landscape. Rivulets of sweat traced their way down his neck and under the collar of his shirt. Although he was no cowboy, he was glad he'd been given the chance today to act as a man—not just a store clerk.

Chapter 19

Emily watched her daughter leave the building. Although she'd tried to act cheerful and normal around Dove, she was still shaking with the news of Zeb's attack. If anything had happened to Dove, Emily would never forgive herself. For eighteen years she'd tried to shield and protect her from being hurt by what others said and did. Despite her efforts, sometimes hate showed its evil, ugly face.

So far life in Barton Creek had been pleasant with only Bea Anderson and Charlotte Frankston making their prejudices public. Now her daughter had been attacked and her son accused of stealing. If not for friends like Mellie Haynes and Marie Fleming, Emily might never come into town, not even to attend church.

"Well, it looks like we have ourselves a thief and a little tart among us today."

Emily spun around at the acid tone of the voice behind her. "Charlotte Frankston, I can't believe you'd say that after what Zeb Fowler tried to do to my daughter today. And my son is innocent. You, however, are as guilty as sin—guilty of hate and lies and prejudice."

Emily stopped to catch her breath then swallowed. Heat rose in her face. She'd never spoken like that to anyone. Several other women had gathered around. Charlotte's face turned red, and veins stood out in her neck. An apology sat on the tip of

Emily's tongue, but she bit it back. She had meant every word said and wouldn't seek forgiveness at the moment.

Charlotte lifted her shoulders and stood tall. "I don't care what you say, Emily Morris. Indians are savages who killed and scalped thousands of people all over this country, including Bea Anderson's very own father and mother."

Emily aimed her gaze at Bea, who stood in shocked silence. "Bea, I'm sorry for what happened to you and your family, but that was years ago. Times have changed. Most tribes are peaceful and only want a part of the land that was theirs anyway. Why, the very ground we're standing on once belonged to the Cherokee Nation. Now all of my people have to live wherever the government puts them. You have freedom to pick out your land and settle wherever you please."

The expression on Bea's face didn't change one fraction. Her clenched mouth and fists told Emily the woman would never listen to reason. Marie Fleming stepped to her side.

"Emily, why don't you go get Dove and take her to my house? We have enough women here to handle whatever customers decide to come in now."

"Thank you, Marie. I do need some fresh air. It's getting to be stifling in here." She spoke to Marie but glared at Charlotte. Her anger made her want to stomp out of the building, but common sense bade her to stand proudly and walk away with her head held high.

"Just wait until Sheriff Claymore captures your son. Then we'll see who the savage is." Charlotte's parting words stabbed Emily with even deeper pain than her heart held before. *Please, God, let Jake and Martin find Hawk before anyone else does.* She stopped in her tracks on the boardwalk outside. Where was Eli? She hadn't seen him since before the commotion with Chester Fowler. *Lord, keep him safe too.*

Bea couldn't believe the scene she'd just witnessed. It broke all the rules of propriety. Smiling at her supposed triumph, Charlotte Frankston walked out of earshot and began talking to one of her cronies.

Marie turned to her. "Emily was right. None of what happened to you is Emily's fault. Can't you see that? Please try, Bea."

"I'm sorry, but I can't." She cast her eyes downward as shame rained down on her. Still, no words of understanding would come.

Aunt Clara came around the table, and Bea steeled herself for the onslaught of words.

The elderly woman planted her hands on her hips. "Bea Anderson, I will never understand how a good Christian woman like yourself can be so stubborn. You volunteered to donate what we needed to make the ice cream to raise money to help the farmers. That shows you do have compassion, but then you turn the cold shoulder to a gracious woman who loves the Lord just as you do."

Although the look on her face was stern, Aunt Clara's words simply told the truth, a truth Bea didn't want to accept. She spoke up, her voice shaking with suppressed emotion. "Her tribe killed my family, took my sister, and left me for dead. I will never forget, nor will I forgive them for it."

"Then I suggest you return home and read your Bible very carefully. I believe you'll find a very different attitude toward forgiveness from our Lord and Savior. Until you forgive, Bea, you will not have peace in your heart." Aunt Clara turned away and walked back to her position behind the cake table.

Bea straightened her back. "I'm going home now. I'm sure you ladies have much to discuss among yourselves."

As she walked to the door, the voices of the women followed her. What they thought didn't matter. How could they know how it felt to lose your whole family to the hands of savages?

Bea trudged up the street to her home. Alice stood behind the counter, going over some figures. "Where are Luke and your father?"

"Pa's upstairs, but Luke went with Jake and Martin to look for Bart and Hawk."

"He's doing what?" Bea spun on her heel and raced out the door. What was he thinking, riding off like some cowboy? She stopped and stared down the street, willing Luke to appear in the crowd. *Oh, Luke, why do you have to go and get yourself involved in things like this?* But she knew why. Because it involved Dove.

People still milled about eating ice cream and visiting as though nothing had happened. Bea turned to head back into the store. All she could do now was to pray for Luke's safe return.

Luke looked down at his hands, growing red from the chafing of the reins. Jake and Eli both wore gloves, and Luke wished he had a pair. He glanced at Martin, who appeared just as uncomfortable in his black trousers and white shirt. Too bad they didn't wear Levi pants like the ranchers did.

Jake kept them traveling at a steady pace. As they neared the Fowler spread, he waved for them to stop. "I think from here on we'd better go on foot. No sense warning them of our approach if they're inside." He dismounted. "We can tie the horses in that stand of scrub trees over there." He walked a few yards and looped the reins around a branch. Luke did the same, followed by Eli and Martin.

Jake shook his head. “I hate to involve you boys in this, but I know Dove and Sarah mean a lot to you, so that’s why I let you come with me. I’m only a few years older than you boys, but I’ve had experience with troublemakers and gun-totin’ cowboys. Don’t do anything unless I tell you to do it.”

He tilted his head and stared at Luke. “You know how to use a rifle?”

“Yes, I do. Pa taught me.” He could shoot, but he prayed it wouldn’t come to that. He’d never fired a gun at anything but tin can targets.

“Good. You take mine. What about you, Martin?”

Martin’s face paled. “I haven’t been around guns of any kind much.”

Jake shook his head. “Then you stay behind Eli. If there’s any shooting, you get on the ground and lie flat until I tell you to move. Understood?”

Martin nodded, but the color didn’t return to his face. Jake motioned for Luke to join him. “We’ll separate here and approach the house from the back. Martin will stay with Eli. He knows what to do.”

Luke licked his lips. His parched throat felt as dry as the dead grass all along the trail. He followed Jake, breathing deeply to calm his nerves. They found little to offer in the way of protection, but Jake circled around to approach the house from the back where there were fewer windows. Luke took note of where the barns and stables were in relationship to the house. They would make good places for cover if needed.

Jake held up his hand then placed a finger to his lips. He motioned for Luke to stay put then began a slow walk up to the back door. Jake held his gun cocked and ready to fire. Luke’s heart pounded in his ears. Everything about today reminded him of the stories he'd read in the dime novels Pa bought for the store, only this time he was in the middle of it all.

Jake stopped by a window then gestured for Luke to come. A ball of fear rose in his throat that he couldn't swallow, but he crept up to stand behind Jake. Voices drifted through the open window. Again Jake put his finger to his lips.

Luke recognized Zeb's voice. "I'd had me an Injun girl if I'd taken care of that Luke feller first. Don't know why I turned my back on him. Guess I didn't think he'd have any fight in him."

The tips of Luke's ears burned. No, he didn't like fights, but he'd stood up to Zeb once, and he'd do it again to protect someone he loved.

Bart snorted. "Well, you were wrong, but that ruined everything. If you'd gotten away with her, they'd all be hunting you and not worrying about the money. Now they're hunting both of us."

A female voice joined the men. "I'm worried about your pa. He should be back by now. Are you sure he's OK?"

Bart said, "Aw, we told you, Ma. He was creatin' a scene out in the streets. That's when I took the money. Then Zeb let that Anderson kid get the better of him and almost ruined it all. We'd a both gotten clean away if he'd hit Luke first."

Blood rushed to Luke's head. This whole thing had been planned, even to attacking Dove. He'd strangle Zeb if he could get his hands around that fat neck. Jake must have sensed Luke's anger, because he reached back to grab his arm.

Mrs. Fowler spoke again. "What if he got himself arrested for starting that riot or whatever in the streets?"

Bart's voice growled in answer. "He kin take care of hisself. You know that, Ma."

"And if the law comes looking for you, what happens?"

"Nuthin'. I've hid the money good and proper. They can't

arrest us without any evidence. But Zeb here might want to leave town for a while."

Luke wanted to rush in, but he and Jake had no real authority and nothing to truly prove what the boys had said was true. If the Fowlers hid the money, then it needed to be found in order to prove they took it.

A movement in the shrubs back from the house where Eli and Martin waited caught his attention. When Luke turned his head in that direction, Hawk Morris stood at the edge of the clearing.

Hawk motioned for Luke and Jake to come back to the cover of the bush and trees. Luke retraced his steps and met Hawk. Jake was close behind.

"What do you have, Jake?"

The three moved back to the cover of the brush. Jake hunkered down, and Hawk knelt beside him. "Zeb and Bart and their mother are inside. Chester hasn't come back yet. You want to tell me what happened to make you leave town in such a hurry?"

"Soon as I heard what happened to Dove, I went after Zeb. By the time I got to the creek, though, he was gone. Then I saw Bart hightailing it out of town on his horse. I got my horse and took off after him but lost him. I came here on the off chance they'd be around. Can't believe they're so dumb as to come back home."

Luke crouched beside Hawk. "Where are Martin and Eli?"

"I told them to stay out of the way. Eli knows how to use a gun, and he protested and wanted to come with me, but he's too young to make quick decisions and could get hurt again. Martin looked white with fear, so he was all for staying back by your horses."

For the moment, Luke wished he were back with the horses, but he couldn't leave without doing whatever it took to protect Dove. "What's the plan, Jake? Can we take Zeb and Bart in?"

Jake shook his head. "Remember, Claymore told us to wait until he came. He didn't deputize us, so we can't do anything." He looked back at Hawk. "You know about the missing money?"

Hawk's eyebrows raised in surprise. "What money?"

Jake pushed his hat back from his forehead. "That's what we thought. We overheard Zeb and Bart talking. With the distraction his pa created, Bart was able to grab the money box and get away." He hesitated a moment and frowned. "Mrs. Anderson and Mrs. Frankston are convinced you took the money and started getting the town all riled up."

Hawk let out his breath in a huff. "Those women...I didn't touch the money."

"We know that."

Again Luke's face burned with the idea that his mother could be so thoughtless as to agree with Mrs. Frankston. Her very silence gave support to the mayor's wife.

Hawk peered over Jake's shoulder. "We could go in and take them now, but since we don't have any real authority, I don't want a fight with them. Those boys are trigger happy, and I don't see any sense in giving them a chance to shoot."

"You're right." Jake stood and headed toward the horses.

Luke's mind went into motion. He'd listened long enough. "Why don't Martin and I go back for the sheriff and tell him what we heard? We can try to find your pa too so he can come out here with the sheriff to arrest the boys. Once they find out their pa's in jail, it shouldn't be too difficult."

Hawk stood. "That's a good idea. Take Eli with you. I'm sure Martin will be glad to be headed back to town. Jake and I will wait here and keep an eye on what's going on. If they try to leave, we'll either follow them or stop them."

Luke jumped up. He'd be glad to get away from here. "I'm

going now." Without a backward glance, he raced to the clearing where Martin and Eli waited.

"Come on. We're going back to town and get the sheriff to come out and arrest Zeb and Bart. Jake and Hawk are staying here to keep watch." Martin wasted no time climbing up onto his horse.

Eli shook his head. "No, I want to stay here."

Hawk grasped his brother's shoulder. "No, Jake and I will handle this. You go back and reassure Ma that we're OK."

Eli frowned and looked like he wanted to protest further, but a sharp nod of Hawk's head sent Eli onto his horse to follow Luke.

"Before we go, Luke, tell me what you heard."

"Zeb and Bart were talking about the attack and the robbery. Sounds to me like both of them and their pa were in on it." Luke swung his leg up and settled into his saddle. "I'll tell you all about it later, but right now we need to find the sheriff."

Bea walked back into the town hall. No matter what others thought, she did care about the success of the ice cream social. It had been an hour since the men had gone looking for Zeb and Hawk. The ice cream containers were empty, and most of the desserts had been sold. If not for the disappearance of the money, this would have been a most profitable day. If what Marie said was true, then Sheriff Claymore could go about getting it back from whomever did steal it. Deep down, relief that it wasn't Hawk nudged at her conscience, but Bea chose to ignore it.

Marie Fleming and a few other women wrapped leftover cake to be taken home by the wives of the farmers for whom the social had been held. Bea strode over and began to help. Her hands busied themselves with the task. The other ladies ignored her and continued to chat. That didn't bother Bea, her mind kept busy with worry about Luke. If he got hurt chasing Zeb, she didn't know what she would do.

Marie tapped Bea's arm. "You've had a long, hard day, and we appreciate all your help and your donations for the ice cream. Why don't you go on back to your place and wait for Luke. I'm sure he and Martin will be back any minute, and they'll both be fine."

Bea gazed into the woman's eyes and saw no condemnation or pity, only true concern. Marie Fleming was one of the few women in town who truly loved everyone. Sometimes Bea wished she could do the same, but then the memories of the past always came back to interfere.

"Thank you. I am rather tired. I hope this whole thing is resolved very soon. It'd be a shame if the money isn't recovered and all our efforts are for nothing."

"I think it'll be found."

Bea trudged back to the store. Just as she reached out to turn the doorknob, the sound of galloping horses made her turn. Luke rode in with Martin and Eli. She lifted her skirt and raced down the steps. The horses stopped at the jail, and she ran over as Luke slid down from his saddle.

"Oh, thank God, you're all right. I prayed those boys wouldn't hurt you." Bea hugged Luke's neck and fought back tears.

Luke, looking embarrassed, disentangled himself from her arms. "I'm fine, Ma. Nothing happened. But I do have to talk to the sheriff right away."

Bea watched in disbelief as her son entered the jail. Sometime in the last few hours, he had turned into a man. He was no longer her little boy.

Luke strode into the jail office. Sheriff Claymore, Ben Haynes, and Sam Morris stood looking over some papers. Eli and Martin followed Luke inside.

"Sheriff, we found Bart and Zeb. They're at their place. Jake and Hawk are keeping watch. Jake and I heard Bart and Zeb talking about the robbery and the attack on Dove. It sounded like the whole thing was a ruse to cover up Bart's taking the money. Jake and Hawk are waiting for you to come out so you can arrest the Fowler boys. We have to hurry and get back."

Claymore raised his hands. "Whoa, boy, slow down and catch your breath."

A voice from the jail cells hollered. "My boys is innocent. They ain't done anything. He's lying."

The sheriff frowned and gazed back at Eli and Martin. "Were you two with him?" At their nod, he asked, "Did you hear Bart and Zeb?"

Martin shook his head as did Eli.

Claymore turned back to Luke. "Are you sure of what you heard?"

"Yes, sir. Jake and I heard it all. Mrs. Fowler is there too." Luke started for the door, but the sheriff grabbed him.

"Wait a minute there, Luke. You're not going anywhere. We'll take care of this."

Again Chester hollered, "He's lyin', sheriff. You gotta let me outta here."

"Shut up, Fowler. You're staying right there." He looked back to Luke and the others. "And that goes for the three of you too. We don't need you out getting hurt."

Martin nodded. Color returned to his face. "That's fine with me. I'm going home."

Luke shook his head. Martin was too much of a town boy to want to be involved in things like this, but then he was supposed to be too. He stifled his desire to return and help arrest the two men and stepped back as Claymore left the office followed by Mr. Haynes and Mr. Morris.

Eli remained behind for only a moment or two after the men walked out. He shoved his hat onto his head. "I know a shortcut to the Fowler place. They're not doing this without my being there."

Luke nodded as Eli slipped out the door and then onto his horse. Luke ran outside as Eli rode away. He shouted at Luke. "Find Dove and Ma, and tell them what's going on."

Luke nodded, but he had no idea where to look for Dove or her mother. He surveyed the streets but saw no sign of them or his mother. His mother would be concerned, but he needed to make sure Dove was all right first. He spotted several ladies leaving the town hall and hailed them. "Mrs. Fleming, do you know where I can find Dove and her mother?"

Mrs. Fleming nodded. "Yes, they're at my house." She peered down the street. "We heard a lot of noise and horses a few minutes ago. What's going on? And where's Martin?"

"Sheriff Claymore took Mr. Morris and Mr. Haynes with him to arrest Zeb and Bart. Martin's most likely home by now."

Her hand went to her throat. "Oh, thank You, Lord." Then she peered back at Luke. "I knew it was Bart who took the money. Hawk wasn't anywhere around when it disappeared, and I'll testify to that." She reached for his elbow. "Come, let's go give Emily and Dove the good news."

Dove stood on the Flemings' front porch and peered down the street but could see nothing but more houses. The noise had come from the direction of town, but with the angle of the Fleming house, she couldn't see Main Street.

Martin had returned and told her what happened. Once again Luke had proved himself to be a hero in her eyes. She prayed now that he had obeyed the sheriff and stayed in town. Worry for him and her father filled her mind.

She paced across the porch and back again before she spotted Luke and Mrs. Fleming turn the corner toward the house. Her heart pounded with relief that Luke was safe and coming to see her. She lifted her skirts and flew down the steps. In a moment she reached him and threw her arms around him in a hug.

"Oh, Luke, I was so worried about you. Martin told us what happened out at the Fowlers' ranch. You could have been hurt."

Luke hesitated a moment then his arms wrapped around her back. "I was fine. Jake was with us, remember? And then Hawk showed up. Sheriff Claymore will take care of them."

Dove shoved back from him, heat rising in her face. He must think her to be a terrible person to be so bold as to embrace him like that in public.

Mrs. Fleming cleared her throat. "Hmm, I think we need to go inside out of the heat." She went up the steps and into the house.

Dove turned to walk away, unable to speak or look at Luke. He reached for her hand. "Dove, wait." He grasped her hand. "I'm so thankful you're all right. I...I wanted to kill Zeb for what he tried to do to you. When I heard him talking, my anger nearly overwhelmed me, but Jake kept me from doing anything that might have gotten us hurt."

She raised her head to gaze into his gold-flecked eyes. Love for him filled every ounce of her being. "Thank you for taking care of me and for being willing to go after Zeb."

His grip tightened on her hand. "I'd go to the ends of the earth and back to make sure you are safe." He caressed her cheek with his fingers and bent his head toward her.

She sucked in her breath and stepped back. She wasn't quite ready for him to kiss her if that is what he planned. His words rolled over her like a wave but crashed on the shore of knowledge that he may go to great lengths to save her, but he wouldn't stand up against his mother. She blinked, not really wanting to know the answer that would spoil this moment and most likely any hopes of their future together.

Chapter 21

Luke followed Dove into the parlor where Mrs. Fleming, Mrs. Morris, and Martin discussed the events of the day. Dove sat down next to her mother on the sofa and grasped her hand. Luke took a stance by the window. Color had returned to Martin's face, and he now talked of their trek out to the Fowler ranch as though it had been an everyday occurrence.

"Luke and Jake stayed up at the house a long time, so we knew they must be finding out what had happened. Eli wanted to barge in and take the Fowler brothers, but Hawk showed up and convinced him not to do something foolish."

Mrs. Fleming patted her son's arm. "I'm glad Hawk was there. I tried to tell people that he couldn't have taken the money, but nobody wanted to listen to me until the sheriff told them himself."

Martin nodded. "He told us he'd gone straight to the creek to find Zeb when we told the sheriff what had happened."

Luke's thoughts rambled like tumbleweed skittering across the prairie. So many things could have gone wrong this afternoon, and it still could. If Zeb and Bart decided to shoot it out, death might still come to Barton Creek today.

Mrs. Morris spoke his name. "Luke, where is Eli? Martin said he came back with you and was still at the jail when he left to come home."

Luke glanced at Martin, who didn't have any idea what had

transpired after his departure. Eli's instructions had been to tell Dove and his mother everything, but Luke hesitated to let her know both of her sons were in danger. She continued to stare at him, waiting for an answer. None of the others spoke. They too wanted to know.

Finally he gave them the answer. "Eli said he wanted to be there for the arrest, so he followed after."

Mrs. Morris frowned and bit her bottom lip. "Both my boys and Sam. I pray nothing happens to them. Those Fowlers are mean men."

Mrs. Fleming knelt beside Mrs. Morris. "Then let's pray together right now for all their safety." She reached her hand toward Martin, who moved beside his mother. Luke joined them and grasped Dove's hand in his.

When he squeezed it, she responded with one of her own. Luke closed his eyes, but Dove's hand in his led him to his own prayer. *Lord, give me the words that will soften Ma's heart.*

Mrs. Fleming concluded her prayer and stood. "I think we could all stand a cool drink. I have some lemonade ready in the kitchen."

She left the room, and Luke sat down beside Dove, still grasping her hand. She made no effort to move away, and his heart filled with joy.

Mrs. Morris glanced at their clasped hands and then at their faces. She smiled and leaned toward Dove. "I see a little more than saving Dove from Zeb took place this afternoon. I pray that all will be well, but your father doesn't approve and will not give his permission for Luke to call on you as long as his mother feels the way she does. Again I plead with both of you to be careful so that neither of you will be hurt."

Luke squeezed Dove's hand again. "Thank you, Mrs. Morris. I make a promise to you that I will do everything I can to change

Ma's heart. Until then, we'll remain friends and see each other only with Sarah and Martin."

Martin nodded his head. "And we'll do all we can to make sure you two have some time together."

Luke stood. "I'm so thankful to have friends like you and Sarah. Tell your mother I have to leave. Ma's going to worry until she knows what happened. I should have gone right home, but I wanted to see Dove first."

Dove's cheeks turned pink. "I'm so grateful you did. But I know your ma needs to see you now."

"Good afternoon, ladies." On the porch, the set of the sun in the western sky told him suppertime was near, and hunger pangs rumbled in his stomach as if in agreement.

The aroma of frying chicken wafted from the kitchen when he climbed the stairs to his home. With nothing but a bowl of ice cream and a piece of cake since breakfast, his ma's chicken would be most welcome.

When he walked through the door, his mother dropped her spoon on the table and ran to him. She grabbed him in a hug that took his breath away. "Luke, I've been so worried. What happened? Where have you been?"

"Jake and I found the Fowler boys." As he related what had happened at the ranch, he debated with himself as to whether or not to tell her about being with Dove at the Flemings's home. Finally he opted for the truth. "I've been at Martin's house. Dove and Mrs. Morris were there to wait for news of Hawk and Eli."

Ma's lips set in a firm line. He braced himself for the anger he expected to explode from her lips any moment.

"You went to see that girl and her mother before you came home to let me know you were all right? Do you have any idea how worried I've been? I thought you were still with the sheriff or down at the jail. How could you do this to me?" Her words, quiet and deliberate, shouted louder than any tirade could.

Something seemed to burst within Luke. All the frustration he'd bottled up for so many weeks spewed forth like lava from a volcano. "I understand you were terribly hurt, Ma, but I don't understand how a wonderful Christian woman like yourself can't forgive something that happened over thirty-five years ago. I love Dove, and I believe she loves me. That is something you're going to have to accept. If it means I have to move out of this house, I will, because I will not stand around and let you blame Mrs. Morris, Dove, or her brothers for something in which they had no part."

His mother's eyes opened wide, and she stepped back. "I'm sorry, Luke, but I can't. I've tried, but my heart won't let me forgive or forget." She grasped his arm. "Please don't move out. I won't say anything else. You know how I feel, but if this is what you want, do it. Just don't expect my blessings."

"Ma, listen to yourself. You won't say anything else against Dove or her family, but you won't give your blessing or change your feelings. That just doesn't make sense to me. I'll stay here for now, but I don't want to hear any more talk about the savages you think Hawk and Eli are." He turned to leave the room and found his father standing in the doorway from the store. Alice and Will were with him.

At the stricken look on Pa's face, remorse filled Luke, but he had to be strong and let them know he was making his own decisions about his life now, and that life would include Dove if she'd have him. He strode into his room and closed the door.

Luke's departure created a void in Dove's heart. Mrs. Fleming returned with lemonade and cookies, but they had no appeal for Dove. Her joy went right out the door with Luke. Without him beside her, the memory of the afternoon crept back into her thoughts.

Mrs. Fleming peered at her. "My dear, you seem to be troubled about something. I sensed something between you and Luke. Is that what is bothering you?"

Sadness formed a lump that filled her throat and prevented her answering. She blinked back tears and wished this day to be over and her family safe at home.

"My dear, Martin has told me all about the plans he made with you, Sarah, and Luke to give you time together. I think it's a wonderful but very dangerous idea. Your mother says she knows about it too, and for that I am most thankful. I wouldn't want my son to be a part of any deception."

Ma grasped Dove's hand. "Yes, she did tell me, and at first I wasn't sure it was a wise thing to do, but then I decided that since Dove is going off to school soon, it wouldn't hurt for her to see him."

Dove swallowed hard. "Ma, I've been meaning to talk to you about that."

Mrs. Fleming stood. "Come with me, Martin. Let's see to supper. Your brothers came in and went upstairs to get cleaned up, and your father will be home shortly." She smiled at Dove. "You stay here and talk. If the men aren't back soon, then you will have supper with us."

"Thank you, Marie. That is most kind of you."

When the two left the room, Ma raised her eyebrows. "Now, what is this thing you want to tell me?"

Dove moistened her lips then plunged ahead. "I don't want to go off to school." There it was said, but she held her breath waiting for her mother's reaction.

Disbelief filled her mother's eyes, and she pursed her lips. "I see. What about your dream of being a teacher?"

Words spilled forth from Dove like water over a dam. "It's not a dream anymore. I love Luke, and I want to be his wife. I want to have children I can teach to love God." How quickly her dreams had changed once she'd fallen in love. Her only goal for the present was to love Luke and support him in whatever he decided to do with his life.

Ma hugged her. "That's a wonderful ambition, but you know how difficult that will be with Mrs. Anderson and her prejudice."

"Yes, I do, but if God wants us to be together, then we can rely on Him to get us through any problems we have. That's what you and Pa have always taught me." That principle had been ingrained in her as long as she could remember. God hadn't let any of them down yet, and she believed with all her heart that He never would.

"Oh, my precious child, I pray you never lose that faith. Mine has been tested severely through the years, but God keeps His promises and will give us the strength to overcome whatever the future holds."

Ma's arms and words brought great comfort to her heart, a heart now full of love for Luke Anderson. The memory of his arms around her turned her inside out as though every part of her had been laid bare and every emotion exposed for all to see.

"Dove, we must consider your father and how he feels about Luke. I think after today he will see that Luke truly cares about you, but I'm not sure it will convince him that you and Luke should be together."

If ever Dove had to choose between Luke and her parents, her heart would be with Luke, but she'd have to find the courage to go against their wishes. She blinked. That's exactly the choice Luke would be making. The idea caused her to shiver, and the chill remained despite the warmth of the room.

The front door slammed and Dove jumped. Mr. Fleming burst into the room, his face red and his breath coming in short spurts. "The sheriff's back, and he has the Fowler boys with him. They're in the jail now."

Ma gasped. "What about Hawk? Is he with them? And Eli?"

"Ben Haynes and Sam are with Hawk and Eli. So is Jake Starnes."

Mrs. Fleming ran into the room. "George, did I hear you say the Fowlers are in jail? Did they find our money?"

"Yes and no. Bart won't tell where he hid it. Claymore seems to think he can get it out of Chester, but we'll have to wait until he does."

Ma and Mrs. Fleming hugged each other. Dove fell back onto the sofa. Hawk and Eli were safe, and Hawk was no longer accused of stealing the money. She wanted to shout and jump up and down, but such behavior was not fitting to an eighteen-year-old young lady. Still her heart could leap with joy.

Someone knocked on the door. Mrs. Fleming hurried to open it. Pa, Hawk, and Eli stood on the porch. Ma ran to them and embraced Pa. "I'm so thankful my men are all right and everything's over."

Pa held her mother's head to his chest and bent to kiss her hair. "It's not all over yet, Emily, but at least the Fowlers are behind bars for now."

"Sam, won't you and your family stay for dinner? I have plenty for all of us."

"Thank you, Marie, but I think it's time to get my family home. This has been a long day."

Ma stepped back from Pa and swiped at her cheeks with her fingers to remove the tears. "Yes, I'm ready to go home." She turned and hugged Mrs. Fleming. "Thank you, Marie. You've been a true friend today, and I appreciate your letting us come here."

"Oh Emily, I'm so glad you did." She peered over at Dove. "A lot more happened here today than we can ever imagine. I thank the Lord it all turned out as it did."

Dove didn't dare look at her father. He might see what she had not been able to hide from Ma or Mrs. Fleming. This was not the time or place to have a discussion concerning her feelings for Luke or her desires concerning going to college.

Ma reached for Dove's hand. "Come now, we're going home with our men."

Once she and Ma were settled in the seat of the wagon, Pa went around to tie his horse to the back. Ma leaned over and whispered, "Don't worry about your father. I'll find the right moment to tell him your decision about school, and I'll talk to him about Luke. He's a fine young man, and I can see that he cares for you deeply."

Tears threatened Dove's composure. What a day this had been. Had it been only this morning they had ridden into town for a day of fun and raising money for the farmers? So much had happened to fill her heart with fear as well as joy, but she decided to dwell on the joy. Even now she pictured Luke as he'd said good-bye, and her knees felt weak, making her glad to be sitting down. She'd hold on to the memory of his arms around her until the time came when they could embrace without fear.

She pressed her fingers to her lips, imagining what it might feel like to have Luke's kiss there. If she had not stepped away earlier, she might know that feeling now. She understood why Lucy had waited for Jake to return. The flames of love could not be doused by separation, and Dove would wait for Luke however long it took for him to break away from his mother or for her to have a change of heart. She prayed it would be Mrs. Anderson who would find the heart to forgive and welcome Dove into her family.

Chapter 22

Sunday had been quiet with the arrest and jailing of Zeb and Bart Fowler on Saturday, and Dove and her family had not come to church. Luke covered his disappointment and consoled Alice because she had missed seeing Eli.

Now on Monday, Luke checked the stock in preparation for the week ahead. So much excitement on Saturday had taken its toll on Pa, and Luke would be in charge today. Alice came down the stairs.

"Ma will be down after she cleans up the kitchen, and I think she plans to send Will over to Mrs. Porter's to let him play. She says Pa needs rest and quiet today."

He nodded but didn't reply as she went about turning the sign on the door and preparing to open. His words with Ma still lingered in his mind. Luke had never intended to be so sharp with her, but his anger had taken over.

Forgiveness came hard for Ma, and his apology yesterday had been accepted in silence. Perhaps she knew he was sorry to have hurt her but that he had meant what he'd said. Pa and Alice, who had caught only the end of the conversation, had made no comments about his actions.

If this is what the next days and weeks would be like until Dove left for school, then he couldn't stay here. Perhaps he could move in with the Flemings until Martin had to leave.

How fortunate Martin was to have parents who understood their son's need to have a life of his own.

Half an hour later his mother made her appearance in the store. He untied his apron. "Ma, I have some errands to run. I'll be back sometime later today."

He hung his apron on the hook and caught a glimpse of his mother's face. The sadness there almost destroyed his resolve, but he steeled himself against it and continued on his way. If he could see Dove and tell her what had happened with Ma and that he planned to see her as often as he could, then perhaps Mr. Morris would not be so angry with him and would give his permission.

After he saddled his horse, he headed back to his room to change his clothes and get his hat. When he stepped into the kitchen, he heard voices from downstairs. He tiptoed across the room to go to his. If he walked softly, they wouldn't know he was there. Another encounter with his mother was the last thing he wanted at the moment.

The sound of his name and Dove's stopped him in his tracks at the top of the stairway. They were discussing him.

"Bea, I warned you about what would happen if you didn't let up on Luke and his feelings for Dove."

"I know, but I can't help it. I see what's happening, and I can't do a thing to stop it."

"Then why try? Didn't Mrs. Morris say that Dove was going off to school in the fall to become a teacher? I don't see any harm in letting Luke be friends and see her until then."

"Because if they're in love, no telling what will happen between those two. Sometimes young folks their age have no idea of the foolish decisions that can come with those feelings."

Luke envisioned his mother standing with her hands on her hips and a stern look on her face. She worried he'd do something rash with Dove. As much as he loved Dove, he would never do anything that would hurt her or bring shame on her.

"I don't think you need to worry about that, love. Luke has a good head on his shoulders and he's well grounded in his faith. He'll do what is best for Dove, just like I always want to do what is best for you."

At least his father believed in him, but his mother didn't answer for a moment. When she did, her tone of voice had turned to one of resignation.

"All right, I won't say anything else about Dove or stand in the way of his seeing her for now. When she's gone off to school, he'll find someone else." She hesitated again then said, "I only wish he'd decided to go on to school himself, but I understand his wanting to stay here and help you expand the store. We do have a fine son, and I am proud of him even if I don't approve of what he does all the time."

His mother's anger had disappeared, and hope that she had forgiven him filled him with determination. He would not forget Dove just because she was off learning to be a teacher. He fought against the desire to argue with his mother and concentrated on her final words instead. Not only was Ma proud of him, but she also had agreed not to stand in his way of seeing Dove.

His mission this morning became even more important. He went into his room and closed the door. Luke changed into a pair of denim pants and shirt, grabbed his hat, and headed back to his horse. He couldn't get to the Morris ranch fast enough.

Dove helped her mother in the kitchen. Today Pa and her brothers had headed out on the range to check for more fences.

They had said they'd be back for the noon meal, and Dove decided to make a berry cobbler with the berries canned from the last picking.

She made her way down into the dirt cellar below the house where they stored bounty harvested from the garden. Jars of fruits and vegetables she and her mother had canned earlier now lined the shelves as did bags of potatoes. Although the sun shone bright above, the cellar remained cool. Dove collected what she needed and headed back up into the sunlight.

The two one-quart jars of berries should be enough for a good-sized cobbler. She set fruit on the table. "Ma, do we have fresh cream for the cobbler?"

"Yes, Eli milked Bessie this morning." She reached into the cupboard for the supplies to make the crust for the cobbler. "I know you're not happy about skipping church yesterday, but Pa and I decided it was best not to attend. After everything that happened on Saturday, he and I didn't feel like facing the people of Barton Creek again."

"Yes, Ma, I understand." And she did, but that didn't make staying away and not seeing Luke any easier. Even now the memory of his arms about her caused her knees to buckle. She grabbed the edge of the table for support. She would love to feel them around her once more.

Dove sighed and began preparing the pastry. Half an hour later the cobbler sat ready to pop in the oven. She stuck a fork into the top to make a few more vent holes then shoved it into the hot stove.

Ma returned to the kitchen. "Hmm, I can smell those berries already. Pa and your brothers will be so pleased." She picked up her paring knife and started peeling potatoes.

With the last of the baking dishes cleaned up, Dove sat down at the table. "Ma, do you think Pa will ever let Luke call on me?"

"Only if his mother approves and Luke asks. Pa doesn't want you to be hurt any more than you have been by Mrs. Anderson's hateful words."

"But I understand her fears and her memories. It's not really me she's angry with; it's her past and all that happened to her. I don't dislike her for that, and I admire Luke for not being disrespectful and going completely against her wishes."

Ma stopped her peeling and turned to Dove. "My dear, that's exactly what he's doing by letting you and Martin and Sarah make those plans with him and change partners in secret. Don't you think that's being disrespectful and secretive?"

That thought had entered her mind weeks ago, but it had been shoved aside as the plan had worked and she'd spent more time with Luke. Still, Ma had a point, and one that Dove must consider. She'd been thankful because her mother knew of the arrangement and didn't go against it, but Luke had no such support from his family. Of course Alice understood because of her feelings for Eli, but she was only his younger sister.

Dove picked up her needlework and headed for the living room. There she could work on her sampler and think about Luke as well as pray for their relationship. How she'd like to have a visit with Lucy right now. Her friend could always manage to encourage and cheer Dove, but Ma warned her about too many unannounced visits, so she'd have to wait until she could see Lucy and set a time for a good long session of woman talk.

After an hour, the aroma of the cobbler drew her back to the kitchen. Ma removed it from the oven. The browned crust with a sprinkling of sugar bubbled now with the reddish blue of the juices. Oh yes, Pa would be pleased.

The sound of horse's hooves drew Dove to the front door. She peered out to find Luke hitching his horse to the rail. She held tightly to the door frame to keep from running into his arms again.

He turned to find her standing in the door, and a smile lit up his face that sent her heart racing.

"Dove, just the person I came to see." He stepped up onto the porch and removed his hat. "I have so much to tell you."

Her voice lodged somewhere in her throat, but from behind her, Ma welcomed him on the porch. "Hello, Luke. You're the last person we expected here today." She patted Dove's arm. "Don't stand there, dear; invite the boy in."

Dove swallowed hard. "Yes, please, do come in." She stepped back to allow her mother to enter then followed her with Luke right behind. Dove's hands burned with desire to reach out and touch him, but she clutched them in front of her.

Ma sat on the sofa and gestured for Luke to sit down. He chose one of the chairs made from cow's hide and sturdy pine. Dove sat next to Ma, clasping her hands together to keep them from trembling. Something must have happened for Luke to ride out here in the middle of a workday.

"Is your father here?"

Dove blinked at the sound of his voice. This wasn't what she expected to hear at all. He wanted to see Pa, and the idea sent butterflies flapping in her stomach. Did she dare hope he'd come to ask permission to call on her?

Ma answered for her. "He and the boys are due in shortly for dinner. Would you like to stay and dine with us?"

Luke twisted his hat in his hands. "Thank you, Mrs. Morris, but I will need to get back to town and help Ma with the store this afternoon. Pa's not feeling well after all the excitement on Saturday."

At that moment Pa stepped through the door, followed by

Hawk and Eli. Pa stopped short when he saw Luke and scowled. "What are you doing here, boy?" Before Luke could answer, Pa's frown turned to a smile, and he said, "I suppose we never did properly thank you for what you did on Saturday. Jake said you were a good partner, and he was glad you were along with him."

Red seeped into Luke's face. "I only did what needed to be done to see that Zeb and Bart were brought to justice."

"Well, I do appreciate it. Now what brings you out here on a Monday?" Pa sat in his favorite chair and leaned back.

"Well, sir, I've come to speak with you about Dove."

Hawk snapped to attention, and Eli smiled. Pa shook his head at them. "I think you boys better get washed up for dinner."

Both started to protest but closed their mouths when Dove pleaded with them with her eyes. Relief filled her as they headed upstairs.

Luke cleared his throat. "I came to seek your permission to call on Dove. My mother has decided not to stand in the way of our relationship."

Dove's heart pounded. Her most cherished dream could come true. She silently pleaded with Pa to say yes.

Pa stared at Luke for a few minutes before answering. He leaned forward, elbows on his knees, his hands clasped. "What brought about this change?"

"Sir, she still doesn't approve, but she has said she won't stand in the way. I told her I was old enough to make my own decisions and would move out of the house and in with Martin Fleming if she made any further protests. She decided to let me make my own decisions about my relationship with your daughter."

Dove had cared for Luke before now, but her heart soared with love as she realized the implications of what he said. No more secret meetings, and he'd challenged his mother's attitude. She reached over and grabbed her mother's hand.

"I see. So there will be no more planning with Martin and Sarah? You are going to be honest with your parents."

Dove shot a glance at Ma. She must have told Pa about those meetings. She bit her lip; at least Pa hadn't scolded her and forbidden her to meet Luke like that.

"Yes, sir, they wanted me to go off to school at Stillwater, but I explained how I wanted to stay here and help Pa expand the store and make it the best one in these parts. I have lots of ideas for that, and then someday, when Dove returns, we can continue our relationship. She can teach here, and I can run Anderson's Mercantile."

Dove's eyes opened wide. He didn't know she had decided not to attend college. She prayed that wouldn't change his plans or his mother's acceptance.

"That sounds like you have mapped out everything for your future. When Dove returns from college, then we can discuss your future plans with her."

Dove's stomach lurched, and she locked gazes with Ma. Her mother shook her head slightly. She hadn't told Pa yet about her wanting to stay here in Barton Creek.

"I have no objections to your calling on her between now and the time she leaves. As long as your mother accepts what is going on, you can come at any time."

Luke's face beamed with happiness, but Dove's soul ached with the idea that Pa and Mrs. Anderson might both change their minds if they found out she wanted to stay here.

He stood and stretched his hand toward her father, and Pa grasped it in his with a firm handshake. "Thank you again for defending my daughter against Zeb Fowler. That was a brave thing to do. My prayer now is that nothing else will happen to put either of you in danger, and I don't mean from the Fowlers, although I'd be careful around them too."

"Yes, sir, I understand." Luke nodded at her, and again she wanted to run into his arms.

When Luke was gone, Hawk returned to the room and shook his head. "I don't like it. Luke may have stood against his mother now, but when the real challenge comes, what will he do?"

Dove gasped and whipped around. "You were eavesdropping. How could you?"

Hawk shrugged. "I love you, little sister, and don't want to see you hurt." He and Eli went back to the kitchen, and Pa followed.

Dove bit her lip. "Ma, what are we going to do? You should have told Pa I don't want to go to college."

Ma patted her hand. "I know, dear, but let's say nothing right now. We need to see how this relationship proceeds. If Mrs. Anderson keeps her word and doesn't interfere, then we can tell Pa you're staying home this fall."

Dove's emotions bounced up and down like a greenhorn on an unbroken horse. Her heart filled with happiness at the idea of Luke calling on her, but she feared what would happen when Mrs. Anderson and Pa learned no college loomed in Dove's immediate future.

Chapter 23

Luke rode back to town with a lighter heart. Hot, thirsty, and hungry, he headed straight for Dinah's rather than confronting his mother. The delightful aroma of meat loaf and potatoes beckoned him. He waved at Dinah then headed for a table where Martin sat.

"Mind if I join you?" Without waiting for an answer, he sat across from his friend.

Martin laughed. "I'd say from the look on your face you have happy news."

"Maybe, but you look like you have something to share too."

"I do. Yesterday I asked Sarah to marry me. She said yes and that she would wait for me while I'm away at seminary. My folks are happy about it; hers are too. So it's good all the way around." He leaned forward. "Now what about you?"

He glanced up at the woman who came to take his order. "I'll have the same thing he's having." When she left, he unfolded his napkin. "Not as good as yours, but promising. Ma has said she won't stand in the way of my seeing Dove from now until she leaves for college." Martin's eyes opened wide, but he waited to comment until the server placed a glass of water and more biscuits on the table and left again. "Does that mean your mother is willing to accept her?"

"No. She's still against a long-term relationship, but I had to let her know that if I had to choose between her and Dove, I'd choose Dove."

"Wow, Luke, you really are stepping out of your circle. I didn't think you would stand up to her because you've always respected your parents."

"I still do, but I have a life to live, and it's time for me to make decisions about it. Ma tried to send me off to Stillwater for school in the fall. Fortunately Pa and I talked her out of that."

Martin said nothing but studied Luke for a few moments. "I know God wants us to respect our parents and honor their wishes, but sometimes the two just don't fit together. I'm very fortunate that Father decided a ministerial career would be good for me rather than the world of banking. You want to be a merchant, and that should please your father."

"It does. He has great plans for the next year in regards to the store. Soon as the post office next door moves into the new city office building, Pa will buy that property and expand the mercantile to a larger first floor, then he'll eventually build our home and have a second floor for the store." Pride for his father's vision filled Luke. Anderson Mercantile would be the largest store in the area, with merchandise ordered from Montgomery Ward and Sears Roebuck catalogs to give people an even greater selection of goods.

Luke's meal arrived, and after a brief blessing, he dove into the meat loaf topped with a tomato sauce that tickled his taste buds. Dinah sure knew how to please a man's appetite.

Martin shoved his plate back and laid his napkin on the table. "The hard part is pleasing our parents when we fall in love. I've had my eye on Sarah for several years, but only this past spring got up the courage to speak to her. Ma did encourage my relationship with Dove, but we were only good friends, and she knew of my interest in Sarah."

"So you said. Sarah is a very trusting woman to let you continue to call on Dove."

Martin grinned. "That was only because Sarah knew how much Dove liked you. I'd say Dove has had a crush on you for several years."

Luke shook his head. "And I never paid any attention to her even when she and her mother came into the store. Pa always took care of them, and I was usually busy doing something else. She was just another girl from school."

This summer she had become so much more than that. He sipped from his water glass then shoved his own plate away. "Martin, I intend to try and dissuade her from going down to Texas in September. If she stays here, we can have a proper courtship."

Martin's breath expelled in a whooshing sound. "Then it looks like I need to be praying extra hard for you in the days ahead." He laid some coins on the table and rose. "If you're finished, let's walk back to the store together. I want to pick up some of Mother's favorite chocolates. She's been like a rock these past few days with all that happened."

His appetite had fled, so he nodded and placed some coins beside Martin's. "I'm ready if you are."

When they reached the door, Martin touched his arm. "I forgot to tell you. When I came into the restaurant, I saw Mrs. Fowler going into the sheriff's office. She looked terribly distraught."

"I imagine she would be with her husband and sons in jail. She knows what they did because she was with them while they were talking. I wonder if she came to visit or plead for their release."

Martin followed him to the street. "Your guess is as good as mine, but it seems like she'd be glad to be rid of them for a few days. I've seen how Mr. Fowler treats her when they're in town. No woman deserves that kind of abuse."

"I don't think so either, but Pa spoke to Claymore about it, and he said unless Mrs. Fowler filed a complaint against her husband, he couldn't arrest Mr. Fowler." Luke removed a handkerchief from his pocket and wiped his brow. "Whew, this heat is almost unbearable today."

"That ain't all that's unbearable."

Luke recognized Mr. Fowler's voice and turned around. Mr. and Mrs. Fowler stood only a few feet away. Martin's face blanched, and Luke's throat tightened. He would not let this man see his anxiety.

Mr. Fowler spit toward the street, a stream of brown shooting from his mouth. "What's unbearable is seeing the two boys who accused Zeb of attacking that Injun girl."

Luke straightened his shoulders. "He's guilty, Mr. Fowler." He glanced at Mrs. Fowler, whose eyes were wide with fear. Fear of whom, he wasn't sure, but he refused to let Mr. Fowler frighten him.

"That's jest your word agin' his." He narrowed his eyes. "I warn you, boy, you better not be goin' around and spreadin' lies about my family." He grabbed his wife's arm and yanked her as he walked away. "And you can tell them Morris boys they'd better watch their backs."

He shoved his wife up into the wagon and climbed up beside her. The woman's hands shook as she cowered next to him. Luke's anger boiled. At the moment, he wished he was strong enough to pull the man from his seat and give him a taste of his own medicine. Common sense prevailed, but he gripped the hitching rail as the couple made their way out of town.

A few moments later Claymore left the office and climbed on his horse. He headed out of town at a trot.

Martin cleared his throat, but it still squeaked. "I sure don't want to meet up with Mr. Fowler again anytime soon. You think Claymore is following him?"

"Yes. I still wonder, though, why he let Mr. Fowler go. He may not have taken the money or attacked Dove, but he must have been a part of it."

Martin set his hat on his head. "If I were the sheriff, I'd let the man go so he'd lead me to the money they hid. If I was a betting man, I'd bet you a dollar he leads the law to it before the day's out."

"And I'd take you up on it. I say he'll wait awhile, and when they can't prove anything, Claymore will have to let the boys go too."

Martin shook his head. "It'll be a sad day for this town when he does that."

This was one time Luke hoped he was completely wrong about Fowler, but his instincts led him to believe the man would keep the money hidden away until his sons were released. Then a new idea dawned. If Mr. Fowler didn't lead the sheriff to the money, Claymore just might let the boys go free just so he could tail them and eventually find the money that would convict them.

In the meantime, Luke planned to avoid all contact with any of the Fowler family.

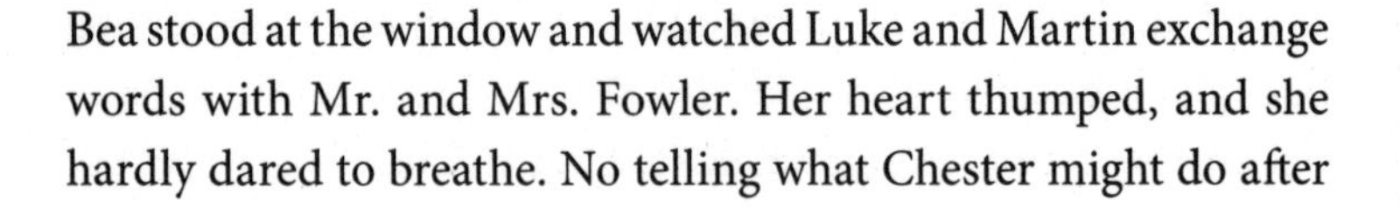

Bea stood at the window and watched Luke and Martin exchange words with Mr. and Mrs. Fowler. Her heart thumped, and she hardly dared to breathe. No telling what Chester might do after the accusations by Luke and Martin against Zeb. Although she could not hear the actual words, she clearly saw the man's anger in his facial expression and the tone of his voice that carried to her ears.

A few minutes later, Fowler pushed his wife onto the wagon and they left. Bea breathed deeply and forced calm to return. Her son was all right, but she still wanted to know where he'd been for the past few hours.

When he and Martin headed toward the store, she turned and rushed to the back and began examining the shelves. No need for them to know she'd been watching. The boys entered, but Luke didn't speak to her. From the corner of her eye she saw him remove his hat then reach for his apron on the hook near the counter.

Martin nodded in her direction. "Good afternoon, Mrs. Anderson. I stopped by to see if you had any more of those chocolates Mother likes so well."

Bea placed a can back on the shelf. "We certainly do. Mr. Anderson got a shipment in last Friday." She hurried to an open box and pulled out several bars of chocolate.

"Tell your mother that we also have another shipment of that cocoa powder she and Lucy Starnes like so much. They both like to cook with it. In fact, I believe that's the secret ingredient your mother uses to make her chocolate cakes so delicious." Bea reached for a can of the powder. "Of course I won't tell anyone else that."

Martin laughed. "She'll be glad if you kept the secret. You know how much Mother likes to experiment, and now her chocolate cake is the best around. I'll take another can of it to her."

Bea set a dark brown can of cocoa on the counter along with two bars of sweet chocolate. It came all the way from a company in Pennsylvania. The cocoa powder had only been around three years or so, but it had quickly become a favorite after Lucy Starnes asked Carl to order it for her. Being from Boston, Lucy had a good deal of knowledge about new things they could order from back east.

Martin completed his purchase and left. Luke busied himself with adjusting displays. Apparently he didn't want to talk to her, and she couldn't blame him after their confrontation Saturday evening. The idea of Luke moving out sickened her every time she thought of his declaration.

Finally, she swallowed her pride and stepped toward her son.

"Luke, I saw Mr. and Mrs. Fowler leave town. Do you know what that was all about?"

He continued working and didn't turn around to face her. "Not really. He's angry with Martin and me because we accused Zeb of attacking Dove and Bart of taking the money."

She reached out and touched his shoulder. "He's a dangerous man."

His shoulders tensed but he remained still with his back to her. "I know that. He warned us and told us to warn the Morris boys that we wouldn't get away with accusing his family."

Bea's heart skipped a beat. No telling what Fowler would be capable of doing after all that happened at the ice cream social. She didn't want to think about that. "Will came back from play not feeling well, so I sent him up with Alice. I need to go check on him, but with the noise he's making, he can't be too sick."

Luke shrugged and continued moving canned goods. "If she's trying to give him some of that stuff Doc Carter gave you for fever, I don't blame him for making a ruckus."

Bea removed her hand from his shoulder. "Yes, that syrup does have a bad taste. I'll take him up a piece of candy. That should help." She started for the stairs but stopped, her curiosity getting the better of her. "Um, where have you been the last few hours?"

Luke spun around to face her. A look of defiance crossed his face. "Out to the Morris ranch. I asked Mr. Morris for permission to call on Dove. He gave his approval, and I plan to escort her to the big party for all the ranchers that Ben Haynes is having this Saturday."

A lump formed in Bea's throat, but she remembered her promise to Carl. Once again she swallowed hard to squelch the anger she felt rumbling in the pit of her stomach. Anger was one emotion she didn't need at this moment. It would serve only to drive Luke further away from her.

"I see. You know I don't approve, but I won't stand in the way of your taking her."

Luke's expression didn't change. "That's good, Ma, because I don't want to go against your feelings or your wishes. All I want is for you to be civil to Dove and her mother and not give them the cold shoulder like you always do when you see them."

Bea shuddered. It would be difficult, but she could do it for one day if it would make Luke happy. Besides, as big as the Haynes's place was, she may not even encounter Dove or her mother. "I will do that for you," she promised.

She turned to the stairway as the bell over the door signaled the entrance of a customer. Bea had no desire to speak with anyone at the moment. She trudged up the stairs. Who was she trying to fool? Even with the size of the ranch, contact with Emily and Dove would be inevitable. If it wouldn't look so bad for Carl, she might suggest that they decline the invitation, but that would resolve nothing between Luke and her. Next Saturday would be a most difficult day.

The noon meal proved to be a quiet one with only talk of work around the ranch among her brothers and father. Ma glanced at Dove several times but said nothing. The food had no appeal for Dove. Her stomach churned with all that Luke had said. Perhaps she shouldn't tell him that she didn't plan to leave Barton Creek at the end of August. Then again, that may not be necessary, since Pa hadn't given his permission for her to stay at home.

Dove shoved her potatoes with her fork. Their buttery goodness usually tempted her to eat more than her share, but today they grew cold with the butter congealing around them. The most unappealing sight finally caused her to push back from the table.

"Excuse me, Ma, Pa. I'm not really hungry right now." She hugged Ma. "I'll return to help you with cleaning up." She nodded to her father and brothers then retreated to her bedroom.

She flopped across the bed and picked at the tufts of yarn on the quilt. Her mind raced with all that had happened in the past three days. Luke had shown how much he cared about her by saving her from Zeb's attack, and then he'd had words with his mother about those feelings. Questions whirled for which she had no answers. What if Mrs. Anderson hated Dove even more for alienating her son? What if she didn't really mean what she'd told him? What if Luke decided not to go against his mother's wishes?

The thunder of horses' hooves outside drew her to her window overlooking the front yard of the house. The ranch foreman and another cowboy jumped from their horses and ran toward the house. Dove raced back downstairs as Pa strode toward the front door. He opened it and stepped out onto the porch. Dove hurried to follow behind her mother.

The ranch foreman swung down from his saddle. A frown creased his face and sent a shiver of fear through Dove.

"Boss, I've just come from town. Chester Fowler is out of jail."

"He's what?" Pa's words exploded through the air. Red and purple mottled his face. Ma reached out her hand to his arm.

Dove sensed Hawk and Eli behind her. She turned to see thunderclouds of anger raging across Hawk's face. Eli stared as though in shock.

Pa shook off Ma's hand. "Tell me what you know."

"Mrs. Fowler came into Barton Creek and went straight to the jail. I didn't think anything of it because a wife has a right to visit her husband and sons in the jail."

"True, but how did Fowler get out of jail?" Pa set his jaw in a way familiar to Dove. She'd seen it enough times when he'd become aggravated with her or one of her brothers.

"The sheriff let him go. When I finished my business at the bank, I walked out to see Fowler walking with his wife to their wagon. They stopped and had a few words with Martin and Luke. I heard him warn them about spreading lies about his family, and then he told them to tell you and your boys to watch your backs."

Pa pounded his fist into his hand. "What in the world was Claymore thinking? Letting that man go free is about the worst thing he could do."

"I thought so, boss, but I spotted him following Chester Fowler on horseback. I bet he's hoping Fowler might lead him to where the boys hid the stolen money."

Hawk stepped forward and spit out his words. "And what if he doesn't?"

"Well, I'm guessing Claymore will then release Bart and let him lead him to the money."

Pa's hands clenched at his side. "And let him cause more trouble too."

"Yes, sir. I came back soon as I could to warn you so we can be on the lookout in case Fowler decides to come nosing around here."

"I'm glad you did. He's not going to mess with my family and think he can get away with it." He turned and strode into the house followed by Hawk and Eli.

The foreman nodded to Dove and Ma. "I'm sorry you had to hear about this, ladies, but you can be sure that me and the boys will make sure you all are safe."

Ma nodded, and Pa reappeared with his hat secure on his head and a gun belt strapped around his waist. He marched out to the stables. Ma started to follow but stopped when Eli and Hawk both barged out of the house and across the yard.

"Hawk, Eli, take care of your father." She then turned pleading eyes to the foreman. "Please don't let them do anything foolish."

"I'll try, ma'am, but we can't let the Fowlers get the upper hand or think they have it. Me and the boys will try to make sure no one gets hurt, but I can't guarantee anything."

Dove bit her lip. Her father and brothers walked their horses from the stables and mounted them.

"I'm leaving two men here to watch you and the house," Pa said. "If Fowler comes around here before we catch him, you'll be safe." He spurred his horse. "Come on, boys, we've got work to do."

Dove clutched her mother's hand and watched them gallop down the road in a cloud of dust.

Chapter 24

Luke worked in virtual silence for the next several hours. His ma's agreement regarding Saturday sent mixed emotions through his bones. Joy should fill him at the thought of spending time with Dove, but the hurt look in his mother's face as she waited on customers gave cause for remorse. This was a huge sacrifice for her.

He sighed and headed for the section where household items were on display. Ben Haynes had finally ordered a sewing machine for his wife, and Jake had ordered one for Lucy. Both had arrived this morning and awaited delivery. Lucy and Mellie would probably be in later today to pick them up. He checked the contents and made sure all parts were included and each order complete.

Charlotte Frankston burst through the door and sent the bell jangling. She patted her chest to catch her breath. "Sam Morris and his boys just rode into town and headed for the sheriff's office. I smell trouble."

Ma rushed around the counter and peered out the window. Luke joined her. Sam, Hawk, and Eli dismounted and headed into the jail. Luke itched to be there and know what was said.

"What's going on?"

Ma spun at the sound of Alice's voice. "Nothing, dear. Sam Morris is going into the sheriff's office."

"I know that. I saw them from upstairs. Why are they in town?" She joined them at the window.

Charlotte Frankston sniffed. "*Humph*. Up to no good, I'd say."

Luke ground his teeth and bit back an impulsive retort. She had no cause for her prejudice. Ma said nothing either, but Luke stole a glance, and the emotion in her eyes clearly said that none of her feelings had truly changed.

A noise on the stairs drew Luke's attention. Will jumped from the third step up. "Is there going to be another fight?"

Ma jerked around from the window. "No, there's not going to be a fight. Alice, take your brother back upstairs, and keep him there."

Alice sighed in frustration. Luke knew she wanted to be here, but if she had to know what was going on, she could watch it from up in her room. She grabbed Will's hand and led him back upstairs with the boy protesting all the way.

A few minutes later the three exited the office. Eli and Hawk climbed back on their horses, but Mr. Morris strode their way. Ma and Mrs. Frankston backed away from the window as though they'd been bitten by a snake. Mrs. Frankston hastened to leave before Mr. Morris made it across the street and to the store.

Ma's hands shook as she finished putting her customer's goods into a bag. She didn't look up when Mr. Morris pushed open the door.

He gazed about the room until his eyes rested on Luke. "Son, my foreman told me how Chester Fowler threatened you and Martin as well as my boys. I'm here to tell you that nothing will happen to either of you or my sons. Chester Fowler will pay for his part in what happened Saturday. If not today or tomorrow, then sometime in the future. We'll let Sheriff Claymore take care of that. And I told him that I'm sending one of my cowboys to keep an eye on you and Martin here in town."

He tipped his hat. "Good day, Mrs. Anderson. You have a fine young man for a son." With that he turned and strode from the building.

Luke's mouth gaped open, and Ma blinked her eyes. She turned to him and blinked again as the light revealed the dampness there.

Suddenly, love and pity for his mother overwhelmed him. He hurried to her and wrapped his arms around her.

"Ma, I know you're worried, but I'll be all right. Martin and I will be extra careful and pay attention to everything around us." He stepped back and grinned. "Did you know Martin asked Sarah to marry him?" Changing to that subject should make her smile, and it did.

Ma wiped her cheeks with her apron. "Yes, her mother came in this morning to give me the news. She's already looking at wedding gowns in our fashion catalogs. It'll be a couple of years, but they want to be prepared."

How like Sarah and her mother. They would leave nothing to the last minute. Sarah liked to plan ahead in everything. He must admit her organized ways had been a big help to him and Dove.

Ma sighed. "So much has happened in the past few weeks. I don't think Barton Creek will ever be the same. With all the new people coming into town and the building going on, it looks like we'll be having the same troubles as the larger towns."

"That may be true, but the people we have here now are mostly good people who want to help each other. Just look at the turnout we had at the fund-raiser for the farmers. The town was full of those wanting to help. Martin said even his father was willing to loan money to help them through the winter with the failure of their crops."

Ma nodded. "Yes, we do have caring people here. So many came to bring food when Carl was ill. I just pray that things like that don't change."

He listened to his mother's words that were in direct contrast to her behavior toward Dove and her family. Although he held sympathy for his mother and her fears from the past, her blindness to the hurt she caused in the Morris family puzzled him. Would she ever change?

Dove heard her father and brothers return from where she sat trying to concentrate on her needlework. She tossed it aside as Ma hurried in from the kitchen. The door opened, and Pa strode through and straight to Ma.

He wrapped his arms around her. "Fowler is out of jail, but his boys are still there. Sheriff Claymore will track Fowler to see if he will head for where the money is hidden. We'll have to trust him to take care of things."

Relief and gratitude flooded Dove. In the past he would have defied the sheriff and gone after Fowler.

Pa kept his arm around Ma but turned and stretched out his arm toward her. She stepped to his side and his free arm went around her shoulders. "You two are more important to me than any money that was stolen. I'll let Claymore do his job, but if Fowler comes around here, I'll do whatever it takes to protect you."

Love for her father flowed through her heart along with the warmth of the security he brought to his family. He had shown more than a few times the length he would go to protect them.

He kissed Dove's head. "And don't worry about Luke and Martin. I've sent a ranch hand to town to watch over them, and those two boys have good heads on their shoulders."

His words brought some comfort, but as long as Mr. Fowler felt the way he did, no one, especially Luke, would be truly safe.

Her mind jumped ahead to the party at the Haynes's ranch on Saturday. Only a few weeks remained until she was supposed to leave for school. Maybe Saturday would be a good day to discuss her staying home. She would be able to spend more time with Luke at the party, and that filled her with anticipation, but her instincts warned her not to be too optimistic. It'd be just like Mr. Fowler to show up and spoil all the joy of the day.

Saturday arrived with clear skies and sunshine. Although the farmers and ranchers needed rain, the sun meant a good day for an outdoor celebration. Luke whistled as he dressed to ride out to the Haynes's ranch for the party.

No suits and ties for this day out at the ranch. Levi pants and lightweight shirts were the order for the day. Luke buttoned his tan shirt then smoothed back his hair. Pa had taken the scissors to it last evening and the ends no longer tickled his neck, not that he minded, but a sharper image was what he wanted for today. He reached for his wide-brimmed light brown hat and headed downstairs.

With the closed sign on the door, Pa would miss more business today, but he didn't mind. People in town had known for a week and had stocked up yesterday. He filled a small bag with peppermints to take to Dove.

"Sweets for your sweetheart?"

Luke jumped at Alice's question. Caught red-handed. Heat rose in his cheeks. "I just thought it would be nice to take her something." He raised an eyebrow. "You look very nice. Eli will pay you special notice today."

Now her cheeks bloomed. She smoothed imaginary wrinkles in her blue skirt. "I hope we have a chance to visit. I thought perhaps with Ma letting up on you and Dove, she wouldn't be upset if I talk with Eli."

Luke shook his head. “I wouldn’t count on it, but for today she may be more lenient. I know she’s only doing this because Dove is leaving in a few weeks for school. She believes I will forget about Dove and find someone else while she’s out of town.”

Am impish grin filled Alice’s face. “Now that’s not about to happen, is it? Besides, there’s no one else your age around. You wouldn’t start seeking friendship with one of my friends, would you?”

“No, but don’t you go putting ideas in any of their heads, you hear?” He reached out and nudged her. “Now I’m off to get my horse.”

Ma appeared at the end of the steps. “Pa will be here with the carriage in a few minutes. Will is already at the Porters’ house with Jimmy. He has a new set of marbles, so that should keep them busy this afternoon.” Her talk was light, but her eyes bored into Luke.

He swallowed hard and hurried out the door. He prayed Ma hadn’t heard the end of his conversation with Alice. If she had, then he’d hear about it later. Until then, nothing would spoil this day.

After mounting his horse at the stables and riding back to the store, he followed along with the family to the ranch. Several other families in wagons and buggies met them on the trail. Alice had been right about the lack of young ladies his age. With Lucy and Jake married, that left only Sarah and Dove.

He chuckled. Just who did his mother expect him to court in Barton Creek? An abundance of boys and girls sixteen and younger filled the school and church, and new families coming into town had children even younger. That’s why Ma had such high hopes last winter when he courted Lucy and everyone believed Jake was gone forever.

Sarah would make a wonderful minister's wife with her friendly demeanor and love for everyone, and Dove would be the perfect wife for him if only his mother could see it. God had put six young people together in town, and now that four of them were paired off, he believed Dove was God's choice for his bride. All the Bible verses he'd learned about patience came to mind and gave him hope that perseverance coupled with prayer would bring Ma to her senses.

As they arrived at the ranch, people from both farms and ranches greeted them. Luke climbed down from his horse and immediately scanned the area for Dove.

"Hey, Luke, you beat us here." At the sound of his name he turned to find Martin and Sarah arriving in the Flemings' runabout. Martin's parents followed in their buggy.

Luke admired the open vehicle and horses Martin drove. The banker and the mayor were the only two men in the area with more than one mode of transportation, except for the ranchers who had extra wagons for working.

Then his attention turned to the surrey now arriving. Mr. Morris handled the reins. Dove offered a shy smile as the vehicle came to a stop in front of him.

"Good afternoon, Miss Morris." He reached up to grasp her hand and to assist her to the ground. She was beautiful in the red and white checked dress she wore. He recalled the day she had come to buy the fabric.

When her feet settled on the ground, she gazed into his face and made no attempt to remove her hand from his. "It is a good afternoon, Luke, and I'm sure it will get only better."

"I hope so." He nodded to Mr. and Mrs. Morris and, still holding her hand, led Dove to where Lucy and Jake conversed with Martin and Sarah.

Bea narrowed her eyes as she watched Luke and Dove. It pained her to admit they made an attractive couple, and Dove did look beautiful today. Still, that wouldn't change her mind about his pairing up with a girl with Indian blood.

Mellie joined Bea. "I'm so glad you and Carl were able to make it here today." She turned her gaze toward Luke and Dove. "They're a fine-looking couple. Luke was such a comfort to Lucy last spring when Jake was in Texas."

"We appreciate your asking us." And if Jake hadn't returned, Lucy could be her daughter-in-law today. Bea glanced back at where the young people gathered. Even from this distance she could see that Lucy and Jake were very much in love. It shone in their eyes and the way they responded to each other. "Your niece and her husband appear to be a very happy couple."

"Oh, they are. After Jake became a Christian, their love blossomed like my roses in the spring. Of course we had a few tense months there when he left to face those murder charges back in Texas."

"Lucy was fortunate to have you and Ben to take care of her through that ordeal." Bea envied the love and pride in Mellie's voice as she spoke about her niece. Of course she had plenty of reason to be proud. When the tornado devastated so many homes and businesses last March, Lucy had stepped in and used her inheritance to set the town back on its feet. No one would forget her generosity anytime soon.

Mellie said, "I'm glad to see Luke find someone else after his disappointment with Lucy."

Bea swallowed the words of objection. She would keep her promise to Luke today and not say one word against Dove, but she wouldn't promote anything between them either.

Aunt Clara joined them. "Bea, I tried some of that cocoa powder Carl ordered for Lucy. It's quite good. Will you be getting any more of it? I'd like to have some for my baking."

"Yes, we will, but we have several cans on hand right now. Charlotte and Lucy both wanted it, so we ordered extra. I can have Luke bring some out to you next week if you don't want to come in for it."

"Thank you. I'd like that very much. Lucy made some chocolate cookies with it, and they were quite tasty." She turned to Mellie. "And didn't you use some in a cake recently?"

"Yes, I did, and it turned out beautifully."

Bea listened as the women continued to discuss recipes. Usually she'd be interested, but her thoughts were only of Luke and Dove today and her promise to him. He'd grown so in the past few years and had passed his father in height last year. He'd filled out too. Maybe that was due to her cooking skills as well as his increased appetite. All that aside, she had to admit he was growing into a fine young man.

Her only concern now was the fact that he no longer wanted to be under her rule. At nearly twenty, it was time he stood on his own, but his words from last week still pierced her heart and caused great pain. All these years she thought he had understood the pain from her past, but apparently he saw it only as intolerance and prejudice on her part.

Luke walked away with Martin and Jake. Dove's hand still contained the warmth of Luke holding it as they talked. Jake had said he needed to speak with Luke and Martin, but Dove wished they had not had to leave to do it. Still, it was good to be with her best friends, Lucy and Sarah.

Lucy wrapped an arm about her shoulders. "I see you and Luke are growing closer. Has his mother changed her attitude?"

Dove shook her head. "I'm afraid not. He says she's agreed to be civil and accept his calling on me as long as I'm leaving for school at the end of the month."

"But you're not. Have you told Luke that?"

Sarah gasped. "You're not going to Texas?"

"No, but we haven't told Pa yet, and I haven't told Luke and won't until Pa knows. Sarah, please don't say anything to Martin. I want to tell Luke when the time is right."

Sarah flattened her hand to her chest. "Of course I won't mention it." Then she frowned. "This could get a little unpleasant when Mrs. Anderson finds out."

"Yes, I know, but for right now, I want to enjoy every minute I can with him. The end may come soon enough."

Lucy hugged her. "I don't think it will end. I see the way Luke's eyes light up when you're around. It's the same as Martin's are for Sarah and Jake's are for me. With love like that, God has to be in it." Then she grinned. "I'm glad my little scheme with Aunt Clara paid off. Between her and Sarah, I say we did a good job of getting you two together."

Dove's eyes opened wide. "You and Aunt Clara? I knew Sarah and Martin were in on the plans but had no idea anyone else was. I just thought Aunt Clara was being Aunt Clara and trying to fix things her own way."

Lucy laughed. "Exactly. I just put a bug in her ear, and she was off and running. She even managed to get Doc Carter in on it."

Dove remembered the day they had gone riding with Aunt Clara and Doc Carter. When that sweet little woman got an idea in her head, she didn't let go until she did something about it. Right now Dove welcomed all the help Aunt Clara, Lucy, Sarah, or anyone else could give her to keep her relationship with Luke going forward.

At that moment the three men returned. Luke once again grasped Dove's hand. She smiled at him and said, "Have you three solved all the problems of the world with your discussion?"

"Not all; just a few. But we have decided that we have the three most beautiful women at this party by our sides."

Heat rose in Dove's cheeks once again as Lucy and Sarah laughed. They could afford to laugh since one was married and the other pledged to be. Still, the compliment warmed her insides and gave her hope for a future with Luke.

Jake wrapped his arm around Lucy's shoulders. "If you don't mind, I'd like to have a little time with my wife." Lucy grinned at the girls and shrugged, and Jake led her away.

Luke squeezed Dove's hand. "Martin and I have decided a little stroll down by the creek would be a welcome relief from the crowd here. We can be back in plenty of time to eat."

"That sounds nice. I'd like that." The nerve endings in her hand and arm tingled with the continued pressure of his hand on hers. She wished he'd never let go.

Sarah picked up her parasol and opened it. "I wish I were as fortunate as you, Dove, with your olive skin. The sun burns me so quickly."

"I may be darker, but I still keep out of the sun as much as possible." She placed a wide-brimmed straw hat over her dark hair. It would also keep the sun from her eyes as they walked.

As they strolled hand in hand, Luke remained silent, but every few minutes or so, he glanced down at her and smiled. For once the silence lent comfort rather than uncertainty about what to say. If she looked hard enough, a tiny dimple could be seen at the corner of his mouth. She'd noticed it for the first time last week when he'd stood so close to her at the Fleming home. Perhaps she'd see a lot more of it in the days ahead.

Sarah and Martin ambled on ahead, giving Luke and Dove more privacy. From the look of bliss on Sarah's face, they must be discussing their future. Dove swallowed a lump in her throat. How she longed for that same bliss with Luke.

Luke stopped and turned her toward him. "I must say, Dove, the thought of your leaving for Texas in a few weeks is almost more than I can bear. I know you want to be a teacher, and I respect that, but my selfish heart wants you to stay here. Please don't be angry with me and think I have no thought for what you want to do with your life, because I do. And if going away to school is what you want, then that is what you should do."

Dove's heart swelled with the love she had for him, and it ached to tell him the truth. She wanted him to know that the plans for college were forgotten for now, but until her father knew, it must be a secret.

"Thank you, Luke. Ma has said that true love wants what is best for the one who is loved." But what was best for her at this moment was her desire to stay and to be courted in a proper manner by Luke.

He wrapped his arms around her in a hug that filled her with so much joy she thought she might burst. Her head rested against his chest. Then he reached down and lifted her chin and bent his head toward hers. This time she didn't intend to shy away from a kiss. His lips met hers, gentle at first, but as she responded, the pressure increased.

When he moved away from her lips, his hand caressed her face.

"You are so beautiful."

She blinked her eyes to keep tears of joy from spilling over. At that moment Martin and Sarah returned, and she moved away from Luke in embarrassed confusion. Glancing up at Sarah, she saw her friend's eyes suddenly open wide with fear.

"So now that little Injun girl is yours, hey, boy?"

The voice sent a chill through Dove. Luke's arms tightened about her as he turned his head to face the man standing behind him. "Go on about your business, Mr. Fowler."

Martin and Sarah now stood beside Dove and Luke. Martin waved his hand. "This is Mr. Haynes's property, and we're here by invitation. You have no right to be here."

Mr. Fowler sent a stream of brown liquid to the ground and shifted the shotgun held in his arms. "I might not have been invited, but you two boys are the reason for my boys being in jail."

Martin started to respond, but Luke stopped him with a hand to his friend's chest. "Mr. Fowler, we told the truth, and I'd truly appreciate it if you would turn around and just go on about your business." He pushed Dove behind him, and Martin did the same with Sarah.

"My business is here with you two lying city boys who think you're better than anybody else."

Luke leaned down and whispered, "Grab Sarah's hand, and run back to the ranch where you'll be safe. We'll handle Mr. Fowler."

Dove shook her head. "I don't want to leave you with that awful man."

"Whispering sweet nothins' in her ear, Luke boy? What would your mother say to your snuggling up to an Injun girl?"

"That's none of your business, but I wanted the girls to leave so Martin and I could talk with you."

"So they can go run for her pa and Mr. Haynes? They stay

right here." The man reeled and advanced a few steps toward them.

He laughed in a high-pitched sort of way that was more a cackle than a laugh. Dove shuddered as she caught the smell of alcohol coming from his body and breath. A drunken man with a gun was not someone to reckon with. She'd seen enough incidents in the past to know that no good would come of this situation.

Sarah's face had paled to a ghostly white. Dove reached toward her, afraid she might faint at any moment. Martin hugged his sweetheart tightly to his chest. Luke released Dove and started toward Mr. Fowler.

"I'm not telling you again. Get off this property and go back to where you belong." His hands clenched to his sides.

Martin stepped away from Sarah, and at that moment Mr. Fowler staggered forward, his gun up and pointed at them. A second later a shot rang out and Dove screamed. Martin's eyes opened wide, and he clutched his arm.

Luke lunged for Mr. Fowler and knocked him to the ground. "Run, girls! Go get Jake and the others. Martin's been shot and needs help quick."

Dove grabbed for Sarah's hand as sobs wracked the girl's body. Dove had a difficult time getting her to move but finally managed to pull her partway up from Martin.

Sarah yanked away. "No, I'm staying with Martin." She lifted her skirt to tear a piece from her petticoat.

Dove glanced once more at Luke, who sat on top of Mr. Fowler, holding him firmly to the ground. He jerked his head toward the ranch. "Go! Go now!"

Her fears had been realized. Mr. Fowler had spoiled the joy of this day. She didn't wait for another command but picked up her skirts and ran for help.

Chapter 26

Luke used every ounce of restraint to keep from bashing Chester Fowler's head against the ground. He tightened his grip on the man's shoulders. Fowler's arms lay pinned at his sides by Luke's knees. He glanced over at Sarah tending to Martin's wound. "How's he doing?"

"He'll be all right. It appears the bullet went through the fleshy part of his arm." She checked the strip of cloth around his arm. "The bleeding's stopped, but I wish Doc Carter would hurry and look at it to make sure."

Martin tried to sit up, but Sarah pushed him back down. Martin groaned. "Sarah, I'm not hurt that bad. Let me up."

"Not until the doctor gets here and I'm sure you're all right."

Luke laughed, relieved that his friend hadn't been more seriously injured. "Listen to her, Martin. No sense in taking chances, and besides, you have a pretty girl's arms around you. Enjoy it while you can."

The man beneath him grunted and tried to toss Luke off, but Luke just pushed Mr. Fowler's shoulders harder into the ground. "You're not going anywhere until we can get you tied up and into town, so just sit still."

Fowler turned his head, and his eyes narrowed. "Just you wait, boy. I'll take care of you yet."

A retort sat on Luke's tongue, but a thrashing in the bushes caused him to cut it short. Jake and Ben Haynes burst through with Doc Carter close behind.

The doctor ran toward Martin, and Jake hurried to help Luke subdue Fowler. "Dove told us what happened. I sent Matt and Eli in to get the sheriff." Jake grabbed Fowler's chin. "You've fooled with the wrong bunch this time. You'll be in jail with your sons before this afternoon."

Doc Carter called out to Jake and Luke, "Martin's wound is only in the flesh and went straight through. We need to get him back to the house and get some alcohol to keep infection from setting in."

Mr. Haynes handed Jake a rope. "Here, you and Luke get him tied up, and I'll help Doc with Martin."

Jake made quick work of securing the rope around Mr. Fowler. Luke stood and stretched his legs. "Looks like you won't be getting away now." He clapped Jake on the shoulder. "Thanks. Wish I'd had something to tie him up with."

Jake grinned and yanked Fowler up to his feet. "You did a good job. I'm proud of you, and so is Dove. That makes twice you've saved her."

Luke pressed his lips together. "I only did what instinct told me. I had to protect her."

"Good instincts." Jake shoved Fowler toward the brush. "Let's go. I'm sure Claymore will take care of you."

What a day this had turned into. Luke shook his head. So many evil things had happened in the past few weeks, and they'd all revolved around the Fowler family. He remembered Mrs. Fowler and her husband's treatment of her. He would ask Lucy and Mrs. Haynes if they could check on her. No matter what her husband and sons did, Mrs. Fowler didn't deserve to suffer because of their ways.

Ma ran toward him when they emerged from behind the

stables. "Luke, oh thank the Lord, you're all right. Dove told us what happened." She wrapped her arms around him.

"I'm fine, but how is Martin?" Luke watched over her shoulder as Jake led Mr. Fowler to a group of men nearby.

"Mellie took him in the house. His mother and father are with him now, as are Doc Carter and Sarah. Sarah's skirt is stained with blood. He must have bled a lot."

Luke removed his mother's arms but continued to hold her hand. He guided her back to the ranch yard. "He did, but Sarah tore off part of a petticoat and tied it around his arm. I think that helped curb the bleeding."

Ma nodded. "Smart girl, that Sarah Perkins. She'll make Martin a fine wife." She tilted her head and peered at Luke. "Marie tells me that Martin plans to be a preacher."

"That's right." A ruckus and loud voices sounded from the men near the corral.

Fowler's voice rose above the others. "I tell you, that boy is lying. My gun went off accidental like. I was hunting me some rabbit for supper. I didn't threaten nobody."

Luke's fists clenched, forgetting he still held Ma's hand. She yelped and he let it go.

She grasped his arm. "Don't listen to him, Luke. Just stay away and let the sheriff do his job."

At that moment Claymore rode up. Luke swallowed hard but determined to do as his mother wanted and let the law take care of Fowler.

Dove stood to the side with Ma. Pa and Jake helped get Fowler up on a horse while Sheriff Claymore questioned Luke.

Lucy hugged Dove. "I'm so glad you were not hurt. What a terrible thing for you and Luke."

Dove blinked back tears. "It was awful. I could smell liquor on Mr. Fowler, and he was wild-eyed, almost like he was out of his mind." She shuddered with the memory. "I don't know how the gun went off. I only remember Luke and Martin telling Sarah and me to run home, but Fowler said no, and the next moment Martin was kneeling on the ground bleeding."

"I'm glad Doc Carter was here and could get to Martin so quickly. I'm sure that will help him to get through this without infection."

Aunt Clara clucked her tongue. "This town has seen more excitement in the past week than I've seen in two years. I thought Barton Creek was a quiet place, but it's getting more like the towns I've heard about in the Wild West."

Lucy said, "Aunt Clara, it's really not that bad. Remember, the Fowler family is only one of hundreds now in the area." Her facial expression changed, and she frowned. "I haven't been here a year, but I've heard Uncle Ben and Jake talking about how greedy he is and how he wants more land than he has."

Ma nodded. "That's true. Sam has had trouble with Mr. Fowler trying to put fences where they don't belong just to show he can. He and his boys don't like the fact that I'm Indian either."

Aunt Clara pursed her lips. "I can't understand how some people have to hate others or wish them harm just because of who they are." She lifted her hand in a wave. "Excuse me. I see the doctor coming out of the house. I want to ask him about Martin." With a swish of her skirts, she walked away.

Lucy giggled. "She's not so much concerned about Martin as she wants to be near the good doctor again. Ever since he asked to escort her to the July Fourth celebration, she's been stuck to him like a burr on the pant leg."

Ma nodded. "I noticed that. Well, it's a good thing. He's been at a loss since his wife died last year. He needs a good woman in his life, and Clara is a fine choice."

"Yes, she is. I've really come to love her even though she's no blood kin to me. From what Aunt Mellie told me, she was eighteen when the young man she was to marry was killed in an accident. That's when she went out to Kansas to live with Uncle Ben's father. She couldn't live in Boston with the memories of her love there."

Dove could only imagine what it would be like to lose the one she loved. Her heart would break if anything happened to Luke. A chill coursed through her as she realized how close they had come to just that today with Mr. Fowler. Her love for the woman everyone called aunt grew as she recognized the loss suffered at such a young age. Aunt Clara never married after the death of her beloved. Dove didn't want that to be her own fate, but if Mrs. Anderson continued to oppose a deeper relationship with Luke, then Dove might be facing choices she didn't want to make.

Pa walked up with Jake and hugged Dove to his side. "Good to see my girl is all right. I had to practically hog-tie your brothers to keep them from beating up on Fowler. I thanked Luke for taking care of you."

Jake kissed Lucy's temple. "I'm going to ride in with the sheriff. Do you mind staying here with your aunt until I get back?"

"Of course I don't mind. She'll need help cleaning up anyway." She reached up to touch his cheek. "Please be careful."

"I will." Then he was gone.

Dove sighed. If only Luke would love her like Jake loved

Lucy, without any fears or inhibitions. So far the Lord hadn't deemed the time to be right, so she had to be satisfied with the temporary truce from Mrs. Anderson. As soon as the news that Dove would not be attending college was learned, that truce would be ended.

At that moment Luke stepped to her side. "I've told the sheriff exactly what happened. Martin is going home with his parents, and Sarah's going with them." He grasped her hand.

Dove peered up at him. "I'm so sorry this day was spoiled by that awful man."

Luke smiled. "Don't worry. It's not over yet. Mrs. Haynes says there's too much food to let it go to waste, so we'll all be eating in a few minutes. The Flemings and Sarah are the only ones who have left besides Jake, and he'll be back."

Lucy gasped with her hand to her mouth. "Then I must go and help Aunt Mellie get the food ready for serving." She lifted her skirt and ran toward the ranch house.

Luke turned to Dove. "I'm thankful things turned out as they did. We could have been in real trouble."

"How can a man be so blind to what his sons did? I thought he was a part of it."

"I'm beginning to think we made a mistake about that." Luke stroked her hand with his thumb and looked down.

Dove squeezed his hand in hers. "I don't understand. I thought it was all planned by the three of them."

"I'm beginning to believe the sons acted on their own. They saw the commotion caused by their father, knew everyone would be paying attention to that, so they took the opportunity to steal the money. Zeb saw the four of us go off together and in that saw an opportunity of a different kind."

A shudder coursed its way through Dove. Never had fear been more real than when Fowler threatened them. Different scenarios rushed through her mind. She shook her head. Thinking about what could have happened made matters worse, not better. Concentrating on the good in Luke and Martin and their bravery presented a better image to remember, but this day would be forever etched in her mind.

Dove gasped. "I just realized something. Twice I have been frightened by one of the Fowlers. If something terrible had happened, my memories would be even worse than they are now. Every time I see them, I'm reminded of what they did."

"And I'm truly sorry for that. I wish none of it had happened."

"So do I, but don't you see? That's what happened with your mother. She can't get the images of those Indian warriors out of her mind. All that she witnessed and experienced is far worse than anything that happened to me. She'll never be able to truly forget."

"But neither you nor any of your family caused that."

"No, we didn't, but we bring back those memories. And as long as she sees us in that light, she can't have peace." Dove wanted nothing more than to bring that peace to Mrs. Anderson. No one should have to live with such horrible memories, but only God could help her, not so much as to forget the images, but to forgive what happened and recognize that not all Indians were like those of the past.

Luke remained quiet for a few moments. "Dove, you have more insight and understanding than anyone I've ever met except maybe the preacher. I see that I've been going about this whole thing the wrong way. I love Ma, and I've been quite harsh with her."

Dove's heart sank. She had turned Luke back to his mother. Not that it was a bad thing, but it could mean he would no longer seek to court her. She bit her lip.

Luke must have sensed her dismay because he grabbed both her hands in his. "Dove, I promise you that my feelings will not change. God will work all things for good for His faithful servants. We must be faithful and believe in the Lord's promises to us."

She swallowed hard, but the tears formed anyway. "I care about you so much, Luke, and you are one of the finest people I know. Your respect for your mother means more to me than you can know. You're right in saying we must let God be in control of this situation. People are praying for us, and God will answer."

The future looked so uncertain at this point that Dove could only trust that whatever happened from this day forward was ordained by God and would be the best for her and Luke. At that moment, the clouds rolled away from the sun and brilliant light again shone down on the party. Dove lifted her face to the warmth.

She still had today, and today was one of celebration, not moping around about what might have been. She was safe, Martin was all right, and Luke was by her side. The heat was no longer unbearable, and the dust no longer a nuisance.

She pulled her hands from Luke's and spun around with her arms outstretched. "Today is a beautiful day." She grabbed his hand again and tugged. "Let's go celebrate. I see tables laden with wonderful things to eat and people gathering for a blessing."

Happiness bubbled forth like a brook after spring thaw. Her fear of Mrs. Anderson and even the Fowlers disappeared. After the events and realizations of the day, a brand-new plan for dealing with Luke's mother took form in her heart.

Chapter 27

Dove placed the last of the breakfast dishes on the shelves and wiped perspiration from her brow. She gazed out the window of the kitchen. Everything as far as the eye could see was brown. The few trees in the yard drooped in the heat. No rain for more than five months made this the hottest and driest summer she could remember. The last really soaking rain had been the tornado last spring. Farmers had time to replant the crops destroyed by hail, but then the drought came.

She had seen devastation like this only once before, but then not so many families lived in the Territory. Now so many lives would be affected by the lack of rain. Still, more families continued to move to the Territory. The increase made for more customers at the mercantile in town and kept the Anderson family busy.

It had been almost a week since the incident at the Haynes ranch, and she had succeeded in putting the worst parts in the far corners of her mind. She wanted only to remember the best part...Luke's kiss. Her fingers touched her lips. How she would love to have the feel of his lips on hers again.

Her mother came into the room. "I know it's going to be a warm day with the heat like it is already, so I want to go into Barton Creek this morning and pick up the two dresses we had made for you. Mrs. Weems said they'd be ready this week. We can pick up any supplies we might need too so we won't have to go in tomorrow with Pa."

A trip into town today meant she could begin the first phase of her plan with Mrs. Anderson. "That sounds like a good idea. If we leave now, we could still be back before the real heat of the afternoon."

Ma smiled. "That's what I thought. Now get your bonnet and parasol. I've already asked to have the surrey ready."

Dove scurried to fetch her things and joined Ma on the porch. The surrey stood ready and waiting for them. Although it was rather big for just two people, the fringed top would offer more protection from the sun.

As they rode into Barton Creek, Dove considered what she wanted to say to Mrs. Anderson. She had rehearsed her words every day for the past week. Her prayers for Luke's mother had changed. No longer did Dove pray for the woman to simply change her attitude and allow Luke to call on her; now she prayed for God to touch Mrs. Anderson's heart and help her to forgive. The anguish seen in the woman's eyes every time she saw Luke and Dove together could only be relieved with the peace God could give her through forgiveness of those who had harmed her family.

When Ma stopped the surrey in front of Mrs. Weems's Fashions for Ladies, she stepped down and turned to her mother. "I have an errand to run. I'll be back in a few minutes to try on the dresses." Before Ma could reply, Dove strode across the street to Anderson's Mercantile.

The large new sign, recently added to sport the new name for the store, creaked on its chain. Dove stopped beneath it and breathed deeply. God would get her through this, no matter what Mrs. Anderson's reaction might be.

She walked through the open door, no jangling bell to

announce her arrival. Dove stood for a moment to let her eyes adjust to the contrast from the bright sunshine. Alice and her mother had their backs to her, one with a pad and pencil, the other looking up to the shelves.

Dove cleared her throat. "Mrs. Anderson?"

The woman turned with a smile of welcome that turned to a frown upon sight of Dove. She worked her mouth a moment then turned her back. "Alice, see what Miss Morris needs."

Dove stepped forward. "I need to see you, Mrs. Anderson." She glanced around the store. Neither Luke nor his father were anywhere in sight. Relief washed over her. This would be easier without Luke.

Mrs. Anderson didn't turn around, but Dove plunged ahead. "I just wanted to let you know how grateful I am to Luke for standing up to Mr. Fowler and to Zeb. He showed great courage and restraint in protecting Sarah and me. I believe he is the brave, kind young man he is because of you and Mr. Anderson. You have taught him well and have every right to be very proud of the man he is."

Alice smiled and grasped her hand. She mouthed the words, "Thank you." Mrs. Anderson didn't turn around, but Dove noticed her shoulders move.

"That's all I have to say. Good day, Mrs. Anderson, Alice." She hurried back to the street and crossed over to Mrs. Weems's store. She stepped inside and leaned against the door after closing it. Her heart raced in her chest, and she patted her chest to catch her breath.

Ma rushed to her side. "I saw you go into Anderson's. Did that woman say something that upset you?" Her eyes narrowed, and she peered over Dove's shoulder and toward the window.

"No, she didn't say anything. I said something."

Ma's eyes opened wide. "You said something? What?"

"I...I told her how grateful I was for Luke's bravery and that he was a fine young man because she and Mr. Anderson were good parents."

"My dear, sweet girl." Ma wrapped her arms around Dove's shoulders. "That took courage." She stepped back. "I'm proud of you."

"I decided that by being very nice to Mrs. Anderson at all times, I could do more to help her see who I am than by fretting over her attitude. I...I've been praying in a selfish manner and for my own desires, but I realized I needed to be praying for her."

Ma pushed a wayward strand of hair off Dove's forehead. "When did you get to be so wise?" She hugged Dove again. "I'll pray for her to have peace too." She blinked her eyes. "Now, I think it's time to try on those new dresses."

As Mrs. Weems fitted the bodice and made adjustments, Dove fingered the ruffles on the blouse. At least bustles were no longer popular, and the gored skirts fit so much better. They didn't need all the petticoats worn under the full skirts she usually wore on the ranch.

Mrs. Weems spoke through the pins in her mouth. "Even with your tiny waist, I think a corset would help to make it even smaller."

Dove grimaced. A corset was the last thing she wanted to wear. If becoming a young lady meant wearing one, maybe she'd rather be just a young girl. She sent a pleading look to Ma. "Do I have to wear one? Lucy told me how she wore one in Boston to a party and couldn't breathe. I don't think I'd like to be bound up like that."

"It may be the fashion in the larger cities, Mrs. Weems, but I don't think Dove needs that right now. We're still a small town, and fashion isn't as important here. I think the fuller sleeves and gored skirts are as much style as we need."

Dove breathed a sigh of relief then tried on the other outfit they had chosen. She turned so that she stood facing front. She could see the mercantile across the way. How she wanted to go back and see what Mrs. Anderson said or felt about the declaration Dove had made. She prayed it hadn't angered the woman further.

"Ma, are you all right? Can I get you anything?"

Bea shook her head. "No, I'm fine." But she wasn't. Her heart raced with the emotion that filled her soul. Her first impulse had been to race after Dove and tell her to stay away from Luke, but that would then break her promise. Besides, she'd pledged to herself to never make a public display of her feelings toward Dove and her mother, and running after her and catching her in the street would do just that.

She sighed and swallowed the anger but couldn't get rid of the bitter taste in her mouth. Dove had never spoken directly to her before, and her soft words in praising Luke rang in Bea's ears. Luke was a fine son, and yes, he was brave and kind, all the things that a good son should be. However, Bea could see no reason why Dove would come now and say those things when every time before she stayed in the background and never said a word.

"Alice, go upstairs and check on Will. He should have been back down by now. No telling what he's getting into."

Her daughter bit her lip but headed up the steps. Will didn't really need to be checked, but Bea needed a moment to think about Dove's visit. The more Bea thought about it, the more she believed that Dove had come simply to play on the sympathies of a woman who loved her son. If that girl thought she'd get favor by doing that, then she'd better think again. Still, Bea couldn't help but admire the girl's courage.

Bea walked over to the window and stared across the street. The Morris surrey sat hitched to the post outside of Mrs. Weems's shop. Dove and her mother must be there getting new clothes for Dove to wear at college in September. That thought brought a smile to Bea's heart. In just a few weeks Dove would be miles away in Texas. Luke would soon forget about her and concentrate on helping his pa with the store.

Luke and his father rode back to Barton Creek with their wagon loaded with supplies picked up in Guthrie. Noise from the railroad crew greeted them a few miles from town. Soon the section would run through Barton Creek, then down to Stillwater, and on to Oklahoma City. Barton Creek would no longer be cut off from all the trade and commerce now taking place in the Territory. All the activity and growth bode well for a bid for statehood. Growth meant more people, but that was a good thing for businesses such as Anderson's Mercantile.

Pa handed Luke the reins as they entered Barton Creek. "I need to make a stop at the bank. You take the wagon on to the store and start unloading. I'll be there shortly."

"If you don't mind, I'll stop with you for a few minutes. I need to speak with Martin."

"All right, son. Just don't be long."

Pa hopped down at the bank and went inside. Luke tied the reins around the post. He glanced up and spotted the Morris surrey and team down the street. Joy filled his heart. If Dove was in town, perhaps he'd have a chance to speak with her. A week was a long time to go without seeing her.

He followed his pa into the bank but stopped short. Mr. Haynes, Mr. Morris, Mr. Dawson, and another man stood talking with Mr. Fleming. Luke's feet rooted to the spot as he overheard the conversation.

Mr. Dawson shook Mr. Haynes's hand then Mr. Morris's. "I can't thank you men enough for all the help. We'll be heading back to Kansas by Monday."

Mr. Haynes nodded. "We're glad to do it, and let Mrs. Dawson know that my wife and Mrs. Morris will be over to help her pack and do anything else she needs them to do."

They shook hands again, and Mr. Dawson turned to leave. When he saw Pa, he stopped. "I'll be in to settle up my bill this afternoon, Mr. Anderson. Thank you for all you've done to help me and my family."

"You're welcome. If I'm not in, Mrs. Anderson will take care of you."

Pa waited until Mr. Dawson closed the door behind him and the other man. "What was that all about? He's the second farmer to leave this week, and that was Elmer Jasper with him."

Mr. Morris set his hat on his head. "Dawson came to Ben and me and asked if we would buy his land. His brother back in Kansas has a good wheat crop this year and needs an extra hand. We were glad to help him out. It's a shame he has to give up, but it's good he has an opportunity waiting for him. Ben and I divided the acres between us. Jake bought out Mr. Jasper."

Ben furrowed his brow. "The only problem I see is how mad Chester Fowler is going to be that we have more land."

"I don't see why. Dawson's property isn't anywhere along Fowler's, and Jasper's is next to Jake's ranch, not Fowler's.

Besides, he'll be in jail a good while yet." Mr. Morris shoved his hat on his head.

Mixed feelings filled Luke. He was sorry to see the Dawsons leave Barton Creek. His family had been regulars at church, and Will had made friends with Billy Dawson. Still, if he had opportunities back home, it would be good for the family to have money for travel and settling in when they arrived there. He didn't know as much about the Jasper family, as they kept pretty much to themselves.

Men like Ben Haynes and Sam Morris would always be the ones who succeeded in life because they looked out for their fellow man. They'd made sure Mrs. Fowler was taken care of while her husband and sons were in jail by providing food for her. Mr. Haynes even sent Matt over to help with any chores. Of course not everyone knew who was doing it because Luke and Martin had been sworn to secrecy by their fathers. Still, these men set a fine example of what Christians are meant to do in time of need.

Luke waved to Martin. "I'll talk to you later." He turned and left his pa to do whatever business he had at the bank and sauntered down the street toward Mrs. Weems's shop. Then he remembered the wagon and that he should be unloading it. The choice pulled at him. Take a few minutes and try to see Dove or go back and take care of his responsibilities. With a deep breath, he turned and headed back to the wagon. Responsibility over pleasure was more important at the moment.

Pa came out of the bank. "You still here? Thought you'd have the wagon to the store by now."

"Sorry, Pa. I started walking off and didn't even think about it until I was nearly home."

Pa moved to the side and peered over Luke's shoulder.

"Wouldn't have anything to do with the Morrises being in town, would it?"

Heat rose in Luke's face. He turned to see Dove and her mother exit the dress shop and head for the new bakery that had opened last week.

"It's OK. You go on and see if you can catch them at the bakery. You might want to see what kind of breads and things they have while you're there. Fresh-baked bread would give your ma some relief from her baking."

"Thank you, Pa. I'll do that." Not that Ma would want bread she hadn't baked herself, but Pa understood Luke's desire to see Dove. He sprinted down the street toward the bakery.

Delicious aromas of fresh-baked yeast breads greeted his nose as he entered the shop. Luke had met the owner once when he had come in to buy flour. "Good day, Mr. Peterson. Sure smells good in here."

The stout man behind the counter laughed. "That's what pulls in the customers. I'll be with you in a moment."

Dove turned, and her eyes sparkled as she spoke. "Hello, Luke. I didn't expect to see you today."

Luke's insides melted like candle wax at her smile. "I've been with Pa picking up supplies. I'm glad you're here because I wanted to ask you about coming out for a visit Sunday afternoon."

Dove glanced at her mother, who nodded. "I think that will be a fine idea. Pa's going over on Saturday to Guthrie to pick up ice for that new box your father ordered for him. We can have iced lemonade, and I'll bake cookies."

He turned his gaze to Mrs. Morris. "Ma'am, do you mind if I bring Alice with me? She would sure like to see Eli again."

"No, I don't mind a bit. I'll tell Eli." She stepped aside.

"Excuse me, I see Mr. Morris outside, and I need to speak with him. Dove, you can take care of our order."

When she had gone, Mr. Peterson took out a white bag with a picture of his store printed on it. "Say, that looks nice."

Mr. Peterson beamed. "Mrs. Peterson drew the picture, and I took it down to Oklahoma City and they printed the bags for me. Makes for a nice touch, doesn't it?"

"Yes, it does." Something like that would be good for Anderson's too. He'd have to tell Pa about it. He turned back to Dove. "I've missed seeing you this week."

She lowered her gaze toward the floor. "I've missed you too, but Pa thought it best not to come into town for a while so all the talk about last Saturday would die down."

"I understand. Thank you for allowing me to come see you on Sunday."

"It will be nice to have you visit and bring Alice." She reached for the bag on the counter. "I must go now. Ma will be waiting." She flashed one last brilliant smile before leaving the store.

Luke sucked in his breath. One more day before Sunday, and then he could spend several hours in the company of one Miss Dove Morris.

Chapter 28

Bea gazed around the store Saturday morning. The place filled with customers coming into town for their weekly supplies as well as those in town who came to do their shopping. Business had been good for the past two months despite the drought, and several of the accounts charged by the farmers had been paid. Though sad to see families leaving the land, she was glad they had been taken care of and had opportunities where they were going.

Will ran around the end of a counter and bumped into his mother. She grabbed his shirt. "You know better than to run in the store with so many people."

"I'm sorry, Ma. I gotta go pee." He pranced around in a circle, and Bea bit her lip to keep from laughing. "Then hurry, but don't trip yourself." She shook her head as the boy scampered off on his errand.

A glance at the clock Carl had hung reminded Bea that it was time to prepare a noontime meal for her family. "I'll be upstairs if you need me. I'll let you know when lunch is ready." At the foot of the stairs she stopped. "Send Will up as soon as he returns." May as well get him out from under their feet.

The noon stage would be arriving soon, and Bea hoped the new fall catalogs from Montgomery Ward and Sears Roebuck would be in the mail. She and Carl had discussed some of the new inventions and conveniences that would be available when the electric lines were finished and connected to the Guthrie electric supply. Of course, that was still a ways in the future, but it didn't hurt to plan ahead.

She set about making a pan of corn bread to go with the stew she put on to cook earlier in the morning. Will came bounding up the stairs.

"Ma, I'm hungry. When is it going to be ready?"

"In just a short while. Go on into your room and play. Be sure to wash your hands."

"I smell stew. Did ya' put in lots of potatoes? I want all potatoes and no carrots. I don't like carrots."

Bea smiled and turned the boy to his room. "You'll eat whatever lands in your bowl. Now scoot."

He skipped away, and Bea finished the corn bread. When it was in the oven, she wiped her hands on a towel then walked to the window overlooking the street. She spotted Sam Morris and his son Hawk down at the stables. That brought to her mind the encounter with Dove yesterday.

If only the girl's mother were not Cherokee, Dove would make a lovely daughter-in-law. Everything Bea had seen of the girl had been good, but family background was too important to be ignored. Just look at how Eli and Hawk had been involved in trouble this summer. It was in their nature. Memories of that time long ago began to surface, but Bea refused to let them emerge fully. She didn't want to think about them today as they would only serve to weaken her promise to Luke, and she was having enough trouble keeping it now.

She checked the corn bread and removed it from the oven then rang the bell to summon her family upstairs.

Luke and Alice's teasing voices reached her before they appeared at the top of the steps.

Her son greeted her with a kiss on the cheek. "Something

smells really good, and right now I think I could eat it all." He reached over for a slab of corn bread.

Alice slapped his arm. "Wait for it, just like the rest of us."

Luke grinned and shrugged. "Always worth a try." He yanked one of her curls, and she hit at him again.

Bea grinned at her two oldest. Their antics filled her with joy. Too soon they'd both be leaving home to lead their own lives. She intended to enjoy every minute they were under her roof.

Carl stepped into the room. "Sounds like a war up here." The twinkle in his eye betrayed the stern tone of his voice.

Will came in and joined in the melee. Luke swung his brother up in the air, and Will squealed in delight. "Enjoy it while you can, little brother. You're getting too big for this and too heavy." Luke grinned and set him back on the floor.

Bea shooed them all to gather around the table. After they were seated, Carl said grace. At the moment he finished, the sound of horses on the street below came through the window. The stage had arrived. Bea jumped up and hurried to the window. A large bag with the letters US MAIL stamped on the side was tossed to the waiting postmaster. The catalogs should be in a bag that size.

Two women stepped down from the coach. Both were nicely dressed and aroused Bea's curiosity. Most of the people arriving in Barton Creek were either families or single men. Rarely did they have women visitors. The two ladies glanced toward the store, and Bea stepped back from the window.

"Carl, were you expecting any visitors? Two women just arrived on the stage and are looking toward the store."

"No. They're probably just visiting someone in town like Mrs. Frankston or Mrs. Fleming."

Bea nodded. Or they could be two new girls for the saloon that had opened down the block from the store. That was one thing she wished had not come to town, but some men had to have their whiskey. They had two saloon girls now, and Bea could only pray these two weren't additions.

When she peeked again, she realized the women were much older than they first appeared. Bea expelled her breath. No saloon girls, just two ladies in town for a visit. When they turned to walk across to the store, she jumped aside.

"Carl, they're headed this way."

"Then they'll see the sign and know we're closed. If they want something to eat, they can go to Dinah's." He nodded toward her empty chair. "Now come and sit down and eat before the stew is cold."

All through the meal Bea's thoughts returned to the two women. She wanted to know who they were so badly that she couldn't eat. Something about them made her insides feel like jelly.

Finally she pushed back from the table. "Alice, please clean up for me. I'm going down to open up."

Carl laughed. "You can't fool me. You want to see who the women are. What if they don't come back?"

Bea waved her hand. Her dear husband knew her better than she thought. "Then I'll have to do some asking around, I suppose." She hurried down the stairs.

She turned over the sign and opened one side of the door so that the bell jangled. The ladies were nowhere to be seen. Perhaps they had gone to Dinah's. She grabbed her bonnet and headed for the post office.

"Good afternoon, Mrs. Anderson," the postman said. "I have your mail for you, and those catalogs did come. A few letters arrived also." He handed her the stack of letters. The two catalogs sat on the counter.

"Thank you, Mr. Gleason." She retrieved the mail and headed

back to the store. Just after she stepped inside, a voice from behind her called out.

"Are you Beatrice Poole?"

Bea stopped cold in her tracks, the letters and catalogs falling from her hands. No one ever called her by those names. She hadn't been Beatrice Poole in over twenty years. She turned to stare into eyes as blue as her own. "I'm Bea Anderson. My name was Poole before I married."

Something about the woman sent a chill through Bea. She knew this woman. "You have the advantage. Do I know you?"

"It's been a long time, Beatrice, but I'm your sister, Catherine."

Luke stopped at the bottom of the stairway. His breath caught in his throat. That woman just said she was Ma's sister! He stepped into the store as his mother staggered and grasped the counter. He rushed to her side. "Ma, what's going on?"

His mother's face paled, and she fought to control her breathing. She grasped Luke's arm and squeezed. "My sister is dead. You can't be Catherine."

Tears streamed down the stranger's face. Her blonde hair, streaked with gray, showed beneath her blue hat that intensified the blue of her eyes. Luke swallowed hard. She did look like Ma.

He peered again at the woman. "My name is Luke Anderson. What did you say your name is?"

"I'm Catherine Poole, your mother's sister."

"But Ma said those Indians dragged you off after they killed everyone else, so she thought you were dead too." He tried to remember the details Ma had related to him. As many times as he'd heard the story, his mind went completely blank.

The woman with Miss Poole handed Luke some smelling salts. "Here, this may help her."

Ma took a sniff and waved her hand. "I can breathe now; thank you." She continued to stare at the woman calling herself Catherine Poole.

"What happened to you? Where have you been all these years?" Ma's hand clutched the front of her dress.

"It's a long story, Beatrice, and one I'll be glad to tell you, but not all at one time. I will say I've been searching for you for the past fifteen years. No one knew where you had gone after your new family left Nebraska. I did find a woman in the town who said she believed you had moved to the Oklahoma Territory, but she didn't know exactly where. It took awhile, but I finally found you."

By now Pa and Alice had both come down. Pa hurried to Ma's side. She blinked and gazed up at him. "This is Catherine. She's my sister—the one the Indians took away."

Pa peered at the woman and nodded. "I see the family resemblance, Bea." He stretched out his hand. "I'm Carl Anderson. Welcome to our home."

Luke's mind whirled with the information he heard. So many questions raced through his brain, the main one being where she had been all these years. Then a scary thought came to mind. If this really was his aunt, she could turn Ma even more against Dove and the Morris family. Being dragged off by Indians and taken to their camp must have been a horrifying experience.

He didn't want to hear any more of his aunt's story at this moment. All he thought about was Dove and how this might affect their relationship.

"Ma, excuse me. I have an errand to run." He had to see Martin and prayed he'd be home this Saturday afternoon.

Ma tilted her head. "But Luke, your aunt is here. Please stay so we can find out where she's been all these years."

That was the problem. He didn't want to hear that story. No tales of how savage the Indians had been and how they had hurt his aunt would change his mind about Dove, but he could think of no really good reason to give his mother for his need to leave.

"All right, I'll stay." But his heart wanted to be anywhere else but in this store looking into the face of the one person who could ruin all chance he had of helping Ma overcome her feelings against Dove.

Ma clapped her hand to her mouth. "Where are my manners? Please, let's go up to our home where you will be more comfortable." She pointed toward the stairway just as the bell over the door jangled to announce a new customer.

"Go ahead, Ma. I'll stay down here and take care of business." That way he wouldn't have to listen. He could keep busy and not think about what was happening upstairs.

"No, son, go on up with your mother. I'll close again for an hour as soon as I take care of these ladies who just came in."

Luke had no answer but to follow his mother and the other two women up to their home. Ma led the women into the parlor, where the ladies removed their hats. They sat on the sofa, and Alice sat beside Luke in a chair near the door. Will, for once, kept very quiet and sat on the floor at Luke's feet.

Aunt Catherine removed her gloves. "This is my traveling companion, Mrs. Taylor. She's been like a mother, sister, aunt, and grandmother all rolled into one. Her husband is a retired army colonel. He was in command of the post where I ended up many years ago."

Ma smiled and nodded. "How nice of you to accompany my sister on this journey."

The older woman, whose hair was whiter than Aunt Clara's, patted Aunt Catherine's arm. "It was my pleasure. I am so thankful she found you. When the Indians gathered at the fort, we made sure they were treated well. But I didn't know they had any white girls with them until one of the women who left with a white man told me. We immediately found Catherine and took her into our home."

Aunt Catherine placed her hand over Mrs. Taylor's. "The Taylors were very good to me. I've been with them for over twenty years now."

Ma bit her lip. "Then you weren't with the Indians all this time."

"No, I lived with them until Mrs. Taylor took me in."

Mrs. Taylor grasped Aunt Catherine's hand. "They called her Yellow Hair because of her beautiful blonde hair, but she never forgot her real name was Catherine Poole."

"And they treated me very well, or as well as could be expected. I lived with an Indian family and wore their clothes and braided my hair like they did and became one of them."

Ma's eyes opened wide. "You lived with an Indian family and they didn't hurt you?"

Aunt Catherine smiled and shook her head. "Yes, I did live with them, and no, they didn't hurt me. I learned later that they were fascinated by my yellow hair and thought I was someone special."

Luke could see his mother's mind working over that. The way her lips twitched back and forth told him she had trouble believing the story. He believed it. Stories of how Indians had raised white girls in the Indian way of life had been passed around for years, but this was the first time to see it in person.

Now the story captured his attention. If anyone would understand Dove and like her, it would be Aunt Catherine.

Ma continued to ask questions, and Aunt Catherine patiently answered them with Mrs. Taylor adding bits and pieces of information. Pa joined them and sat beside Ma.

"I still can't believe you went back to Nebraska where all that happened. I never wanted to see it again." Ma shuddered and grasped Pa's hand.

"I didn't go back to the homestead. I went to the town and learned a family named Whitley took you in. Then the preacher at the church looked in some old records he had and found where you had married a Carl Anderson, but he had no idea where you were now. The Whitley family left Nebraska not long after you and Carl, and I had no idea how to find you."

Mrs. Taylor leaned forward. "My husband retired from the army and we moved to Missouri, our old home. That's when we decided to start looking for you. He made inquiries, and they finally led us to Barton Creek."

Such an amazing story set Luke's heart to racing. Family ties were so strong that years couldn't keep members from trying to find each other. It reminded him of the parable of the lost sheep—of how the good shepherd always searched until he found the one lamb who had strayed. Ma had been lost to her family, and now, thanks be to God, Aunt Catherine had found her.

Chapter 29

On Sunday morning Bea gathered up her Bible and reticule to take to church. Carl would be waiting with the carriage and team. So much excitement yesterday left her feeling somewhat disjointed today. She and Catherine would have sat up until the early morning hours talking, but Carl had the good sense to remind Bea that the ladies had a long day and trip behind them and needed a good night's rest before church today. Bea wanted to know so much more about Catherine's years since she had been taken from her home, but at least she had some idea of her life the past few years. Not wanting to hear about the years with the Indians, Bea avoided questions about those times. Instead she concentrated on Catherine's search and her time with the Taylors.

Bea headed down the outside stairs. Mrs. Taylor already stood at the foot. "Catherine will be down in a moment. We both appreciate Luke and Will giving up their room for us."

"They didn't mind, but we'll have to make other arrangements for you to stay with us." Bea frowned. "You will stay with us awhile, won't you? I can't bear the thought of her leaving right away since we just found each other."

"I'm not going anywhere for at least a month." Catherine stepped down the last stair into the store. "And I'll be happy to stay at the hotel."

Bea shook her head. "No, that will never do. We have a store room we can empty and use for a spare room."

At that moment Carl pulled up with the carriage. The women hurried out, and he hopped down to help them up to their seats. Bea settled her skirts on the front bench while Carl called up for the children. Luke and Alice hurried downstairs with Will close behind.

"Alice and I are going to walk," Luke declared. "You can go on ahead."

Bea eyed him with a practiced eye. He and Alice were up to something. She read it in their faces. She shook off the idea. Nothing would take away from this day and introducing her sister Catherine to her church family.

When Carl drove the carriage into the churchyard, several members stopped talking to stare at the Anderson family. Bea smiled and waved. When she stepped down, Catherine followed her then Mrs. Taylor.

Mellie Haynes greeted them first. "Good morning, Bea. I see you have guests with you today."

"I do." Bea slipped her arm through Catherine's. "This is my sister, Catherine Poole, from Missouri." She lifted her hand toward Mrs. Taylor. "And this is her friend, Mrs. Taylor."

Mellie's eyes opened wide. "Your sister? But we all thought she was..." Her fingers touched her lips. "I'm sorry. It's a pleasure to meet you."

"Yes, we did think she was lost, even dead, but she ended up at an army post, and Mrs. Taylor took care of her." She turned to her sister. "Catherine, Mrs. Taylor, this is our friend Mellie Haynes, one of our ranchers' wives."

Bea beamed as other women arrived and welcomed the guests. She noted a few raised eyebrows as she introduced Catherine. She'd probably have some explaining to do later, but for now they simply greeted her in welcome.

Bea gazed around the grounds and spotted the Morris buggy, but she didn't see Emily anywhere. Then Luke came into view, and he started talking with Dove. She bit her lip. Perhaps it would be best not to say anything about the Morris family and their Indian heritage until she had a better understanding of Catherine's experience. Letting her know that half-breeds lived in the area might bring back painful memories.

"Come, Catherine, Mrs. Taylor, let us go into the building." Bea noted that Carl had gone ahead and talked on the steps with Ben Haynes. Neither Sam nor Emily were anywhere around, but she spotted Hawk and Eli in the crowd. She hoped the boys' parents had stayed at home.

Catherine leaned close. "I see Luke over there with a beautiful young woman. From the looks on their faces, they are very much in love. Am I right?"

Bea swallowed hard. She debated what to say then opted to say nothing and only nodded. Her voice might betray her feelings, and she didn't want to explain that to her sister at the moment.

The preacher's sermon that morning may have been good, but Bea barely heard a word of it. Her mind filled with how she would answer the many questions her friends would have about how Catherine came to be in Barton Creek. They all knew her story and that she believed her sister to be dead. In her mind the Indians had taken Catherine away, tortured her, and killed her. Seeing her here now and alive caused the images of the past to tumble and toss in Bea's brain.

After church, Bea introduced her guests to the preacher, who welcomed them and invited them to return anytime. Anxious to get home and spend more time with Catherine, Bea hurried them along.

Finally, after dinner, she occupied Will with some new wooden toys Carl had ordered for him. Luke and Alice had been given permission to visit the Morrises this afternoon. Although Bea still had misgivings about that, she decided Alice could tell her exactly what went on between Dove and Luke as well as find out why Emily was not at church. Not that Bea cared, but she was curious.

Now came time for more answers to what had happened during these long years of separation. Questions she'd avoided last night must be asked today.

They settled in the parlor with tea while Carl retired to their room to read and probably take a nap. Bea cleared her throat. "Catherine, tell me what happened when they took you away. Did you know I was alive?"

Catherine stared into space a moment before answering. "Yes, I had seen you move. That's when I jumped up. I didn't want them to see you."

Bea gasped. "They could have killed you too."

"I didn't understand what they were saying, but from the way they handled me, I didn't think they'd kill me. Sure enough, one of them pulled me up onto his horse, and we raced away. My last view of our home was the smoldering ruins of the house and Pa, Ma, Billy, and Ray all lying on the ground and your little head sticking out from under Ma's apron. I prayed you'd be all right."

Tears filled Bea's eyes as the horrible images once again rose in her memory. She brushed at the tears on her cheeks. "I'll never forget that. I saw them take you, and I knew you were going to die. That's why I've thought you were dead all these years. There was so much blood, and the fire had destroyed everything."

Catherine knelt close to Bea and grasped her hands. "I know how hard it must have been for you to see all that, but I'm not dead, and my story is the most amazing one you'll ever hear. When we got back to the Indian camp, the young brave who had taken me handed me over to a woman. I don't know what he told her, but she took me into the shelter where she lived and started tending to the cuts and scrapes on my arms and legs. She was most gentle but kept looking at me with those dark eyes as though she knew something I didn't, and, of course, she did."

Bea sat in stunned silence as her sister related more of the care they had given her. This was not how she had imagined things all these years.

"After five years, when I was fifteen, I was to become the wife of the young brave who took me. All the preparations were made, but then there was a battle and our men went out to fight. My warrior didn't come back, so I didn't marry. Not long after that, the army came and attacked and gathered us all up and herded us to a fort, where we were put with some other tribes until they could send us all to the reservations the government was setting up for all the Indians they'd rounded up. I have no idea where we were then. The Indians kept me hidden from the white men because they didn't want me to go back to them, and at that point I was afraid of leaving my Indian family."

Bea made the mental calculations in her head. "But that was almost twenty-five years ago."

"That's when I met the girl I was telling you about. I think she may have been my age or perhaps a little younger. I'm not sure because I never asked her. She had no family because the soldiers had killed them. She was there less than a year before a white man claimed her and took her away as his wife. That happened a great deal while I was there."

Mrs. Taylor set her teacup and saucer on the table. "Before she left, the young woman told me about Catherine. She said a yellow-haired young woman lived among the Indians. She asked me to find the girl and take her back to her people. I did, and that's how Catherine came to live with the colonel and me."

Catherine returned to her chair and clasped her hands to her chest. "I'll never forget the girl's name. She was so sweet and kind to me. We were much alike in that neither of us had families. Indians killed mine, and white men killed hers. She was called White Feather."

The world swirled around Bea, and her heart raced. It couldn't be the same person. That name had to be a common Indian name. She refused to let the possibility settle in her mind, but the walls of her defense began to crumble.

Dove pulled on Luke's hand. "Come on into the barn and see Calico's new kittens. They were born a week ago, and they're so sweet." She turned to Alice. "Do you think maybe your mother might let you have one? We'll have to give them away, but I do want to keep one for myself."

"I'd love one. I'll ask Ma when we get back to town."

Luke shook his head. A kitten would be nice, but Alice would have to watch Will to keep him from smothering the poor thing to death.

They entered the stables that also served as a barn with a large storage room for equipment and stalls for two cows as well as the horses. Hay and straw lay strewn about the wood floor, and the odor of the place surprised him because it wasn't as offensive as it was at the stables in town. The Morrises kept their stalls clean and their stock well cared for.

Dove pulled open the storage room door. "I don't know how she managed to get in here. The door is usually closed."

Eli, who had followed Alice, grinned. "Ma said to leave it open in case Calico needed a safe place for birthing."

Dove knelt down and stroked the mama cat. "I should have thought of that." She turned to Alice. "Calico won't let us touch her little ones just yet, but aren't they adorable?"

Alice knelt beside her, and Luke's heart swelled with love for Dove and his sister. Their heads together, they giggled like schoolgirls at the antics of the kittens vying for feeding space. He glanced at Eli and recognized the admiration in his eyes as he watched Alice. The story of his Aunt Catherine rolled through his mind as he contemplated Dove and Eli's reactions if they knew.

Dove stood. "Let's leave them alone for now and go for our ride."

"I think I want that little yellow and white one with the brown feet. I'll name him Boots."

Luke chuckled. "And what if it's a girl kitten?"

"Boots is a good name for either one. Don't you think so, Eli?"

Eli grabbed her hand and led her back to the horses. "Whatever you say. I think it's a fine name."

Luke and Dove walked hand in hand to the corral. They mounted and followed Eli and Alice. They rode in silence for a few minutes. Luke drank in the beauty of the girl beside him. Her thick, dark hair had been pulled back and hung in one long braid down her back, and her white hat sat at a jaunty angle on her head.

Although hot, the high blue skies with huge cotton clouds and the sunshine made for a perfect day to be outdoors. Dove riding beside him would make the day perfect even if rain poured on them. Then he surveyed the clouds in hopes that they might carry rain the land so desperately needed.

He turned to gaze at Dove, and her black eyes sparkled with amusement. "What makes you so happy today, Miss Morris? It's spilling out of your face like water from a bucket."

She laughed and raised her face to the sun and closed her eyes. "I don't know. It just feels like today will be an extra special day."

Any day he could be with her was a special day as far as Luke was concerned. They stopped near a grove of trees. He glanced up at the sky and the clouds. "Sure would be nice if those clouds held rain."

"Yes, but not for a little while. I don't want it to spoil our day." She dismounted, as did Alice and Eli.

Eli looped the reins of his and Alice's horses around a drooping crape tree whose fallen cherry-red blossoms dotted the ground with a blanket of color. "We'll leave you two here and go over that way. We won't get out of your sight; I promise."

Luke grinned and waved them on. After securing Lightning and his horse Smokey, he spread the blanket he had brought on the ground.

"Don't you love these beautiful trees? Pa planted several more to go along with the ones he found here. I love the crapes because of their flowers, but the oaks do provide more shade."

Luke agreed, but trees were not a topic he wished to discuss at the moment. He had so much to tell Dove about what had occurred in his home only yesterday. "Dove, I have something that I want to tell you. It's a miracle."

Dove leaned against the tree and tucked her legs beneath her. "Now that sounds like a story I want to hear."

"You won't believe this, as I didn't either at first, but Ma's sister has found us."

Dove's face paled, and her dark eyes were luminous. "But I thought she was taken away by the Sioux back when her family was killed."

"So did we, and that's the miracle. The Indians took her back to their camp and raised her among them. When they were all taken to one of the forts, Mrs. Taylor, the colonel's wife, found her and took her to be a part of their family." Even on retelling, the story sounded more like a tall tale than an actual event. His heart hammered in his chest as Dove let the words sink in.

After a few moments, she crossed her arms over her chest and squeezed her arms. "That's amazing. It gives me chills just thinking about it."

"I don't know the whole story yet, but she and Ma are probably sharing it all now back at our house." He imagined them sitting around in the parlor drinking tea and recapturing all the years that had been lost between sisters. Ma would tell him and Alice all the details when they returned, but at the moment he wasn't sure how her experience might affect his mother. He could only hope for the best.

"So those were the two ladies with your mother this morning. Ma didn't feel well and stayed home, but she wanted to know all about church. I told her you had two visitors with you, but I had no idea they were so important."

"And the good thing is that I think Aunt Catherine's experience with the Indians was a good one. I'm praying she'll be able to help Ma overcome her attitude toward your family." He had seen a change in her expression last night as Aunt Catherine talked, but it had been as unreadable as a book in a foreign language.

Dove smiled then looked up with a furrowed brow. Luke turned to see Eli and Alice racing toward them. Their faces carried fear that grabbed at Luke and turned his blood cold.

Eli yelled, "I think there's a fire coming. I see smoke way off on the horizon. We have to get back and tell Pa."

Luke jumped up and put his hand above his eyes. Sure enough a haze appeared to the north. There was nothing but grass and trees between here and there. "Looks like it's heading this way." And that meant danger for everything in its path.

Eli untied the reins. "And it's widespread." He helped Alice up then mounted himself and hit his horse's side. He galloped away with Alice close behind.

Luke scrambled to get Lightning and Smokey. "We have to get back and warn everyone. Even those in town will have to get out if it's as big as it looks." They both mounted quickly and took off after Eli and Alice.

When they arrived at the ranch, Eli jumped down and ran toward the house yelling for his pa. Mr. Morris raced outside followed by Hawk.

"There's a fire heading this way. Looks like it might hit the Fowler place first then sweep on down this way. How are we going to stop it?"

Mr. Morris headed for his horse. "We probably can't, but we need to warn Mrs. Fowler and help her."

He waved toward Luke. "You head back to town with your sister. Tell everyone we have a fire out on the prairie and we need all the help we can get. And tell Claymore to let the Fowlers go. They need to get home and protect their property. Eli, you stay with your mother and load up our wagons to save what we can. Round up our men, and send one to tell Ben and

Jake. Hawk and I will head over to take care of Mrs. Fowler till her boys arrive."

Luke wasted no more time. He kicked Smokey into action and sped away with Alice close behind. Gratitude for her riding ability filled him because he didn't have to worry about his sister falling or getting hurt. Admiration for Mr. Morris grew. His first concern had been for the woman alone in her home to the north of his. The fire would reach there first, and Mr. Morris had rushed to help the wife of the man who held so much hatred for his family.

Mr. Morris was doing exactly what a Christian man should do in caring about his neighbor as himself, but Luke doubted that Fowler would respond in the same manner. His own feelings for Mr. Fowler and his family were less than charitable at the moment, but the man did deserve to protect his property and his wife.

He rode like the wind, and Alice managed to keep pace as they barreled into town. Luke dismounted in front of the jail and ran inside. "Sheriff, there's a fire coming on the prairie. Mr. Morris said to let the Fowlers go so they can go home and take care of their property."

Chapter 30

Sheriff Claymore grabbed his hat and keys. "Luke, run to the stables and tell Jonah to get horses saddled for these men." He headed back to the cell area where Mr. Fowler now screeched at the top of his lungs to be let go.

Luke took off for the livery and burst through its doors, hollering for the owner. "Jonah, a fire is heading in from the prairie straight toward the Fowler ranch. The sheriff said to get horses ready for the Fowlers to go protect their home."

Jonah raced from his living quarters next to the stables and rushed over to where he had stored the horses when Mr. Fowler was arrested. Luke grabbed a saddle and slapped it over the black stallion belonging to Zeb. The three Fowler men burst through the door, and Zeb grabbed the bridle of his horse.

"Don't know why you're helping, but thanks." He tightened the cinch strap.

"Mr. Morris went over to help your ma, and one of Morris's men went for Mr. Haynes and Jake Starnes. We're going to need all the help we can get."

Zeb cast a suspicious look his way, but Luke ignored it and headed for his own horse. He met his father out on the street along with dozens of other men. Alice had spread the word quickly.

"Luke, Alice said the prairie is on fire." He glanced over Luke's shoulder. "And is that the Fowlers getting out of jail?"

"Yes, the fire's headed their way. Mr. Morris sent me to get them. He and Hawk went to help Mrs. Fowler until her men could get there." Luke stood torn between explaining to the people gathered what was going on and racing back to help Mr. Morris. Common sense took over. These people needed to know.

He stepped up on the boardwalk by the jail. "A fire is coming down from the northeast. I don't know how bad it is, but it looks big. The creek running through here might help, but it's been low on water because of the rains."

Mayor Frankston stepped up beside Luke. "It's time to get organized. I want all men who can ride and are able to go out to see if we can do anything to slow the progress. The rest of you and the women stay here, but get your horses and carriages and whatever else hitched up and ready to go in case we have to leave in a hurry."

The crowd scattered in various directions as Ma dashed across the street. "Luke, I was so worried about you. Alice told us what happened." She clutched at his arm.

"I'm OK, Ma." He loosed her hands from his arm. "I have to go back and see what I can do to help Mr. Morris with whatever needs to be done."

Pa led his quarter horse from the stables. "I'm going out to help. I think you ladies can take care of the store."

"Oh Carl, do you have to go?" Ma wailed. At Pa's grim expression and nod of his head, she conceded. "Of course you do."

Luke followed his father out of town. While the men headed off toward the road, he turned toward the shortcut taken by the Fowlers. "I'm going this way to get to the Fowler ranch and see if they need any more help."

Before his father could stop him, Luke raced after the Fowlers. Without a road, the ground was uneven and brush got in the way, but it still cut precious minutes off the time it took to reach Fowler's ranch. The whole way Luke prayed for a way the men could stop the fire. He'd heard of one that had completely destroyed a town and several hundred people. He couldn't bear the thought of that happening to Barton Creek.

He reached the ranch just after Mr. Fowler and his sons, who scrambled from their horses and ran to the house. Their wagon sat out front hitched to a team, and Mr. Morris and Hawk carried items from the house. Mrs. Fowler ran out to greet her husband and boys.

Luke's heart went out to the woman. She must have been frightened to see Mr. Morris and Hawk riding up and then to hear about the fire. Her frail form shook as she clutched Mr. Fowler's arms. He whispered something to her and then led her back to the house. His gentleness at the moment came as a surprise. Maybe the old man had sobered up and realized the real danger in the situation.

Bart carried out a trunk and slid it onto the wagon bed. He grabbed Mr. Morris's arm. "I don't know why you're doing this, but thanks for helping Ma. After all we've done, I figured you'd be glad if we got burned out."

Luke set a chair in the wagon and listened for Mr. Morris's reply. He'd wondered the same thing himself.

Mr. Morris wiped his brow with his bandana. "Son, when people are in danger, it's our duty to protect and help. Your ma was all alone and needed you. Now let's get everything we can out of the house. We'll take care of the other problem later."

They continued to work until two wagons were loaded down with goods and furnishings. Luke leaned against the side of one as sweat trickled down his face. "Mr. Morris, is there anything we can do to stop the fire?" He'd only heard of wildfires and never seen an actual one.

"I don't know. I've been in more than a few, and some we stopped and some we didn't. I don't want to even think about what's going to happen if it isn't stopped or contained. None of us are safe if we don't."

"Hawk! We're moving out!" he called to his son. Hawk nodded and ran to his horse.

Mr. Morris swung up over his saddle. "Luke, I'm going back to our place now that the Fowlers are safe. My men went to check the progress of the fire. You should go on back to Barton Creek. Your family may need you."

Luke grabbed the reins of Smokey and climbed into the saddle. "No, sir, I'm coming with you."

"All right. Now's not a time to argue, but be careful." Mr. Morris and Hawk galloped away at full speed.

Luke tried to keep up, but his horsemanship couldn't match theirs. When he arrived back at the Morris ranch, Luke's heart lurched, and his mouth went dry. The smoke was closer. Two wagons stood in the yard piled with household goods. Dove ran out of the house with a box in her hands. When she saw Luke, she dropped the box onto the wagon and ran to him. "Oh, Luke, I'm so glad you came back."

He wrapped his arms around her. "I'm here to help. It's going to be all right." Luke prayed that would be so and grabbed her hand to hurry back to the house.

Mrs. Morris emerged with another load; a grim expression filled her face. "Thank you for coming back. Eli is helping the men try to contain the fire, but it's getting closer."

To the northeast flames appeared on the horizon. At that moment Eli galloped in with his face reddened by the heat. "Pa, we can't stop it. I figure we have about half an hour before it'll be at our back door. The cattle have already stampeded and are headed southwest out across the old Dawson property."

Mr. Morris spun around to the barn. "I'm going to make sure all the livestock is out. We'll have to let them run loose or they'll slow us down on the road." He ran to the barn and threw open the doors, shooing the cows out into the yard. For a moment they stood, uncertain where to go, and Mr. Morris yelled and slapped at their flanks. Hawk joined him, and together they yelled, waved their arms, and hit the cows on their rumps. Startled, the beasts ran off down the road.

Mrs. Morris climbed into one of the wagon seats. "I think we have enough from the house. I'm ready."

Jake grabbed Lucy. "We have to get back home and take care of our things in case it turns that way." He turned and looked toward the smoke now billowing ever closer. "As big as that is, it may take all of our homes."

The smell of the burning grass filled the air as Eli took over the reins on the second wagon. "We can't go too fast or the wagons might turn over." He glanced over at his mother. "Be careful. We don't want you turning the wagon over. If the fire gets too close, we'll leave the wagons and take our horses. Your life is more important than a few pieces of furniture."

As the two wagons rolled away, Luke mounted Smokey and Dove rode Lightning. Mr. Morris and Hawk followed on their horses. The air around them reeked of the acrid odor of smoke. He had seen the tears in Mrs. Morris's eyes as she left the ranch. He imagined the home she left behind. A two-story structure of logs would catch fire quickly, but he had no idea how long it would take to burn down. At least all the animals had run out of harm's way.

The air around them grew hazy as though a fog had settled in. They had been riding less than ten minutes when Dove jerked her horse around beside him. "Calico. We didn't get her and the kittens." Then she raced away with her head bent low over Lightning's neck.

Hawk and Mr. Morris took off after her, as did Luke. The smoke was as thick as any Luke had ever known. Although he couldn't see flames, he heard the crackling as it consumed trees and whatever else lay in its path ahead.

At the stables Dove struggled to control Lightning because of the smoke and heat. Hawk grabbed the reins. "We have to get out of here. The whole place will be on fire in a few minutes."

She slid from the saddle. "No, I have to get Calico and her babies."

Luke jumped down, as did Mr. Morris. They handed reins to Hawk, who now struggled to control the horses. Finally he was able to lead them out a ways from the heavy smoke and noise. Mr. Morris found a piece of burlap, but Calico wasn't letting anyone touch her kittens. Luke reached over and picked up the mama cat so Dove could gather the five little ones and put them on the burlap her father held.

Luke held the screaming cat out from his body to avoid the angry slashing of her claws. "Hurry, the fire's closer."

She lifted the last one over to the burlap. Mr. Morris bundled them up. "Now get out of here, you two." He ran out with his cargo.

Luke dropped the cat. She'd run to wherever they took her kittens and be OK. He reached a hand down to Dove then heard a crash behind them. The back wall was now in flames that licked up the wall in a blaze of orange and gold.

He pulled his kerchief up over his nose, thankful he'd decided to wear one today. Dove tried to stand but caught her foot in the hem of the split skirt she wore. She freed it and stood. Then her eyes opened wide in horror.

"The whole thing's on fire." She stumbled forward, and

before Luke could steady her, she tripped over something on the ground and fell, her head hitting the side of the storage bin as she went down.

Luke grabbed her up and stumbled toward the door just before a beam fell across the bin and sparks flew. Mr. Morris appeared at his side and took Dove from his arms. Blood seeped from the wound on her head, and her eyes remained closed. Fear rose in Luke's throat like bile, but he managed to follow Mr. Morris outside while the fire raged behind them.

Luke held Dove while her father mounted his horse then handed her up to his arms. He then swung in his own saddle, and Hawk did the same, still holding onto Lightning.

The one glimpse of the house as flames engulfed it etched itself into Luke's memory. The magnificent logs that held the great structure burned and fell like matchsticks. His heart cried for all that would be lost that day, and he prayed that Dove would not be another casualty. He would never forget the sight of her limp form and the roar of the fire behind them as they raced away.

They soon caught up to the two wagons, which had stopped in the middle of the road. Mrs. Morris screamed at the sight of Dove and tried to jump down from the wagon.

Mr. Morris shouted to his wife. "Stay there. I'm taking her in to the doctor."

She slumped back on the seat, her face streaming with tears. Hawk nodded at Luke. "I'll take care of Ma and Eli. You go on with Pa and Dove."

Luke wasted no time in following that order. The only place he wanted to be at the moment was beside Dove.

A new roar filled the air. Luke glanced behind him to see if the fire was gaining but saw only smoke. Then a drop of water hit his hand, then another, and another. He lifted his head toward the smoke-filled heavens. Thunder! It must be thunder and blessed rain.

"Thank You, God. Thank You." He slapped the rear of his horse into a greater speed, welcoming the rain as it grew heavier.

Bea paced the room, wiping her hands on her apron. It had been hours since Luke and Carl had left. Visions of the fire taking their lives filled her with a fear she hadn't known in years. Not even the time Carl had been thrown from his horse had she been this afraid.

She and Catherine had packed up many of their belongings, and both the wagon and carriage stood ready for a quick departure. This room and all its furniture may be lost, but if Carl and Luke were all right, none of these things mattered.

Catherine handed her a cup of tea. "Here, Beatrice. Sit down and drink this. Worrying and fretting isn't going to bring them back any sooner."

"I know that, but it's a wife and mother's duty to worry about her men." She sat down and sipped at the tea. "It's been several hours. Someone should have returned by now and let us know what to do."

Catherine sat up and leaned forward. "I hear rain." She ran to the window. "It is. It's raining, Beatrice."

Bea jumped up and joined her sister. Rain beat against the window. "Thank You, God." Tears streamed down her face to match the rivulets on the windows.

Alice ran into the room. "Ma, Ma, it's raining."

Bea hugged her. "I see it, I see it." Rain meant the fires would go out and the town would be spared. Now if only Carl and

Luke would come home. The only thing she knew to do filled her with energy. Her men would need nourishment. "Who's up for a good hot apple pie? Alice, run down to the cellar and bring me up those apples we dried. I'll get the crust started."

"What can I do to help?" Catherine reached for an apron hanging on the hook by the door.

"If you and Mrs. Taylor could bring some of those boxes back up that we took down to the store, I'd be most grateful. We can have everything back in place in no time. The things in the wagon are covered and will be OK until later." Bea turned to her task with a heart filled with the joy of knowing they wouldn't lose their home and business. But she couldn't help but think of those who lived out several miles from town. Many of them could have lost everything.

Half an hour later, Luke burst through the door with his hair hanging in wet strings about his face and his clothes soaked with rain. She rushed to him. "Thank God you're all right. Are the fires all out?"

"I think so, but I'm changing clothes and going back to Doc Carter's. Dove was injured and won't wake up."

Bea's heart pounded. He'd gone back to Dove, but for some reason that fact didn't bother her today like it usually did. He went into his room and in a few minutes returned in dry clothing. Catherine and Mrs. Taylor appeared at the top of the stairs just as Luke prepared to leave. He'd donned his slicker and boots.

Catherine said, "I'm so glad to see you're all right." She eyed his rainwear. "You're going back out in this downpour?"

"Yes. Dove is badly hurt, and I must get back to her. Leave that stuff downstairs; we can get it later."

Bea stretched out her hand. She worried about how Mr. Morris might react to having Luke there. "Do you think that's wise? Wouldn't it be better to let the doctor treat her first? Aren't her parents with her?" As soon as the words left her mouth, Bea regretted them. Of course he wanted to be with Dove.

Luke jerked away from her. "You're not going to stop me this time. I'm going to be with Dove and her family." He started toward the door then stopped and spun around. "And just so you know, I plan to marry Dove if she'll have me, and none of your talk about Indians and their cruelty will change it. I'm sorry for what happened to you, but it has nothing to do with today and my life."

He pointed to the Bible on the table. "You say you believe in God and Jesus, His Son, but maybe it's not the same loving one I believe in. If your God doesn't tell you to forgive, I don't want any part of Him, and don't tell me that book says we're not to be unequally yoked, because Dove is as fine a Christian as anyone in this room. I won't listen to any more of your anger and your prejudice. If you can't forgive, then I pray God's mercy on you."

With that he turned on his heel and ran out the door.

Bea fell back onto the sofa. Luke had never spoken to her like that. The last time had been hurtful, but this time his words tore her heart in half. She had lost him, and all his trust in her was gone as well. Tears filled her eyes and Catherine sat beside her. Mrs. Taylor brought her a glass of water and sat on the other side. Regret that they had heard the angry exchange filled her, and she searched her brain for a way to explain.

Bea sipped her water, stalling an explanation as long as possible.

But Catherine would have none of that. "What was that all about? It doesn't seem like Luke to be so angry."

"He has a right to be, and it's all my fault." Bea then told her sister about the Morris family and how every time she saw them it brought back memories of what happened in Nebraska.

Catherine listened but remained silent, and her eyes clouded as the story unfolded. At the end, Bea sobbed. "I don't know what to do. I've tried to understand, but it hurts."

Mrs. Taylor nodded to the Bible on the table next to Catherine.

When her sister picked it up, Bea stared at it. How did they think a Bible would help? She'd read it over and over again the past few months but found no peace.

"You know what must be done." Catherine opened the Bible to the sixth chapter of Matthew and handed it to Bea. Catherine's finger pointed to verses fourteen and fifteen.

Through her tears, Bea read aloud. "For if ye forgive men their trespasses, your heavenly Father will also forgive you. But if ye forgive not men their trespasses, neither will your Father forgive your trespasses." The words pierced her heart like a sword. She had read them many times, but they had never spoken to her the way they did at this moment. She lifted her eyes to her sister.

"Beatrice, if Jesus could ask His Father to forgive the men who beat Him and hung Him on that cross, don't you think He'd expect you to forgive the men who killed our parents? I did, and that's how I survived."

Bea swallowed hard. That's what she'd been avoiding, but her anger made her no better than those soldiers who had tortured her Savior. There was only one thing she could do, and she bowed her head. "You're right. I see that now."

Catherine covered her hands with her own. "And what are you going to do about that?" she prodded gently.

Bea lifted her head and spoke bravely, like a child reciting at a school event. "I must go to the doctor's office and find Emily.

Then I must apologize to her." Bea grasped Catherine's hands. "Thank you for helping me to see how wrong I've been. I'm ready to see Dove's family and tell them how sorry I am for my behavior toward them all these years." Then a smile from her heart burst through. "And I want you to come with me. There's a special person I want you to meet."

"Of course I'll come if you think it'll be all right."

"It will be more than all right. Of that I'm sure. Besides, I need your moral support, as this will be most difficult. I only hope they will accept and forgive me." If what she suspected came to be, then more than one person would have a joyous time of reunion and reconciliation.

Bea stood and headed for the door, pulling Catherine with her. Bea's heart pounded, and fear of rejection consumed her. Going down the stairs, she squared her shoulders and stiffened her spine. Apologizing to the Morris family would be difficult, but not as difficult as holding on to hatred and anger and fear.

Chapter 31

Luke's concern for Dove grew as he reached the doctor's office. The Morris family greeted him with grim faces when he entered. Mrs. Morris hugged him. "Thank you for being there for Dove."

Luke choked back his fears. "I'm so sorry I didn't get her out of the barn sooner."

Mrs. Morris's tear-filled eyes bore into his. "You did your best. Dove's tender heart took her back into danger."

Mr. Morris talked in low tones to Doc Carter, and Luke strained to hear. He looked at Hawk and Eli, who both shook their heads. Luke's heart pounded, and fear gripped every part of his body. It was only a gash on her head. She had to wake up soon.

Mrs. Morris patted his arm. "The thing we have to do now is pray. Doctor Carter isn't sure, but she may have suffered a concussion."

Luke shook his head. This couldn't be happening. Mr. Morris motioned for him to come to him. He held back the curtain, shielding Dove. Luke stepped to her side. She lay perfectly still with a definite pallor underlying her olive skin. If not for the gentle rise and fall of the sheet covering her, he would have thought her dead. His lips trembled as he touched her hand.

A portion of her dark hair had been shaved to allow the doctor to sew up the gash. Seven dark stitches now marred her face just above the temple, but they would never mar her beauty. Luke turned to her father. "How bad is it?"

Mr. Morris grasped Luke's shoulder. "It's not good, but Doc says we should know more by morning. An inch lower and we wouldn't be standing here with her."

Luke fought tears. His throat constricted, so he couldn't speak or swallow. He had to get outside. He spun on his heel and ran to the door. "I'm going to the church." Outside he managed to take deep gulps of air and breathed in the fresh smell of rain.

He didn't look back but trudged through the rain and mud down to the church. The rain now fell in a steady but light stream of water. It washed away the dust and grime of the summer and quenched the fires, but it hadn't come soon enough to keep Dove from being hurt.

The quiet interior of the church beckoned him. The soft patter of drops on the roof was the only sound as he sat on a back pew and bowed his head. No words would come. All he wanted was for Dove to wake up.

Images of his times with Dove flashed through his mind in a splash of color and sound. Her crystal clear laugh and her soothing voice rang in his ears. The yellow dress she wore for Lucy's wedding, the red and white dress from the Haynes's party, and her riding attire of today all created visions of the girl he loved with all his heart. If only he could be the one who had fallen.

Then the happy memories gave way to the pale form lying in the office down the street. Tears flowed freely, and he made no attempt to wipe them away. A verse from Romans came to mind. "Likewise the Spirit also helpeth our infirmities: for we know not what we should pray for as we ought: but the Spirit itself maketh intercession for us with groanings which cannot be uttered."

Peace finally consumed his soul. Even if he couldn't say the words, the Spirit knew his heart and interceded for him. God knew, and that was all that counted.

As he sat, the calm assurance that God was in control strengthened his faith. Dove would wake up in the morning, and he would tell her how much he loved her. He refused to think about or believe any other outcome until God proved otherwise.

Bea stepped outside. Only a fine mist was left of the rain, but it gave her the feeling of being washed completely clean. Indeed, her heart, once blackened by the sin of hate and an unforgiving spirit, now beat fresh and new. From the ashes of sin, the glowing embers of restoration and freedom now burned.

On the boardwalk outside the doctor's office, Bea stopped and breathed deeply. A smidgeon of fear threatened her resolve, but she shook it off. She had a mission to fulfill.

Catherine squeezed Bea's shoulder. "I'm right here beside you, and God is with us both. You can do this because it's what He wants you to do."

Bea squared her shoulders and opened the door. As she stepped into the room, Emily gasped. "Bea, what are you doing here?"

Hawk stepped forward. "Please leave us alone. We don't need to hear anything you have to say."

Bea moistened her lips. "But I believe you do. I have made a horrible mistake, and I am here to seek your forgiveness."

No one spoke for a moment, then Emily approached her. "Do you truly mean that, Bea? Have our prayers been answered?"

Bea's head jerked. Emily's prayers? The woman she'd considered an enemy all these years had been praying for her? A knot twisted itself in Bea's throat, and her eyes misted over. She nodded her head. "I guess they have."

Emily's arms encircled Bea. Her head barely reached Bea's chin, but the two women clung together with tears of joy glistening on their cheeks. Bea stepped back. "Here is someone I want you to meet."

She stretched her hand toward her sister. "This is my sister, Catherine, the one I thought was dead."

The two women peered at one another for several seconds. A dawn of recognition flooded Catherine's face. "White Feather, my dear friend, is it really you?"

Emily's voice cracked as she spoke. "Yellow Hair?"

They stared for another moment before reaching out to grab each other around the shoulders. Emily shook her head. "How is this possible? I thought you were with the colonel's wife. And how did you end up here?"

Catherine swiped her cheeks. "Mrs. Taylor did take me in after you left. I've lived with them all these years and just yesterday found my sister here in Barton Creek."

The two women hugged again and began asking questions about the past years. Bea spoke to Sam Morris. "I'm truly sorry for all the unkind things I've said and for the way I've snubbed your family for so many years. Luke is a fine young man, and I know how much he cares for your daughter. I will no longer stand in the way of their relationship."

Sam's mouth worked in a way that a man's will do when he's deciding exactly how to say what he wanted to say. Bea had seen Carl do it often enough after some remark she made.

Finally Sam spoke. "If you're truly sorry, then I can't do anything but accept your apology and forgive you." He glanced over her shoulder. "I see that my wife and your sister have some kind of special relationship. I remember her telling me about a white girl she'd left behind when we left the fort."

"When Catherine told me that the Indian girl who befriended and helped her was named White Feather, I just knew there had to be a connection." She gazed around the room. "Where is Luke? I thought he'd be here."

"He was, but he went down to the church." Sam nodded toward the door.

"Then I will wait for him." She hesitated. "That is, if it's all right with you."

"Yes, you may stay, but we've tried to stay quiet. Doctor Carter is keeping a close eye on Dove. He's taken her into the other room and put her to bed there. We won't know anything until morning."

"How badly was she injured?" Nothing must happen to Dove now that Luke had declared his love for her. God wouldn't be so cruel as to take away that sweet child just as everything was resolved among the parents.

Sam shook his head. "We're not sure. She has seven stitches on the side of her head where she hit a feeding bin when she fell."

"The fire. I...I'd forgotten about that. What happened?"

"We were well away from the ranch when Dove remembered her cat and new little kittens, so she rode back to rescue them. We got them in time, but when we were leaving the barn, she tripped, and that's when she hit her head. Luke was there to get her out just as the barn went up in flames."

Bea blinked her eyes. Just like a girl to go back for a cat and her kittens, but it was just the sort of thing Luke loved about her. Then the implication hit her. "Luke could have been hurt too. Thank God he wasn't and could take care of Dove."

"Yes, and I'd say your son has done enough rescuing of our

daughter the past month that he has earned her love, although I don't think he needed to do anything to earn it."

Bea turned to Emily. "Did you lose the house?"

Emily nodded. "The house and everything we couldn't take out."

"I'm so sorry. You had some wonderful things." Bea thought about how she would feel if she lost her own home and realized how close she had come to having that happen.

"But none are as important as my husband and three children. They were spared." Then Emily stared at the door to Dove's room. "All except for my precious girl, and I believe she will be all right. We just have to wait for God to do His work of healing."

Ideas formed in Bea's head and meshed together like cogs on a machine. She knew what had to be done and the people who could help make it happen.

Luke left the church and headed back to Doc Carter's. Maybe there'd been some change in Dove since he left. Alice ran across the street and called his name. "What are you doing out here?"

"Mrs. Taylor just told me that Ma and Aunt Catherine went to the doctor's office to see the Morris family."

Luke's heart jumped in his chest. He swallowed hard. If Ma took her anger at him out on them, he'd never forgive her. He had to stop her. Alice grabbed at his arm.

"No, wait. Mrs. Taylor said it was a good surprise, so don't be angry again."

His teeth ground together in frustration. Ma should have left well enough alone, but if Aunt Catherine was with her then maybe she could control Ma.

"Are you going to stand here or go with me?" She turned and darted toward the office.

When he burst through the door, he stopped short and took in the scene before him. Ma, Aunt Catherine, and Mrs. Morris sat on chairs in a huddle while Mr. Morris, Hawk, and Eli stood on the other side of the room. Alice ran to Eli.

"What's going on?" Luke approached his mother. "What are you doing here? If you came to cause trouble, then you'd better leave."

Mrs. Morris grabbed his hand. "No, it's nothing like that. The most amazing thing has happened, and it's truly a miracle."

That's when he noticed the tears in Ma's eyes. He knelt beside her. "What's the matter?" He jumped up and spun around. "Is it Dove? Is she worse?" He could think of no other reason why three women would be sitting together with tears in their eyes.

Aunt Catherine wrapped her arm around Ma's shoulders. "Your mother and I have made a miraculous discovery." She peered down at Ma and nodded.

"My dear son, I no longer oppose your relationship with Dove. Through my sister, your angry outburst, and God's Word, I have done what I should have done so many years ago. I've forgiven the men who killed my father and mother."

Luke heard the words, but his mind couldn't believe them. For over two months now he'd prayed for a change of heart. Now that it had happened, the shock left him unable to respond.

Ma stood and hugged him. "I know it's hard to believe after so many years of bitterness and anger, but God showed me the way through your aunt." She stepped back. "But another miracle has happened. Aunt Catherine and Emily Morris knew each other as young girls. They were brought together when her tribe and Emily's arrived at the same army post."

This was more than he could take in at the moment. He

slumped back against the wall, his legs shaking as though made of mush. His heart raced and his mind sifted through all he'd been told. When God had opened the door for his mother to forgive, He'd kicked it wide open with another miracle.

"I can't believe all this. It's like a dream." His eyes darted from one to the other of the Morris family. Each face gave evidence of the reconciliation and acceptance that filled the room. "Now all I need to hear is that Dove is all right."

Doctor Carter shook his head. "We won't know that for another twelve to fourteen hours. She had a pretty deep cut on her head and is still unconscious. I'll be watching her closely through the night." He peered around the room at the number of people there. "I suggest you all go get something to eat, find a place to stay, and come back in the morning."

Emily jumped up. "No, I can't leave my baby alone even with you, Doctor Carter. Please let me stay with her. The rest of you can do what he said."

Luke shook his head. "I don't want to leave either. I have to stay here."

The doctor grasped his shoulder. "Son, I understand why you want to be here, but it will be much better if everyone leaves for now." He turned to Emily. "Go eat, rest a bit, and then come back to sit with her. You'll feel much better, and those are doctor's orders."

Aunt Catherine and Ma both spoke at the same time, but Aunt Catherine stopped, and Ma continued. "I want you all to come back to my house. I'll fix us something to eat, and you can change into some drier clothes."

Luke's mouth dropped open. Another surprise in a day full of strange, terrifying, and miraculous events—and the day wasn't over yet.

Chapter 32

So much had happened since church that morning, and Luke's mind couldn't wrap itself completely around the facts. Dusk fell on the town, signaling the end of the day, but it was a day he would never forget. His eyes misted at the thought of Ma's complete change of heart. He had prayed for it these past months, and now that it had happened, he couldn't rejoice as he wanted because Dove lay unconscious at Doc Carter's, her recovery uncertain. They needed another miracle.

The most wonderful smells filled the kitchen, and Mrs. Taylor waited to welcome them. "I have a pot of soup and corn bread ready for you. I figured you'd all be hungry after the ordeal of this day."

Emily rushed to the woman and grasped her hands. "Mrs. Taylor, I'm White Feather. Do you remember me?"

Mrs. Taylor gasped. "White Feather?" Her gaze darted from Mrs. Morris to Aunt Catherine, then she gathered Mrs. Morris in her arms. "I can't believe this. Oh my, this is wonderful."

The two women hugged, and then both began to talk at once. Mrs. Taylor held up her hands. "You first, White Feather." She led Mrs. Morris to a chair in the corner of the parlor.

Satisfied they were comfortable, Ma smiled, her eyes resting on Luke. "We've had one miracle, and I believe God will give us another one with Dove." She paused a moment then clapped her hands. "Now let's get organized."

Mr. Morris had taken the two wagon loads of possessions down to the stable to have them stored for however long needed. Eli and Hawk were with him. Luke itched to return to Dove's bedside, but Doc Carter probably wouldn't let him near her.

He glanced around the room. His one big question at the moment was where they would put all these people. They still needed to clear the store room and put a bed in there, but that would only take care of Aunt Catherine and Mrs. Taylor. He and Will could go down to the stables and sleep there, and perhaps Mrs. Morris could stay in his room.

Pa appeared at the top of the stairs, his arms laden with goods. "I have more food here and some sheets and things for sleeping."

Ma ran over and hugged him. "I didn't know you were back. I'm so glad the rains came to stop the fires."

He put his load on the sofa. "I am too." Then he grasped Ma's hands. "Mrs. Taylor told me where you were and what you were doing. I'm so proud of you doing something about it immediately." He glanced over at Emily and Mrs. Taylor. "I suppose there's a story behind that too."

Ma nodded and kissed Pa on the cheek. "I'll tell you later." She turned to Alice. "Go over to the Flemings's house and tell Mrs. Fleming we have people who need a place to sleep tonight."

"Yes, Ma." Alice ran out the door and down the outside steps.

Mrs. Morris put up her hand. "Bea, you don't need to worry about that. We can stay at the hotel."

Ma shook her head. "They may be full. I saw several families come in earlier, including the Fowlers. Of course, Sheriff Claymore put the boys back in jail, but he let Mr. Fowler stay with his wife for tonight."

That answered Luke's curiosity about what had happened to

them after he and Mr. Morris left. No matter what they had done, they didn't deserve to lose their home. But then no one did.

Ma led Emily to Alice's room. "Let's see what we can find you to wear."

An image of Mrs. Morris dressed in one of Alice's school outfits brought a smile to Luke. He couldn't imagine the older women in any of them. He shrugged. Let the women worry about that. He'd take care of Eli and Hawk. "Ma, I'm going down to the stables to help Mr. Morris if he needs it."

Just as he opened the door, Alice and Mrs. Fleming burst in. "Alice told me everything." She hugged Mrs. Morris. "I'm so sorry about Dove. Doc will take care of her, and we'll pray extra hard for her tonight. And your home and all your things, Emily. Anything we can do to help we will. There's plenty of room at our house for you." She stopped for breath. That was Luke's cue for a quick exit.

Ma and the other ladies would take care of all the details. He'd wait and get his instructions later. Right now he had a matter to discuss with Mr. Morris.

When Luke reached the stables, he found Mr. Morris talking with the owner. "Thank you, Jonah. Don't know how long it'll be, but I know our things will be safe here."

"Just glad I have the extra room. Fires are horrible things. Tell your missus that my wife and I will be praying for Dove."

"I'll tell her; thank you." He turned and saw Luke then frowned. "Is something wrong?"

"No, no. Everyone's fine. Ma and Aunt Catherine are taking care of Mrs. Morris." Perhaps now wasn't the time to seek permission for what he wanted, but Luke didn't care to wait. "There's something I've been wanting to speak with you about."

Mr. Morris nodded. "Walk with me. The sheriff asked to see me. I'm going that way now."

"Yes, sir." Luke strode beside him.

"Would what you want to say have anything to do with my daughter?"

Luke gulped. Now that the time had come, no words would form on his lips. "I'm praying Dove wakes up in the morning." He groaned. That's not what he intended. Surely Mr. Morris already knew everyone would be praying.

"That's good, Luke. We need all the prayers we can get." He clapped Luke on the shoulder. "But that's not what's really on your mind, is it?"

"No, sir." They reached the jail. "I'll wait until you finish your business here."

Mr. Morris grinned. "This won't take long. Come on in with me."

Inside the office, Claymore shook Mr. Morris's hand. He pointed toward the back. "I have the boys locked in their cells. I deputized one of the men at the hotel, and he's standing watch over Chester."

The sheriff continued, his face serious. "I have struck a deal with the boys—if the money is returned, I will drop charges for the theft. But Zeb will be charged for the attack on Dove, and Chester will be charged for the shooting of Martin. Bart will be released to sell their property and take his mother back to family out east."

Mr. Morris shook his head and frowned. "I'm not sure I agree with your plan, but we'll see." He set his hat on his head and nodded his farewell.

Once out on the boardwalk, Luke hurried to keep up with Mr. Morris. Luke's legs were long, but his strides barely matched those of Mr. Morris.

"Let me check on Dove, and then you can finish that conversation you tried to start earlier." Mr. Morris walked into Doc Carter's place, and Luke followed. The doctor sat at his desk in the corner. He glanced up and removed his glasses. "I figured you'd be back. Can't tell you anything more than I did before. She does seem to be resting better now. Like I said, we'll know more in the morning."

"Mrs. Morris will be over after supper to stay with her. We don't want her waking up in a strange place without a familiar face around."

Alice poked her head around the door. "Ma said she'd bring you a tray over soon as we get everyone settled and eating."

The doctor grinned. "Now that will be most welcome. Your ma's a good cook."

"You two coming, or do I tell Ma you're passing on supper?"

"We'll be there in a few minutes, Miss Alice. Luke and I have a matter to discuss first. Isn't that right, son?"

Luke swallowed hard. "Yes, sir, we do."

Alice hurried back across the street to the mercantile, and Luke stepped out of the doctor's office and onto the front porch behind Mr. Morris. Luke grabbed at a porch railing for support. Now he had to muster up his courage all over again. All the words he'd wanted to say tumbled around in his head. Now was the time or he'd never get them said.

He took a deep breath to bolster his courage. Dark had fallen, but he could still see the set of Mr. Morris's mouth and his narrowed eyes. "Mr. Morris, I love your daughter. Dove is more important to me than anyone else on this earth. I want to marry her and protect her and have her by my side as my wife."

A smile slowly formed on Mr. Morris's lips. "I guessed that was what you wanted to say. I've seen my daughter's face when you're around. Every time she's with you, her face is so full of love that I don't think either her ma or I would be able to stop it."

Luke's heart swelled to bursting. "Ma no longer objects, and I promise to take good care of her."

A chuckle escaped Mr. Morris's throat. "I'm sure you will, but we'll have to wait for the little lady to have her say. You know we've made arrangements for her to go to Texas to attend school at Baylor."

"Yes, sir, but I was hoping she'd change her mind if I ask her to marry me."

Mr. Morris stroked his chin. For the first time Luke saw gray in the stubble now covering the man's chin and jaw. He'd never seen him not clean shaven, and the short whiskers reminded Luke this had been a long, harrowing day for all of them.

"When she wakes up, you can ask her."

Luke wanted to shout with glee but instead stretched out his hand. "Thank you, Mr. Morris. I'll be there when she wakes up, and you know, sir, she will wake up. God is letting her body rest from the ordeal, but she'll be all right; you'll see."

Mr. Morris gripped Luke's hand. "I pray you're right." He grasped Luke's shoulder. "We'll be proud to have you as part of our family. Now, let's go get some supper."

Chapter 33

The sky had just begun to lighten on Monday morning when Luke slipped out of the house and made his way across the street to Doc Carter's. He'd been careful not to wake anyone, but even then he'd heard Ma up already preparing for the day.

When Luke crossed the street, Mr. Morris met him. Luke's jaw worked as he greeted him. "I said I'd be here first thing. I want to be here when she wakes up."

"That's fine, son. We'll all be here when that happens. Eli and Hawk are on their way."

They entered the office just as Doc Carter closed the door to Dove's room behind him. He shook his head. "No change yet." He reopened the door. "You may go in and sit with your wife."

Luke followed Mr. Morris, but the doctor put out his hand to stop him.

"Let him come with me. He has a stake in this too." Mr. Morris stepped aside to let Luke go in.

He stepped to the side of Dove's bed. Mrs. Morris sat with head bowed, holding her daughter's hand. Luke walked to the other side and grasped the other hand. He knelt beside her. *Dear God, please let her wake up soon. I love her so much and want to spend the rest of my life with her.*

He closed his eyes and squeezed her hand. Except for the murmur of Mr. and Mrs. Morris's voices, the room was quiet.

Luke's heart thumped in his chest, each beat willing Dove to awaken from her deep sleep.

All the events of yesterday and last evening rolled through his brain. The flames eating at the walls of the barn, the heavy smoke, and the mewling of the kittens were images and sounds he would never forget. His head jerked up. "Mr. Morris, what happened to Calico and her kittens?"

Mr. Morris smiled. "They're down at Jonah's. He fixed up a special box for her. She and her kittens will be fine."

"Thank goodness. It would be awful for Dove to wake up and find out they didn't make it." He moistened his lips. "I should have gotten her out of there sooner."

"Don't blame yourself. You were there when needed. You got her out before the barn roof fell in."

When Luke opened his mouth to protest, Mr. Morris held up his hand. "None of us should have been there, but Dove wanted to save those kittens. Don't think on what ifs and should haves; concentrate on her waking up."

Luke nodded. Still, he carried the guilt that he should have prevented her fall. If only he'd grabbed for her sooner. No matter what Mr. Morris or others said, he would carry the blame if she didn't get better.

The door opened, and Ma stepped in. She held a basket and coffeepot in her hands. "I thought you might need a little nourishment. There's biscuits and bacon, cups and napkins in the basket, and coffee in the pot." She set them down on a nearby table.

Then she reached down and hugged Mrs. Morris. "Emily, we're all back at the house praying for her. Eat a little something to give you strength. You don't want to become ill yourself."

"Thank you, Bea. I'm not hungry, but I could use some of that coffee." She peered up at Ma. "Bea, I've always thought that

Alice reminded me of someone I knew, and now I realize she looks very much like Catherine at that age."

"My memory of her has grown fuzzy through the years, but now that you mention it, I guess she does."

Mr. Morris poured a cup and handed it to his wife. "We appreciate your prayers and concern, Mrs. Anderson. We'll let you know as soon as anything changes."

"Anything else you need, just let us know." Ma came over and hugged Luke then left.

The three of them sat in silence around the bed. Luke took a biscuit but could barely swallow. He gulped down a cup of hot coffee, trying to fortify himself for the uncertainty of the wait ahead. Doc Carter checked on Dove as the first rays of light streamed into the room.

Sheriff Claymore appeared at the door. "Sam, I need to speak with you a minute."

Mr. Morris nodded and went into the other room with the sheriff. He closed the door behind him.

Luke strained to hear their voices but could not make out any words. A few minutes later Mr. Morris returned. Luke's curiosity got the better of him. "Was that about the Fowlers?"

"Yes, they've handed over the stolen money, and the sheriff will take it over to Mrs. Fleming as soon as he knows they're up and about."

"What's going to happen now?"

"I'm not sure. We'll let the sheriff handle that now."

"What about you? What will you do about your ranch?"

"Rebuild, of course. Most of the herd was spared, so our livelihood is safe. This is just one setback, and God spared our lives, so we have much to be grateful for."

Mrs. Morris covered her husband's hand with hers. "God has been good to us, and I don't believe He'll fail us now."

Their faith strengthened Luke's. Encouraged, he took Dove's hand and stroked it with his thumb. He would wait here all morning—all day, if he had to.

He was staring so hard at her face that when her eyelids fluttered a moment, it didn't register. Then she squeezed his hand. He jumped from his chair. "Doc Carter, she's waking up."

Mrs. Morris bent over Dove and touched her face as the doctor hurried to the bedside. He examined her, and Dove's eyes opened wide. "She's awake!" Luke cried.

The doctor stepped back. "Looks like our girl is coming back to us."

Dove blinked, but all was a blur. Her head hurt. She heard the doctor speak and then her mother's voice. Someone shouted. If only she could focus. She willed her eyes to open again. This time her mother's face was next to hers.

"What happened? Where am I?"

Ma squeezed her hand. "You're at Doctor Carter's. Do you remember the fire?"

The fire…the barn…the images returned. Calico! "Did we save Calico and her kittens?"

Someone squeezed her hand. She turned her head to see Luke.

"We sure did, but we almost lost you." His grin spread wide.

Luke was here, and he'd been with her in the barn. She remembered falling, but nothing after that. She gazed up into his eyes.

He told her what had happened, but she barely heard the words. Then he was on his knees holding her hand tightly in his. He leaned forward and brushed his lips across her hand. Her heart leapt within her chest, and joy filled her soul.

Pa placed a hand on Ma's shoulder. "Let's leave these two alone for a moment. I believe he has something to say to our daughter. I'll go get Hawk and Eli."

Ma squeezed her hand again, then she and Pa left. Dove turned her attention to Luke, her heart eager to hear what he had to say.

Luke's eyes were moist as he held her gaze. "I was so scared you were going to die before I could tell you that I love you with all my heart. I never want to be away from you again."

The words she'd wanted to hear for so long now rang in her ears like church bells pealing good news across the land. "Oh, Luke, I love you too."

"This morning is for you, Dove. It's the beginning of a brand-new life for all of us. And I want to spend every morning of the rest of our lives together. Will you marry me, Dove?"

"Yes, yes, I will." Never had she wanted to do something as much as she wanted to be Luke's wife.

Luke leaned over then and kissed her cheek. Tears filled her eyes. The night may be black with fear and anxiety, but the Lord promised joy for the morning. He'd kept that promise, and now she looked forward to more mornings of joy with the man she loved.

Epilogue

Dove's white dress shimmered in the sunlight from the windows on this October morning. Crystal beads and pearls adorned the neckline, and lace trimmed the sleeves and the short train. Lucy picked up the matching headpiece and attached it with a pearl comb to Dove's hair.

Two months ago Dove couldn't have believed this day would arrive. She lifted her fingers to touch the jagged welt above her temple, a grim reminder of the accident that almost took her life.

Lucy worked with Dove's hair and arranged a curl over the scar. "You are a beautiful bride." Her hand lowered to cover Dove's. "See, it's completely covered."

"Thank you." The looking glass revealed the bloom on her cheeks that rose in anticipation of the day ahead. She gathered up her floral bouquet and buried her face in the petals. Such a wonderful fragrance filled her nose. The deep orange, yellow, and gold blooms echoed the colors of the season, her favorite time of the year. Her heart couldn't contain any more happiness or it would burst.

She set the bouquet aside. "I'm so thankful for God's blessings over the past few months. Mrs. Anderson has been wonderful, Pa is rebuilding our home, and the Fowlers are gone."

A voice from the doorway said, "Let's not even mention

the Fowler family today. They're out of our lives and in prison where they belong."

Dove turned to find her mother entering with flowers for Lucy and Alice. Mrs. Anderson followed close behind with something in her hands.

Alice greeted her mother with a hug. "Doesn't Dove look beautiful? I'm so glad she's going to be my sister."

Mrs. Anderson smiled at Dove, her gaze filled with loving admiration. "Dove, you do look lovely." She approached Dove and handed her a small Bible. "This belonged to Carl's mother and grandmother. They both carried it when they wed, as I did when I married Carl. It would be such an honor if you would continue the family tradition and carry it today."

Words lodged in Dove's throat, and tears threatened. In the time since the fire and her accident, she had come to know Mrs. Anderson as the wonderful woman everyone said she was. While Dove's family lived at the hotel during the rebuilding of their home, Mrs. Anderson had invited them for dinner numerous times. She had even helped with the wedding invitations.

Dove swallowed the lump and accepted the Bible. "Thank you, Mrs. Anderson. It will be my honor to carry it." She caressed the soft leather binding. To think it had seen three generations of women marry and now lay in Dove's hands for the fourth.

Ma grasped her hands. "It's time."

They opened the door to the hallway, and Pa greeted her. "Here's my princess." He offered his arm. "Are you ready for the walk to the altar?"

She grinned. "I am, Pa. I have been for months."

He kissed her cheek, and then they moved to the foyer of the church. Alice walked down the aisle first, followed by Lucy. Then the organ swelled and the congregation stood. Dove and her father prepared to step through the doorway.

All she had endured these past months now served as a lesson in God's faithfulness. The prejudice against her Indian heritage, the unkind words, the attack by Zeb Fowler, and even the fire and her accident were worth every pain and heartache, for they were the very things that had led her to this moment.

The music beckoned her forward, and she took a step onto the aisle leading to the altar and her beloved. Her gaze immediately locked with Luke's, and everyone else in the room disappeared. She walked toward him, his smile and the love that poured from his eyes reassuring her that today was the beginning of a lifetime of love.

BOOK ONE OF THE

Winds Across the Prairie Series

Can LUCINDA learn the power of TRUE LOVE and FORGIVENESS?

OKLAHOMA RANCH LIFE brings seventeen-year-old heiress Lucinda Bishop more than she bargains for in *Becoming Lucy*, book one of the Winds Across the Prairie series.

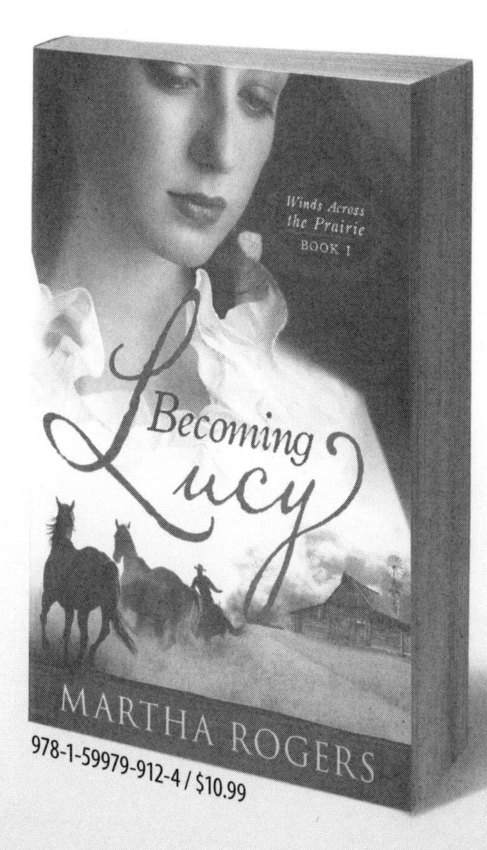

978-1-59979-912-4 / $10.99

Visit your local bookstore.

Finding Becky
Chapter 1

Oklahoma Territory, 1905

Rebecca Haynes slammed her book shut. If those children didn't quiet down soon, she would scream. A mother ought to be able to control her own young ones, but the woman across the aisle and up one seat seemed to have none over the two ruffians in her charge. The baby in her lap was not too happy either. She was just the type of woman Rebecca hoped to liberate in her efforts with the suffrage movement.

The landscape outside the train window sped by, drawing Rebecca closer to home with each clack of the wheels. To this point the journey had been quite pleasant, but when the mother with her brood of three had joined the travelers, all peace disappeared.

Rebecca turned her attention again to the children. They had quieted down some but still roamed the aisles. She loved children, but she just preferred the well-mannered, quiet ones like the cousins she'd met during her stay in Boston. A deep sigh escaped. How she would miss the friends she'd made while in college at Wellesley. Her aunt and uncle had made sure she would have the best education possible, and Rebecca had loved every minute of it, but it was now time to go home and see what difference she could make.

She mused at the similarity of her situation with that of Lucy Starnes, one of her cousins from Boston now living in Barton Creek. Just as Lucy had come to live in Oklahoma Territory to live with her aunt and uncle, Rebecca had traveled to Boston to live with an aunt and uncle there. The difference being that Lucy's parents had died, forcing her to move west to live with family. Rebecca had gone back east to further her education and learn more about her father's family.

Now she was headed home to Barton Creek, where she hoped to begin the steps toward her career in journalism. Mr. Lansdowne, her new boss, had balked at having a female reporter working for him, but then he'd relented and hired her. Her father was bound to have had some influence there, but that didn't matter. She had the job, and if she did it right, she'd be ready for a larger city paper when the opportunity arose.

A hand tugged at her skirt. A blond-haired little boy gripped the fabric with a grubby hand. She glanced over and took in the haggard face of the mother and realized the load carried by the young woman was taking its toll. Instead of scolding the child, Rebecca's heart softened, and she took matters into her own hands. She grasped the boy's hand in hers and removed it from her skirt, thankful for the gloves she wore. His bright blue eyes opened wide in surprise. "And what is your name, young master?"

At first he said nothing. He tilted his head as though deciding it would be all right to answer. A grin revealed a space in his bottom row of teeth. "I'm Billy, and I'm six."

"Hello, Billy. That's a fine name."

A little girl wedged her way next to Rebecca. "My name is Sally, and I'm six years old too. What's your name?"

A smile filled Rebecca's heart, her previous vexation gone. The two were twins. No wonder the mother had her hands full. Her heart filled with sympathy. "My name is Rebecca."

The twins looked at each other then back to Rebecca. As one voice they said, "We like that name. Can you tell us a story?"

"Children, please don't bother the young lady." The mother cast an apologetic frown toward Rebecca.

"That's all right. I'll tell them a story." Doing so would give their mother a much-needed break to take care of the baby.

The mother rewarded her with a relieved smile. Rebecca reached down and lifted Sally to her lap while Billy climbed up beside her. Since she planned to be a writer, Rebecca decided to make up her own story for the two. As she wove the tale of two children on a great adventure across the plains in a covered wagon, Sally's and Billy's heads began to nod.

The young woman across the aisle laid her now sleeping baby on the seat and came to Rebecca's side. "I'll take them now."

Though reluctant now to let her go, Rebecca handed Sally to the mother then picked up Billy. She followed the two back to their seat. The mother laid Sally on the seat facing her own then picked up the baby. "You can put Billy by his sister."

"Do you mind if I sit here and hold him? I know you have your hands full with the three of them."

A tentative smile formed. "That would be nice."

Rebecca settled herself and shifted Billy so that his weight was more evenly distributed. Just as she craved to speak with another woman, the young mother might enjoy the same. "My name is Rebecca Haynes, and I'm going to Barton Creek."

The woman's eyes sparkled with excitement. "I'm Ruth Dorsett, and I'm headed for Barton Creek myself."

Rebecca searched her memory for a recollection of a Dorsett family in Barton Creek. Of course in the four years she'd been gone, many new families had moved to the town. "I grew up there. Are you visiting, or do you live there now?"

A sadness veiled Ruth's face. "My husband passed on a few months ago, so we're going there to live with my parents."

A lump formed in Rebecca's throat. "I'm so sorry about your husband. Who are your parents? Perhaps I know them."

"Their name is Weems. Ma owns a dressmaking shop, and Pa works in the telegraph office."

"Oh, I do know them. I remember when Mrs. Weems opened her business. We were so glad to have someone who could keep us up to date on the latest fashions. She does wonderful work."

"Thank you. They heard about the opportunities in Oklahoma Territory and moved there when Pa learned they would open a new telegraph office in Barton Creek."

"Business is doing quite well for your mother. Will you be helping her?"

"Most definitely. Ma taught me to sew at an early age, and I've been doing it for my family. After Henry had his accident and passed on, I didn't know where to turn. The people in Glasson, Kansas, were so helpful, but they weren't family. After the funeral, Ma insisted that I come live with her. She's delighted to have her grandchildren so close now."

What a small world. Rebecca marveled at the coincidence. The people in Barton Creek were going to love Ruth and these adorable children who had captured Rebecca's own heart with their big, blue eyes and captivating smiles. Now that Aunt Clara lived in town as Doc Carter's wife, she would certainly spoil them if Mrs. Weems didn't, and Ruth couldn't be much older than Lucy. She'd be a good friend for Ruth.

Ruth's desire to work with her mother in business impressed Rebecca. If more women would be willing to take charge and seek careers that didn't include all-day baking, cooking, and taking care of children and husbands, more would be willing to join the movement to secure voting privileges for women. Perhaps she could convince Ruth to join the fight. This year was an election year, and women had as much right to have a say in who ran the government as any man.

That reminded her of the story she wanted to write to show the editor of the *Barton Creek Herald*. If she was going to be a success at the newspaper, she must show her capabilities right away. "Ruth, if you will excuse me, I have some work I must do before our destination. We'll talk again later, and I'm looking forward to having a new friend in Barton Creek."

"So am I. It'll be nice to have someone I can visit with and talk to on occasion."

Rebecca placed the still sleeping Billy beside Sally. "I look forward to it." Someday in the distant future she might have such a family, but at the moment her mission was to become the best reporter in Oklahoma Territory and then on to bigger and better opportunities in a larger city.

A grin spread across her face. No matter that she'd won the traditional Hoop Race at Wellesley. After her dunk in the fountain, she'd declared she would break the tradition and not be the first in the class to marry. Hoots and hollers from her fellow classmates told her they didn't believe that. Let them laugh. She'd prove there was more to life for a woman than being a wife and mother. Although nothing was wrong with that, she simply wanted to see what the world had to offer before settling down, if she ever did.

FREE NEWSLETTERS
TO HELP EMPOWER YOUR LIFE

Why subscribe today?

☐ **DELIVERED DIRECTLY TO YOU.** All you have to do is open your inbox and read.

☐ **EXCLUSIVE CONTENT.** We cover the news overlooked by the mainstream press.

☐ **STAY CURRENT.** Find the latest court rulings, revivals, and cultural trends.

☐ **UPDATE OTHERS.** Easy to forward to friends and family with the click of your mouse.

CHOOSE THE E-NEWSLETTER THAT INTERESTS YOU MOST:

- Christian news
- Daily devotionals
- Spiritual empowerment
- And much, much more

SIGN UP AT: **http://freenewsletters.charismamag.com**

8178